James Eugene Farmer

The grenadier, a story of the Empire by James Eugene Farmer

James Eugene Farmer

The grenadier, a story of the Empire by James Eugene Farmer

ISBN/EAN: 9783743306455

Manufactured in Europe, USA, Canada, Australia, Japa

Cover: Foto ©Andreas Hilbeck / pixelio.de

Manufactured and distributed by brebook publishing software
(www.brebook.com)

James Eugene Farmer

The grenadier, a story of the Empire by James Eugene Farmer

"A ROVING, ROARING, ROLLICKING BLADE WAS THE
CAPTAIN TARJEANTIRRE."

The Grenadier

A STORY OF THE EMPIRE

BY

JAMES EUGENE FARMER, M. A.

Author of " Essays on French History."

NEW YORK
DODD, MEAD AND COMPANY
1898

"Le guerrier qui a suivi Napoléon sous tous les climats de l'univers, le guerrier qui a combattu sous ses ordres en tant de royaumes, qui tant de fois a pris sa part de la gloire et du triomphe, qui a mené cette vie tourmentée pleine de privations, de souffrances, de fatigues et de dangers mortels, ne peut pas, ne doit pas oublier son grand général."—RAMBAUD, *L'Allemagne sous Napoléon Ier*.

𝕿𝖍𝖊 𝕷𝖔𝖗𝖉 𝕭𝖆𝖑𝖙𝖎𝖒𝖔𝖗𝖊 𝕻𝖗𝖊𝖘𝖘
THE FRIEDENWALD COMPANY
BALTIMORE, MD., U. S. A.

TO THE MEMORY OF THOSE WHO WERE FAITHFUL
TO THE END,
LA GARDE IMPÉRIALE

CONTENTS

CONTENTS

PREFACE

Good reader, I'll not burden you with a long preface; nobody likes a long preface. This is a story of the Empire. Follow with me, then, the French eagles, from the towers of Saragossa to the Kremlin's gilded dome at Moscow, in that stirring epoch which, as even the Prince de Metternich was forced to admit, can receive no more fitting appellation than " The Age Napoleon.". If when you have finished you feel that you have derived some pleasure and some profit from my labor, I shall say, like Gaspard in my story, " That will be nice. I would like that "—and so, good-bye.

PROLOGUE

The Post-House of Burgos

Is this the man of thousand thrones,
Who strew'd our earth with hostile bones?
—Byron, *Ode to Napoleon.*

In the month of January, 1809, a dozen chasseurs of
the French army were gathered around a log-fire near
a post-house. This post-house of Burgos was a small
stone structure, one story high, and had upon either
side, in the rear, a long wooden barn, forming a
wing. Through the half-open door of one of these
barns might be seen a couple of rough traveling carriages; one of which, freshly covered with mud, and
with a broken wheel, showed that it had lately been in
service.

In the other barn, the one nearer the fire where the
chasseurs had gathered, were a number of horses;
some standing ready saddled and bridled; others being rubbed down by the grooms, while one in particular, a splendid bay animal whose saddle-cloths
were stamped with an N surmounted by an imperial
crown, was being led slowly up and down the narrow
paved court between the post-house and the barn. In
the door of the post-house stood a large man, dark and
swarthy, with long black hair and beard. On his
head he wore a broad, soft hat, around his waist a
wide, red sash, and a dark red cloak hung from his

shoulders to the tops of his long muddy boots. He was the postmaster of Burgos. He was looking earnestly down the road toward Valladolid; occasionally he turned and looked toward Vittoria, and then his eyes flashed as his gaze rested upon the little group of chasseurs and upon the bay charger with the imperial trappings. The day was cold and clear. It had been raining hard the night before, but it was freezing now, and a thin coat of ice was forming on the water in the deep ruts cut in the roads by the artillery and baggage trains that had passed over them.

The wind blew more sharply and the chasseurs drew nearer to the fire.

" It is true," said one, who showed from the manner in which he had been giving orders that he was in command of the little detachment, " it is true we are to have war with Austria. I had it from De Viry, who brought the dispatches from the War Minister in Paris to the Emperor at Astorga. Austria is arming; she thinks the present a good chance, since the Emperor and the Grand Army are off here in Spain, where it must be allowed we have our hands full."

" Well," cried another, whose bronzed countenance with its two ugly red scars showed that this was not his first campaign, " let us hope it may be so if it will take us out of here. Mon Dieu what a country! Nothing but mountains to climb and rivers to cross, and rain and mud always. And what a people! Their army is nothing—the Guard alone could thrash that; but every peasant is in arms, and they shoot out at you from behind their houses, they lie in wait for you in the mountain passes, they lurk behind every rock We are not fighting an army, but a nation in arms."

So it was. Spain, having looked on while the victorious armies of France traversed Italy and Austria and Prussia and Poland, while the French eagles flew from Milan to Vienna and from Vienna to Berlin— Spain had now met, face to face, the man of Marengo and of Austerlitz, and Spain would not soon forget it.

What mattered it to the Spaniards if their government was imbecile and debased? it was their government; it was a Spanish government. What mattered it if their Prince of the Asturias, whom they admired and who, they knew, was held prisoner in France, was weak and corrupt? He was their Prince and he was a Spaniard. Prince Joseph Bonaparte, whom the French Emperor informed them he had chosen for their king, might be a very good man; they knew nothing about it; they did not want to know. The priests told them that a Frenchman was a devil in human form, and that whoever killed three of them would receive the reward of heaven without purgatory. Joseph Bonaparte was a Frenchman. That was enough for them. Had he been an angel they would have given him all the attributes of hell.

Therefore this proud nation—the national pride of Old Castile and Aragon leaping to its utmost height— rose as one man, drove King Joseph out of Madrid, and proclaimed war to the death against him, and against his brother, the great Emperor, who had commanded them to receive him.

But they reckoned not with whom they had to deal. They were proud, but not so proud as the man who had written, "I shall find the pillars of Hercules in Spain. I shall not find there the limits of my power."

They could fight, but not so well as the victor of Rivoli and Marengo and Austerlitz and Friedland. So he came, with his genius and his glory, his Army of the Rhine and his Old Guard. He beat them at Vittoria; he routed them at Burgos; he drove them from the pass of Somo Sierra; he wheeled his thundering cannon about their capital; and Madrid, like Cairo, Vienna and Berlin, was compelled to open her gates and bow before the conqueror.

Then the red-coated English, under Sir John Moore, came from Portugal, and the French Emperor set off promptly in pursuit of them, and pressed them hard through the steep defiles of the Guadarrama, and across the Seco, as far as Astorga. There he received the news that Austria was arming against him, and, leaving the pursuit to his Marshals Ney and Soult, he returned to Valladolid, where for five days he worked incessantly, giving his orders before setting out for France.

Such was the position of affairs on this January morning, 1809, and in the little group at the post-house of Burgos each had his special rôle to play in the great drama of Empires.

"They say that General Moore and the English have escaped the Emperor," said one of the troopers, addressing the captain.

"Not yet," replied the captain. "De Viry tells me that Ney and Soult are to continue the pursuit, but the Emperor must return to France."

"Again, I say," cried the old chasseur, who had spoken before, "God grant we may all go with him. Give me a good fight on the plains of Germany, and no more chasing of these miserable banditti, who hide among their mountains and shoot you in the back. If the Austrians want another Austerlitz, we'll give it to them. I shall be glad to see Vienna again. I was there in 1805, and I like the town."

At that moment the clatter of hoofs was heard upon the road in the direction of Valladolid, and the chasseurs ran to the front of the post-house, which had hidden their view in that direction, that they might see who was coming.

It was Watteville, one of the Emperor's aides-de-camp, riding at a furious pace. He drew rein at the post-house door, and the captain of chasseurs approached him and saluted.

"Captain Duval," said Watteville, "the Emperor will be here in less than a quarter of an hour; he does not stop, but pushes on to Vittoria. Be ready." With that he galloped on.

All was now movement and animation around the little post-house. The grooms quickly brought the horses out of their stables; Captain Duval inspected them to see that their portmanteaus contained linen maps, paper and telescopes, as the Emperor's orders required; the bay charger was led in front of the post-house door; the other horses were brought to the courtyard gate, and the chasseurs drew up in line beside them. Captain Duval was near the groom, who held the Emperor's horse; all was ready.

They did not have to wait long. Suddenly, around a bend in the road from Valladolid, came a company of horsemen. They rode at a tearing gallop, and their helmets with long horsehair crests, their busbys with waving plumes, and their glittering, gold-laced uniforms made a brilliant show. But they attracted little attention from the group gathered about the post-house door. All eyes were fixed upon him who rode at their head. All knew that short, square figure beneath the plain cocked hat with the small tricolored cockade; his gray greatcoat was buttoned closely over his breast; his riding boots with silver spurs were thickly splashed with mud; by his side was the sword of Austerlitz; it was the Emperor Napoleon. His pale face was calm, but his brow was knit, his lips compressed, and his eyes flashed as he leaned forward, jerking impatiently at his bridle reins as if to quicken his already furious speed.

On arriving at the post-house the Emperor checked his horse so suddenly that the beast was thrown upon its haunches. He flung himself off, bringing his foot heavily to the ground. One of the grooms, who stood ready, led the horse quickly away; another brought up the bay charger. The Emperor seized the reins, sprang into the saddle and gave the highly mettled animal a sharp cut with his whip, which made him leap forward furiously.

"Vive l'Empereur!" shouted the chasseurs. The postmaster stood in his doorway, with his red cloak wrapped about him, silently watching. The staff, having changed horses as rapidly as possible, rode hard after the Emperor; the chasseurs returned to their quarters to await orders from Marshal Lannes, who was in command at Valladolid, but the postmaster still stood, gazing intently down the road toward Vittoria after the great apparition which he, for the first time, had seen.

CHAPTER I

Pierre Pasquin

I hate that drum's discordant sound,
Parading round, and round, and round ;
To thoughtless youth it pleasure yields,
And lures from cities and from fields,
To sell their liberty for charms
Of tawdry lace and glittering arms ;
And when Ambition's voice commands,
To march, and fight, and fall in foreign lands.
—JOHN SCOTT, *Ode on Hearing the Drum.*

IN the Rue Montorge, Grenoble, not far from the famous inn, the Hotel des Trois Dauphins, stood the little house of Widow Pasquin. It was well known to all persons living in the vicinity, and though used now as a humble *épicerie*, showed signs that it had seen better days. The plain stone façade was broken by a low doorway, above which ornamental consoles supported a circular stone balcony with a curiously wrought iron railing, so common in the rococo architecture of the Louis Quinze period. Inside all was neat and scrupulously clean, and a modest stock of groceries and staples was arranged upon the counters and shelves.

Jeanne Pasquin, or as she was called by her neighbors, the Widow Pasquin, was a small, slender woman, now nearly fifty. She had once, no doubt, possessed beauty, but long years of struggle for subsistence and

2

the terrors and anxieties of the Revolution had left their marks in the careworn eyes and sad lines of her face. Her hair, once black, was thickly streaked with gray and her shoulders somewhat bent. People said she had never been the same since the day the news reached her that her eldest son Robert had perished in the war.

Her husband, Amand Pasquin, enjoyed some consideration under the Old Régime, and had been at one time *directeur des postes*, but, unlike many of his fellows, he embraced warmly the revolutionary doctrines of 1789. On the outbreak of the war in 1792 he entered the army, fought bravely at Valmy and Jemmapes, gained the rank of colonel, followed Bonaparte to Italy and perished at the Bridge of Lodi. Robert had entered the army in 1805 and had been killed at Eylau. Left thus to struggle with the world, the Widow Pasquin had managed to derive enough support from her *épicerie* to maintain herself and educate her son Pierre, in whom all her love was centered; Pierre, whose manly qualities won for him the hearts of all, not only of the boys and girls who were his companions, but of old Father Augustin who taught at the college and of Father Morot who preached in the chapel of St. Laurent.

On this day, the second of January, 1809, Pierre was eighteen. The Widow Pasquin, sitting in her little shop, was planning to arrange some surprise for him, when the door opened suddenly. There was a merry laugh, a joyful cry, " Ah! there you are, la petite mère," and Pierre sprang forward and caught her in his arms.

He was a fine-looking fellow as he stood there by her side, with his well-built form, his dark eyes flashing brightly, his cheeks glowing with health and exercise, and his thick black hair, which he still wore long in fashion of the Directoire, tossed back from his forehead. So thought the fond mother as she looked upon him; so too thought many a fair maiden of the Rue Montorge.

"Why do you come so early to-day, Pierre?" inquired the Widow.

"News has come of the surrender of Madrid," answered Pierre, "and the good Father Augustin has gone to the cathedral to assist at the Te Deum. I have hastened home to you because I have something to ask of you. This is my birthday, you know. I am eighteen to-day. Now, mother dear, grant me this favor; it will be your greatest birthday gift to me,—let me enter the army."

The Widow Pasquin did not answer. She sank into a chair and covered her face with her hands. For this, then, she had so carefully watched and guarded her only remaining child! How she had trembled at each decree of the senate which offered to the Emperor new levies of troops! How she had hoped, in 1807, that the Peace of Tilsit would bring repose to France! Now this new war in Spain, with all its terrors; these new levies of men! He too would go like her Amand and her Robert, and she would never see him again.

She raised her head and Pierre saw that her eyes were full of tears. "Do not cry, petite mère," he said gaily. "I shall fight for France and the Emperor. I shall win glory! Think how proud you will be when one day you learn that Pierre has done some brave deed and has received the cross, and he comes back to you in a splendid uniform all covered with gold, and tells you of all the adventures of the campaign, and has enough money to make you happy always! Oh, mother, you should have seen Jean Deteau! You remember Jean who lived near the Place St. André? He was here yesterday. He goes to Spain, for he is aide-de-camp to Marshal Lannes. You should have seen him with his beautiful uniform and gold lace, his great plumed busby, his glittering sword, and his cross which he won for capturing a gun at Jena. The Emperor gave it him at the review in the great square at Potsdam. He gave it with his own hand, saying, ' For the brave Jean Deteau,' and all the drums rolled. Think of that, mother! How they crowded around him yesterday when he came into the Hotel des Trois Dauphins! Old Monsieur Montfort, the rich banker who lives in the Place Grénette, got out of his carriage and talked to him hat in hand. Think of that! You should have heard him tell how they charged the Prussians at Jena! Forty thousand of our cuirassiers, and at their head the Prince Murat; his long hair streaming in the wind, his gold-embroidered uniform shining in the sun, and his great white plume floating over all, as he waved his riding whip and urged his war horse right into the midst of the enemy, shouting, ' Forward, my brave boys! Vive l'Empereur!'"

"I cannot let you go, my son," said the Widow Pasquin. "You are all that is left to me. The père Amand went; he too was to win fame and honor. One day came news of a great victory—Lodi. There were bonfires in the streets and all the people danced and sung, but no husband came back to me. He was lying dead on the plain. Then Robert—noble, brave

Robert—he too must go. Again I heard them crying, 'Glorious victory! Battle of Friedland! Peace
of Tilsit!' There were bonfires in the streets, the
Mayor illuminated the Hotel de Ville, and the Archbishop celebrated mass in the cathedral, but no Robert
came back. My brave boy was dead and cold amid
the snow in Poland! Now you would go. For what?
To win glory, you say. Alas! some day I shall hear
of a famous victory, some Austerlitz, some Friedland,
but no Pierre will come back to me! I shall never
see my brave boy again!"

"But, mother,——" said Pierre.

"This man," continued the Widow, "this Napoleon! What do I profit by his Austerlitz, by his Jena,
by his Peace of Tilsit! Has he not robbed me of
enough? No, No! I cannot let you go! How I have
trembled when I heard of each new levy! How I have
rejoiced when you were not drafted! Now you come
to tell me that you want to leave me. I shall die perhaps of want, for I am getting old to labor, and you
will go to perish."

The Widow Pasquin covered her face with her
hands and sobbed aloud.

"But, mother," cried Pierre, "I shall have better
luck than père Amand and Robert. You shall never
die of want! I shall bring you all things! Everyone
should fight for la patrie, for the Emperor, the great
Emperor who governs all; who gives our France such
glory!"

"You will fall like Robert and père Amand," answered the Widow. "The Pasquins are not lucky.
As for fighting for la patrie; why should they fight at
all now? They do not fight for France; they fight to

make his brother King of Spain. So, if you fight, you do not fight for France, but for Napoleon alone."

"But, mother," said Pierre, "the good priest tells us that the cause of France is just; that God will bless our efforts for the country."

"My son," said the Widow Pasquin, raising her eyes solemnly, "we cannot believe all that even priests may tell us in these days. The Frenchmen of this age no longer worship Father, Son and Holy Ghost. They have created a *new* Trinity—France, Napoleon and Glory!"

CHAPTER II

Henri Jodélle

None but the brave deserves the fair.
—DRYDEN, *Alexander's Feast.*

HENRI JODÉLLE had been a soldier. He gained some distinction in the early wars of the Revolution; led a charge at Valmy, and was in that famous company of Pichegru's hussars who captured the Dutch fleet in the winter of 1795. Later he entered the Army of Italy, but lost a leg at Castiglione, and as misfortunes never come singly, his wife died shortly afterwards. Retired with a small pension, he had made a comfortable living as a restaurateur, and few places were better known to the people of Grenoble than the Café Jodélle. It faced the Place Grénette, and in fine weather the little tables and chairs were placed outside about the door under a broad awning. The interior was of modest dimensions. In the centre stood a large shining urn for making coffee. Against the walls and under the latticed windows were placed the small tables, with four chairs to each. On one wall hung a print of Hennequin's curious engraving representing General Bonaparte with a great plumed hat, his hand on his sword, his horse at a gallop, and underneath the title, "Bonaparte, Général en chef de l'armée d'Italie." Between the windows hung a picture of the Battle of Castiglione, while above the white wooden mantel was suspended a large colored print entitled, " Napoléon distribue les aigles à l'armée," a copy of David's painting which represented the Emperor in his coronation robes giving the eagles to the army on the Champ-de-Mars.

The café was famous for having the best liqueurs in Grenoble, and doubly fortunate was that patron of the place, who, in addition to the viands he received, could obtain a smile from the host's daughter Marie. Though only seventeen, Marie had had many suitors; but Henri, in his double rôle of father and duenna, had frowned upon them all. In Henri's eyes a man who was not a soldier was nothing. To him the Emperor was a god, and the Garde Impériale the apogee of military glory.

If, among the many who had sought Marie's hand, there was one on whom Henri looked with some favor, it was Jean Deteau. He had known Jean from his boyhood; had watched his career with interest; had rejoiced at the bravery he displayed in the Prussian campaign, and now that he saw him return decorated with the Legion of Honor and aide-de-camp to Marshal Lannes, he felt that here was one of whom, as a possible son-in-law, he could be justly proud.

Marie, on the contrary, had never cared for Jean. Perhaps the very reiteration of his praises by her father had wearied her. She admired his bravery, but she could never feel at ease when his keen, restless black eyes were fastened upon her, as they always were when he came to the Café Jodélle. He was bright and gay. He laughed a great deal, but about his laugh there was something so insincere, at times so heartless, that it almost frightened her.

As may be surmised, Jean would not leave Grenoble without paying a visit to Marie and Henri, and about seven in the evening on the day when Pierre had seen him at the Hotel des Trois Dauphins, he entered the Café Jodélle.

Henri gave him a warm welcome, and Marie smiled as she extended her hand.

The clock was striking ten when Jean emerged from the café. Something had evidently occurred to mar the pleasure of his visit. His face was hard and set; his eyes flashed fiercely; he pushed his busby angrily down upon his forehead, and threw his military cloak about his shoulders as he strode across the Place Grénette.

There were few pedestrians in the Rue Montorge when he reached it, and nothing disturbed the stillness of the street save the clank of his sword and the click of his spurs on the cobblestones as he hurried along. As he came under one of the flickering lights that faintly illuminated the gloom, he noticed, in the window of a shop before which he was passing, the sign, " Jeanne Pasquin, Épicerie." He stopped, and glanced up, surveying the façade of the little house, from its curved gables to the circular balcony above the door. The glance was momentary, but it was full of hatred and scorn. Then hurrying on, he reached the Trois Dauphins, and in the gray dawn of the following morning mounted his horse and set out for Spain.

It was four o'clock in the afternoon. Henri had gone to the Place St. André, and there were few people in the Café Jodélle when Pierre Pasquin entered it. A couple of hussars were seated at one of the tables, being served by the garçon Gaspard, while a young fellow in a peasant's blouse and heavy wooden shoes was staring at the engraving of Bonaparte as General in Italy.

Pierre nodded to Gaspard, and passed through the café with the air of one thoroughly familiar with the place. He crossed a narrow side hall and was about to knock at a door, leading into a small sitting room, when he perceived that it was slightly open. Through the crack he could see Marie Jodélle. He thought she had never appeared more beautiful. Her soft brown hair waved about her face, and her delicate color was heightened by the little white cap she wore and the bow of black ribbon about her throat. She was sitting in a chair, her hands clasped in her lap, looking thoughtfully out of the window.

Pierre watched her for a moment, but, as something outside the window attracted her attention, she moved her chair and turned her back toward the door. He entered quietly, and slipping up behind her, put both hands over her eyes, and then, quickly removing them, kissed her on the cheek.

" Oh, Pierre! " cried Marie, jumping up, " I am so glad you have come. I have been hoping you would come to-day. I am so troubled."

" What has troubled you, Marie? "

" Close the door, Pierre," said Marie, " and I will tell you."

He did so, and when he had seated himself, she said, " Pierre, last night Jean was here. He came to say good-bye before he went to Spain. Father was very glad to see him. You know father always speaks well of Jean."

"Yes, I know," answered Pierre.

"Father went away before very long," continued Marie, "and then Jean told me that he loved me, he asked me to be his wife, he—Why, Pierre, what's the matter?"

Pierre was pale; he trembled.

"I told him I did not care for him, Pierre. Of course you know that. I told him I could not marry him."

The boy sprang forward and caught her in his arms.

"He looked at me so strangely," said Marie. "He was so angry when he went away," and she added nervously, "he said—he said he was determined to marry me. I was afraid he would ask père Henri, and if he did I think father would consent, for he admires Jean. I am so troubled about it all."

She had intended to tell him everything, but there was one incident she forgot to mention. Jean had tried to embrace her; she had sprung away from him, and as she did so, her foot had caught in the folds of a rug and she had fallen. A gold chain which she wore about her neck caught in the fringe of the rug, and, as she jumped quickly up again, it snapped, leaving a little picture lying on the floor. Jean had picked it up. It was a cheap miniature, the work of some mediocre artist, but the likeness was fair enough. He had recognized it at a glance and had handed it back to her without a word. It was the picture of Pierre.

"Do not worry, Marie," said Pierre, kneeling beside her and putting his arm around her waist. "Jean has gone to Spain. He will not be here soon again. You know how I have longed to enter the army, to do some brave deed, to win the cross, so that I could go to the père Henri and say, 'See, I am a soldier, I have won honor, I am worthy of Marie!' Only this morning I asked the mère Pasquin to let me go, but she felt so badly and cried so much that I cannot ask her again. I fear I must stay and help at the épicerie. Others will go to gain riches and honor. Oh, Marie, none of them could love you more truly than I! None of them could fight better for France! None of them—"

"What are you doing here, sir?" came suddenly in sharp imperative tones from the doorway. They had been so occupied that they had not heard the door open. Marie started to rise. Pierre sprang up and faced the door. There, leaning upon his crutch, his heavy gray mustache bristling fiercely and his eyes flashing as they might have flashed when he led the charge at Valmy, stood Henri Jodélle.

"Young Pasquin," said the old soldier, who was evidently making an effort to control his temper, "I have let you know before that you have been here too often. What do you mean by being here to-day?"

Pierre saw that the moment which he dreaded had come. He looked his interlocutor full in the face. "I love your daughter, père Henri," he said quietly. "She has told me that she loves me, and I am come to ask you for her hand."

He expected an outbreak. The old soldier's face was very red, his eyes flashed, but he said nothing. He looked at Pierre, a stern, steady glance which surveyed him from the crown of his head to his feet. Pierre did not weaken, and his bearing evidently made some impression upon Henri, for his glance softened a little, but when he spoke his tone was sharp and severe.

" What are you going to do to support a wife, young Pasquin? "

Pierre colored a little, but replied firmly, " I am going to manage my mother's épicerie in the Rue Montorge."

" Mon Dieu! a noble occupation!" cried the old soldier contemptuously. " Here is a brave young man truly! A great, strong fellow, who when the country needs men and thousands are winning glory under the eagles of our glorious Emperor, stays at home to sell butter and eggs! Young Pasquin, my child shall never, with my consent, marry any one who is not a soldier. It will be time enough for you to talk to me when you can stand before me with the Legion of Honor on your breast. Do you think I am going to give my daughter to a poltroon? Now go, and do not let me find you here again."

" Oh, father," cried Marie, " you are unjust!"

" Go, I say!" cried Henri, who had by this time worked himself into a passion.

Pierre, who had blushed while Henri sneered at his occupation, turned pale at the word poltroon, and clenched his hands. Marie had never before seen such an expression on his face. She sprang up and stood before her father and looked at Pierre, so earnestly, so beseechingly. She said nothing, but her eyes said, Oh, go! go!

Pierre bowed his head and left the room. He crossed the Place Grénette slowly, his head still bowed and his eyes fixed on the ground. " Stand aside!"

cried the driver of a cabriolet which was approaching
at a rapid pace. He called twice before Pierre heard
him, and then only in time to avoid being struck by
one of the large wheels. "Sacré!" muttered the
driver, "these idle fellows deserve to be run down."

Pierre wandered on. Suddenly the sharp ring of
horses' hoofs and the clank of sabres made him look
up. He had reached the Place St. André. A squadron of dragoons were crossing it. How grand they
looked, with their glittering cuirasses, their crested helmets, their great boots and long military cloaks!
What a proud, determined, conquering air they had!
Pierre watched them as long as they were in sight,
then he turned and slowly made his way to the Rue
Montorge.

The Widow Pasquin could see, when he entered,
that something had happened. She had never seen
him look so sad. "What is the matter, Pierre?" she
asked.

The tears came to Pierre's eyes and then he told
her all. She listened without a word, but when he
told her of Henri's taunts and of the word " poltroon "
which he had used, the Widow Pasquin sat erect in
her chair and her eyes flashed. When he had finished
she looked at him long and earnestly, and in her look
he read the great love she bore him, and the effort the
words she was about to speak cost her. Then she took
his hand. "My son," she said, "I will not keep you
back. You cannot rest happy here. Go, since you
wish it, and may better fortune go with you than that
which went with Robert and père Amand."

CHAPTER III

SARAGOSSA

The voices are mighty that speak from the past,
With Aragon's cry on the shrill mountain blast,
The ancient Sierras give strength to our tread,
Their pines murmur song when bright blood hath been shed.
Fling forth the proud banner of Leon again,
And shout ye " Castile! to the rescue for Spain! "
                    —MRS. HEMANS, *Ancient Battle Song*.

SINCE the 10th of December, 1808, the French Army
had laid siege to Saragossa. This town was not regu-
larly fortified. Surrounded by a wall of brick and
granite, without either bastions or terraces, it was protected on one side by the river Ebro, and on the other
by the Castle of the Inquisition and the Convents of
the Capuchins, the Augustins, Santa Engracia, St.
Joseph and Santa Monica. These were in themselves
real fortresses which must be battered down, or taken
by assault, before entrance could be gained into the
town.

In every street were barricades bristling with
cannon. Great stores of corn, wine and cattle had
been collected in the city, whose population was now
swelled to more than 100,000 souls by the inhabitants
of the surrounding country. The impetuous Palafox
was their commander, assisted by his brothers Francis
Palafox and the Marquis de Lassan, and in every
public place a gallows warned all of the fate awaiting
those who should speak the word *surrender*.

Thus Saragossa, the last hope of the obstinately resisting Spaniards, defied the power of Napoleon.

Toward evening on the 25th of January a detachment of troops arrived in the French camp. They were conscripts, mainly from the province of Dauphiné, and were destined to form part of one of the newly raised regiments, the 115th of the Line. Some of them now saw war for the first time, and among this number was Pierre Pasquin.

The 26th of January began with a tremendous cannonade, as fifty guns of large calibre poured their shot and shell into Saragossa. The 115th of the Line were stationed in the trench between the Convents of Santa Engracia and the Capuchins. Pierre, who had climbed to the top of the escarpment, could see, far on the left, the Castle of the Inquisition, where were stationed the 40th of the Line and the 13th cuirassiers, who were to repulse any sortie that might be made from that side. Before the centre towered the massive walls of Santa Engracia, now battered and broken in many places by the heavy fire of the breaching battery, and on the right was the Convent of St. Joseph, from one of whose towers floated the tricolor and about which were stationed the Grandjean division, consisting of the 14th and 44th of the Line. In the centre, next to the 115th, was massed the Morlot division, and beyond it the Musnier division, which consisted principally of Poles, fierce-looking men, with their strange uniforms and shaggy beards, who had been brought from the far north to battle here in Spain under the banners of the modern Caesar.

" Down from that escarpment! " cried a corporal of the 115th who was passing. Pierre obeyed.

"Will the Emperor be here to-day?" he inquired.

"The Emperor? No, he has gone to France," answered the corporal.

This was a disappointment to Pierre. He had hoped to see the Emperor and to fight under his eyes. All day the cannonade continued, and the Spaniards, fortified behind their walls, endured it bravely. The soldiers in the trenches became restless and impatiently awaited the order for a general attack. Pierre saw, in the distance, a man on horseback, with a cocked hat, and the broad red ribbon of the Legion of Honor across his breast. He was followed by four aides-de-camp, and Pierre was told that it was the Marshal Lannes.

At noon on the 27th the order was given to assault the town. A detachment of voltigeurs of the 14th and 44th, commanded by the chef-de-bataillon Stahl, and having at their head a company of sappers, crossed the Huerba beyond the Convent of St. Joseph and occupied an oil mill, which stood somewhat isolated not far from the wall. As they advanced, tremendous explosions took place, for the Spaniards foreseeing their approach from that direction, had mined the ground over which they must pass. Then a hot fire of musketry opened upon them from the houses and batteries of the town. Stahl was severely wounded and the detachment fell back. Some grenadiers of the 44th now made their way toward the second breach, mounted it, and, under the command of the intrepid Guettemann, obtained possession of the houses next the wall in spite of the furious fire of the Spaniards. A column of voltigeurs hastened to their aid and strove to enter the streets. The great houses, loopholed and barricaded, flashed fire on every side, as skilled marksmen, hidden behind their walls, shot with deadly effect among the French troops.

The soldiers, opening interior passages from the houses they had captured into those adjoining, were enabled to proceed as far as the Calle Quemada, one of the chief streets which opened into the great boulevard of the Cosso. Here a galling fire from the cannon of the barricades rendered further advance impossible. Meanwhile a furious assault was being made upon the Santa Engracia by the Poles of the Musnier division and the soldiers and officers of the engineers. They made themselves masters of the convent, and pushing on across an open space, approached the Convent of the Capuchins. The carabineers of the 5th light infantry at the same time made a charge upon the Capuchins, and these two forces uniting speedily took the convent and its battery.

And now the 115th of the Line, whose eagerness to rush to the assistance of their comrades had long been manifest, could no longer be restrained. " En avant! " shouted the Major. They dashed forward to the long wall between the Santa Engracia and the Convent of the Capuchins, entered through the embrasures and advanced into the interior of the town. They found themselves in the street of Santa Engracia. On one side stood the enormous Convent of the Nuns of Jerusalem, next to it the madhouse, and opposite, the Monastery of St. Francis. The Spaniards concealed in these great buildings opened a terrific fire upon the French.

The head of the column halted and suddenly fell back as the soldiers, crowded together in the narrow street, endeavored to return the fire of their hidden foes. Pierre was pushed against the wall of the Convent of the Nuns of Jerusalem so tightly that he could not move. The air was thick with smoke, through which came the bright flashes of the enemy's fire. On every side resounded the groans and curses of the soldiers and the shouts of exultation of their adversaries.

Suddenly the doors of the Monastery of St. Francis were flung open. The Spaniards infuriated by the capture of their walls and the taking of the Capuchin Convent, were no longer content to stand on the defensive. They came to battle with their enemies. A body of sharpshooters of Castanos' army, led by forty monks of the order of St. Francis and a number of Spanish women, whose religious fanaticism roused them to frenzy, rushed out. Shouting, " Death to the invaders!" they ran toward the French. The women armed with long knives were even more violent than the men and attacked the soldiers with unwonted fury. It was a hand-to-hand conflict there in the street of Santa Engracia, and all the time the musketry fire continued to pour upon French and Spaniards alike from the Convent of the Nuns of Jerusalem. A part of the monks, who remained grouped upon the steps of the Monastery, shouted words of encouragement to their followers, and the aged white-haired abbot held aloft his great gilded crucifix as though the sight of this holy emblem would paralyze the arms of his enemies.

The French, firing at short range, and using their bayonets with deadly effect, cut their way to the monastery steps, and a fierce contest took place between them and the monks gathered there. As the first grenadier dashed up the steps, the aged abbot beat him on the head with the great crucifix and stretched him lifeless on the stones. In a moment four soldiers pierced the monk with their bayonets, and, dropping the crucifix, he fell dead upon the body of his adversary. The monks defended themselves with vigor, but the soldiers, by this time wild with fury, cut and stabbed them with ferocity, and rushing over their dead bodies poured into the interior of the monastery.

When the first ranks of the French rushed forward, Pierre was freed from the pressure which had held him against the convent wall and charged with the other soldiers. Just in front of him was a great voltigeur, and, as they advanced, a Spanish woman with flying hair, wild, haggard eyes and bare arms smeared with blood, sprang forward and stabbed the soldier in the arm. With a terrible oath the voltigeur turned, tore the knife from her hand and, seizing her by her long hair, forced her to her knees, as he stabbed her again and again. Pierre felt sick at heart and rushed on toward the monastery. The dense smoke choked and blinded him, the tremendous firing almost deafened him. Suddenly he felt a sharp pain in his right side, everything swam around him and he fell to the ground. As he gradually came to his senses, he realized that he was lying on his face. He could not move, a great weight seemed to press upon his legs. He felt the pain in his side, and when he attempted to struggle to sit up, it became so sharp that he fell back helpless. "It is all up with me," thought Pierre. "Soon some Spaniard will come and finish me." The street was full of smoke, and it was so dark that he could see nothing; he thought night must have come.

The firing had ceased from the Convent of the Nuns of Jerusalem.

How different it all was from what he had expected! He had hoped for a grand charge, like the one Jean had described, to the inspiring blast of the trumpet, behind the white plume of Murat, and under the eyes of the great Emperor. The Emperor was far away in France, and here was war stripped of all its grandeur, war in all its horror! Burning houses, women massacred in the streets, unseen enemies pouring forth their deadly fire! Around him were the bodies of the dead and the groans of the dying, and, as he lay there on the rough stones, he remembered the words of his mother, "You, too, will fall like Robert and père Amand. The Pasquins are not lucky!"

CHAPTER IV

THE SURRENDER

The horrid war-whoop and the shriller scream
Rose still; but fainter were the thunders grown;
Of forty thousand who had manned the wall,
Some hundreds breathed, the rest were silent all!
—BYRON, *Don Juan.*

A GHASTLY spectacle was the street of Santa Engracia
in the dawn of the morning of the 28th of January.
On every side lay heaps of dead, while guns, knapsacks, cartridge boxes, and battered timbers were
strewn thickly about the ground.

Before the Convent of the Nuns of Jerusalem the
fire had been fiercest, and there the bodies were most
numerous. The dead voltigeurs of the 115th lay
mingled with the brigands of Castanos' army, while
here and there among the slain might be seen the
corpse of some poor Spanish woman, who, roused to
fury by religious zeal, had perished in defense of all
she held most dear.

The Monastery of St. Francis, with its walls blackened by powder and stained with blood and its great
doors battered and torn from their hinges, remained
in the possession of the French. Before the main entrance lay the monks, and upon the top step the aged
abbot, his white hair stained with blood, while above
him was suspended the great crucifix which some soldier had fastened to the casing of the door.

Two soldiers of the transport corps passed through the Santa Engracia on the morning following the assault. "There is a fine belt on that Spaniard," said one, "I mean to have it." He went toward the wall of the Monastery of St. Francis, where several bodies were lying, and turned over the corpse of a burly Spaniard. As he did so, a deep groan came from the body of a French soldier, across whose legs the Spaniard had fallen.

"Here is one not yet dead," said the transport man to his companion. "We must carry him back to camp. The Marshal has given orders to bring in all the wounded."

"He is a young fellow," said the other. "From his uniform he must belong to the 115th. He has been shot in the side and has bled a good deal," he added, raising Pierre.

The man who had first spoken had meanwhile secured the brilliant belt which had attracted his attention. He joined his companion, and they lifted Pierre, one supporting his head and shoulders, the other carrying his legs. They bore him slowly along the Santa Engracia, out through the embrasures of the wall and across the tête-de-pont of the Huerba. A stone house, which stood opposite the Santa Engracia at some distance from the Huerba, was used by the French as a temporary hospital, and here the transport men conveyed their burden and surrendered him to the army surgeons.

The doctors gave the wounded man some nourishment, and then probed his wound, extracting a bullet which had fastened itself in the muscles of his side. The operation gave Pierre much pain, for the surgeons were in a hurry and did not handle him very gently. At last it was over. They dressed the wound and made him fairly comfortable upon a heap of straw. For some days he suffered a great deal, but finally his vigorous constitution got the better of his malady and by the middle of February he was able to leave his bed.

Meanwhile, the siege of Saragossa was pressed with vigor. The French fought their way from street to street, but every house was a fortress which must be battered down or taken by assault, and there were some houses which cost whole days. Still, Saragossa, with her defenders stricken by fever, famine and the sword, her dead rotting in her streets, and her living wandering about like gaunt shadows, refused Marshal Lannes' terms of capitulation and bade the French defiance.

On the 18th of February, Pierre, who was able to leave his bed, walked toward the Huerba. Near by was a detachment of the Grandjean division. The soldiers were gathered about an old red-faced corporal, who stood gesticulating emphatically, upon a broken cannon. Pierre stopped to listen.

"Was there ever such a war!" cried the old corporal. "Here after forty days' hard fighting we have gained possession of only four or five streets! Are we to capture the whole town in this way? We shall all perish!"

"What is the Marshal thinking of?" said another. "Why does he not wait for reinforcements and bury these devils under bombs instead of sending us to die in taking a few houses?"

At this moment Pierre saw a horseman rapidly approaching, attended by a single aide-de-camp. It was the Marshal Lannes. As he approached, the shout was raised, "Vive le Maréchal Lannes!" but, as he reined in his horse, one voice cried "To France!"

"My friends," said the Marshal, looking over the crowd of bronzed, scarred faces upturned towards him, "my friends, you are suffering, but do you not suppose the enemy suffers also? For every man we lose they lose four. Do you suppose they will defend all their streets as they have defended some of them? They are at the end of their strength. Remember the Emperor is awaiting impatiently the news of our success. Come, my friends, a few more efforts and Saragossa will be ours!"

"Vive le Maréchal Lannes!" cried the soldiers as he rode away.

"Well, Ajax is right," said the old corporal. "Let us finish these Spanish devils."

Pierre had been watching the Marshal intently during the brief harangue, but, as Lannes rode away, the aide-de-camp, who followed, passed near him, and Pierre suddenly recognized Jean Deteau. His first impulse was to spring forward and cry out—the sight of a familiar face was so pleasant—but in a moment Jean was gone, following the Marshal, who rode rapidly toward the Musnier division. Pierre returned to the stone hospital. He was still weak and walked slowly. As he neared the building, Marshal Lannes rode up alone. He flung himself off his horse, and threw the reins to Pierre, remarking, "Hold my horse." Then, entering the building, he dropped into a chair near the door and passed his hand wearily across his forehead, and Pierre heard him mutter, as the old corporal had done, " Was there ever such a war! "

Pierre watched him closely. This was the great Marshal Lannes, the Emperor's right arm, "Ajax" the soldiers called him, the son of a poor mechanic, by his military talents and the fortunes of the Emperor made Marshal of France and Duke of Montebello. The Marshal was well built and of middle size. His gold-embroidered uniform and great boots were stained with mud, across his breast was the red ribbon of the Legion of Honor and the cross hung suspended from his buttonhole. He had thrown his plumed hat on the ground, and his usually open and pleasant countenance, framed by his dark, curly hair and short side whiskers, was now drawn and sad as he sat with oné leg crossed, supporting his head on his hand, absorbed in thought. Suddenly he raised his head and looked at Pierre. " Boy, can you write? " he inquired.

" Yes, Monsieur le Maréchal," answered Pierre. How glad he was that the Father Augustin had taught him well!

" Tell one of those men to hold my horse," said the Marshal, pointing to four soldiers of the Grandjean division who were approaching, " and come here."

Pierre did as he was ordered.

" What is your name? " asked Lannes.

" Pierre Pasquin, Monsieur le Maréchal."

" What regiment? "

" The 115th of the Line."

The Marshal drew out a tablet and handed it to Pierre, who seated himself upon a pile of straw and wrote rapidly as Lannes dictated several orders. As he finished, an aide-de-camp rode up. "Well," cried the Marshal as he entered, "are the mines ready to blow up the university? Have you seen General Gazan?"

"The mines are ready, Monsieur le Maréchal," answered the aide-de-camp, "and General Gazan is organizing the attack on the faubourg."

Pierre recognized the voice and looked quickly up. "Oh, Jean!" he cried.

Jean started, a look of surprise, then of anger passed over his face; it was gone in an instant; he smiled and extended his hand. "Why, Pierre, what do you do here?"

"You know him?" inquired the Marshal.

"Yes, sir, he comes from Grenoble, as I do," answered Jean.

Pierre handed the orders to the Marshal, who remarked, as he signed them rapidly, "You write well, young Pasquin." Then he turned to Jean. "Take these at once to Colonel Rogniat and to General Lacoste and rejoin me at headquarters." Jean saluted and rode rapidly away. The Marshal rose, Pierre sprang forward and picked up his hat. "Young man, I thank you for serving me as secretary," said Lannes. He motioned to the voltigeur to bring up his horse, mounted and rode off toward General Gazan's division.

Soon the cannonade began upon the convent adjoining the bridge of the Ebro, and a tremendous explosion of 1600 pounds of powder announced that the university had been blown up. The attack on the faubourg by the Gazan division, led by Marshal Lannes in person, was successful, while the Grandjean division, grumbling no longer, rushed over the ruins

of the university and gained possession of the Boulevard of the Cosso. Thus the main street of Saragossa
was in the hands of the French. Before such a succession of disasters the Spaniards gave way, and sent
a flag of truce in the name of Palafox to propose terms
of capitulation. Marshal Lannes met the envoy near
the tête-de-pont of the Huerba and demanded an
unconditional surrender, adding that he would blow
up the centre of the town on the following day if his
terms were not complied with.

Of the 100,000 inhabitants who were in Saragossa
at the beginning of the siege, 54,000 had already perished, and the remainder, stricken by fever, were on
the verge of starvation. The junta of defense could
hold out no longer. On the 21st of February they
surrendered the city, and the garrison, passing out of
the Portillo gate, laid down their arms and became
prisoners of war. And when that crowd of soldiers,
peasants, monks, and women, gaunt, ragged, covered
with wounds and stained with blood, defiled before the
French army and the conquerors rode through the
bloody, ruined streets, filled with putrid corpses, they
felt there was little in which to glory. Here, at least,
the Spaniards had atoned for their cowardice in the
field, and maintained against their adversaries a contest memorable in history. It was even as one of her
defenders has expressed it, "Saragossa," cried the
Spaniard proudly, "has spit in the face of Napoleon!"

CHAPTER V

A Letter for the Emperor

Art thou a friend to Roderick?
—Scott, *Lady of the Lake*.

THE envoys, who came to the French camp bringing
to Lannes the acceptance of his terms of surrender by
the junta of defense, were unable to find the Marshal at headquarters. Colonel Rogniat informed them
that he had gone toward the Huerba. They made
their way slowly through the camp. The soldiers of
the Morlot and Grandjean divisions looked at them
sternly; at one point they were almost run down by a
squadron of the 13th cuirassiers coming to take up
position, but, finally, they found the Marshal in the
stone hospital opposite the Santa Engracia. He was
unattended and busy giving orders to the surgeons for
the care of the wounded, who had been brought in
after the bloody fight of the 18th.

Pierre, who was helping one of the surgeons carry
into the hospital a wounded Pole of the Musnier division, passed near the Marshal and the Spanish envoys.
He saw that Lannes was listening to their statements
with evident satisfaction, and as he dismissed them he
remarked, " You may rely upon my word."

The Marshal came into the hospital just as the sur-
geon and Pierre were placing the Pole upon a heap
of straw.

" Young Pasquin, I have some work for you," said
Lannes. Pierre set down his burden and hurried for-

ward. "Come, write," said the Marshal, and he dictated two letters, one to the Emperor at Paris, the other to King Joseph at Madrid.

An aide-de-camp rode up and saluted the Marshal. "Here, Deteau," said Lannes, folding the letter to King Joseph which he had signed, "you are to take this to Madrid at once. Saragossa has capitulated. Where is d'Albuquerque?"

"He is coming, Monsieur le Maréchal," replied the aide-de-camp, "I left him near Santa Engracia. Ah! there he is now," he added, as a horseman was seen rapidly crossing the tête-de-pont of the Huerba.

"Good," said the Marshal, who was signing the letter to the Emperor. Suddenly Deteau uttered an exclamation and hurried forward. The horse, coming rapidly through the works of the tête-de-pont, had stumbled and thrown his rider. D'Albuquerque struck his head with violence against one of the heavy jagged timbers which covered the ground about the tête-de-pont and lay stunned and bleeding. The aide-de-camp, assisted by Pierre and two Poles, raised the wounded man and carried him into the hospital. His head was badly cut and several splinters of wood were sticking in the gashes.

"What a misfortune!" cried the Marshal, stamping his foot impatiently. "D'Albuquerque was to have gone to Paris. You cannot go; you must go to Madrid, you know the road. Marbot is not yet over his wound. This must go to Paris at once."

"Young Pasquin, are you strong enough to ride?" he asked suddenly, turning to Pierre.

"Yes, sir," said Pierre.

"Then you shall carry my letter to the Baron Lejeune whom I sent yesterday to Tudela; he will take it on to Paris. Deteau goes with you as far as Alagon, from there you will go over the road you have already come. Take d'Albuquerque's horse." He sat down and wrote a few lines on his tablet. "There," said he, "that will enable you to get relays at the post-houses. Lose no time. Give my letter safe to the Baron Lejeune and I answer for your promotion."

Pierre was trembling with excitement; his eyes were fixed on the Marshal; the Marshal was engaged in writing his order; had either of them looked at Deteau they would have seen him standing with folded arms, his brows knit in an angry scowl and his black eyes glittering wickedly as he looked at Pierre. "I will answer for that promotion," he muttered.

In a few moments they had mounted, and were riding rapidly through the camp and out into the level open country beyond. The road ran along the valley of the Ebro, and on every side was a vast undulating plain, dry and barren, enclosed in the distance by long chains of reddish hills. Here and there were scattered the ruins of a few miserable villages, whose inhabitants had fled to Saragossa at the commencement of the siege. Upon some of the heights stood the blackened ruins of ancient castles. The Ebro wound in great curves, sometimes near the road, sometimes far away, and in the distance could be faintly seen the white summits of the Pyrenees.

"Oh, Jean," said Pierre, as they rode rapidly along, "to think that I should carry a letter for the Marshal!"

"Yes," said Jean, "they will be glad to hear of it in Grenoble," and he began to whistle the "Partant pour la Syrie" of la reine Hortense which was so popular in the army.

" I had a letter from Henri Jodélle some days ago," he said after a time; " Marie was ill," and he watched Pierre narrowly.

Pierre grew pale. Jean saw that his hand trembled. " I am very sorry to hear it," he said.

" She is to be married before long," continued Jean.

" To whom? " cried Pierre.

" I do not know; some officer of dragoons, I think."

They rode on for a long time in silence. " Marie is to be married! " the words kept ringing in Pierre's ears louder than the clatter of the horses' hoofs upon the hard road. The honor of his mission, the hope of promotion, the eagerness for glory had all vanished from his mind.

It was fast growing dark, and in the distance could be seen the lights of Alagon.

" There is Alagon," said Jean, as they rode rapidly up a rising ground. " I leave you there; I go to Madrid and you go on to Tudela—with your letter for the Emperor! "

As he spoke, he drew his pistol suddenly from his holster and fired at Pierre. The rapid movement of the horses and the darkness rendered his aim somewhat unsteady, but the ball grazed Pierre's forehead. His horse sprang forward, he lost his seat, fell heavily to the ground, and lay there stunned and senseless. Jean reined in his horse, and riding back, dismounted, and stood for a moment looking at the prostrate form. Then he laughed quietly. " My fine fellow, I fancy the Café Jodélle will not see you soon again, and the Marshal will have one less promotion to make." He stooped, and cut the wallet, which contained the Marshal's letter; then springing on his horse he galloped forward in the darkness toward Alagon.

CHAPTER VI

Dolores La Zorillo

O woman! in our hours of ease
Uncertain, coy, and hard to please,
And variable as the shade
By the light quivering aspen made;
When pain and anguish wring the brow,
A ministering angel thou!

—Scott, *Marmion*.

Poor Dolores La Zorillo! Her thirteen years had not been happy ones. She had never known a mother, for the Francisca had died so soon after Dolores was born that she could not remember her. She lived in an old crumbling stone house in Alagon with her granddame Matesca and her father Rafael. The little house was only one story high, its floor was made of baked earth, and about its walls hung coarse pictures of the saints, strings of melons, crucifixes, and dried herbs. When Dolores was younger she had slept in a sack on the floor, but now she had a kind of bed of straw, with a quilt of which she was quite proud.

She saw little of the father Rafael, and it was better so, for when he did come home he quarreled always with the Matesca, and that was hard to bear. What a temper he had, the father Rafael, and how he did swear! And how cross he was if he did not get his mañana, or morning dram of aguardiente flavored with rosemary and a chew of garlic bulb, which could

4

be bought at the ventorillos or reed huts along the road.

Sometimes he would take too much, and perhaps when he came home the door would stick. How angry he was then! "Carajo!" he would cry, kicking the door, "you won't open, won't you! Dios mio (my God) qué poineterra! Santa Barbara bendita! (Blessed be Saint Barbara). Come down with all the saints in heaven and open this door!" And when, finally, by Saint Barbara's aid, the door flew open, he would cry, "Alavado sea Dios!" (God be praised.)

The Matesca was somewhat old to work, and so it was always "Dolores, light the fire; Dolores, fetch the water," for it was little indeed that the father Rafael would ever do. "I prefer to smoke and eat and sleep," said he. "Por mi eso es bastante (that is enough for me). Had I a stew with meat in it every day of my life, then should I be happy!"

So little Dolores would rise early, when the whistle of the sereno, or night-watchman, sounded to call the peasants to pannier their donkeys, and laden with fruit, be off to the nearest fruit market. And she would go to the small brick shelf with its two little holes, called hornillas, or cooking-stoves, and put in the charcoal and fan it into a flame by shaking to and fro a wisp in front of the outlet from the hornilla. Then she would mix together the oil, salt, red bird pepper, and water, and pour it into the brown jar half full of beans or potatoes to make the stew, for they were poor, pobre de solemnidad (solemnly poor) and could afford only the cheap stew called potaje, and not any of those finer stews that some of their neighbors had. The stew would go on simmering until it turned to a thick soup.

and then they would sit about and eat it out of the same dish, each dipping in with a wooden spoon. Thus there was always work for the little Dolores, and some mornings, when the Matesca had had a bad night or the father Rafael not enough to buy his mañana, there was the stick too.

So it was a hard life, and there was only one friend, and that was Beppo the donkey. When the stick had been laid on hard and the little back ached dreadfully, Dolores would run out to the dirty stable and throw her arms about Beppo's neck and say, " You love me, don't you, Beppo? " Beppo never answered; he stood meekly, as was his wont, occasionally wiggling his long ears. But Dolores knew what he meant without his answer.

She was a comely little girl, Dolores La Zorillo; her features were delicate, her small hands and feet beautifully shaped, and she wore her thick hair rolled up at the back in a square, spreading plait. And sometimes, when she went to the Plaza de Fruta, or Market Square, and saw the titerero, the comedian from the capital, her pensive, melancholy face would be brightened by a naïve smile.

She liked to go to the Plaza de Fruta, and would put on her tiny green shawl and short red gown and go there sometimes to dance the boléro, hoping to earn a few cuartos (farthings). And it often happened that a majo, or dandy, who passed by in his tight black jacket and trousers, crimson sash and plaited pigtail, saw her dancing, and said, " There is a pretty girl, dancing the boléro," and threw her a real.

It was a great place, that Plaza de Fruta. A wide-spreading stone quadrangle divided into portions for the tiendas, or shops of the venders of meats, dried fish and vegetables. In the meat stalls were pork, lamb, and goat's flesh cut into all manner of odds and ends for stewing in the savory olla. There were bacon and sausage in abundance, too, and in the grocers' stalls were lentils, garbanzos, haricot beans, rice, garlic, oil, dried figs, quinces, turnips, hard and stringy beet-root, the acelga or white vert, gourds, tomatoes, sage, mint and green parsley.

Though the Aragonese were mainly agriculturists, yet some of them were soldiers and smugglers, and all were guerrilleros par excellence. The men wore breeches of common cotton, ornamented about the pockets with filigree buttons and old medios reales in silver, blue woolen stockings and sandals, and short black waistcoats which showed the wide red cotton faja, or sash. Gay-colored cotton or silk handker-chiefs were tied about their heads, so that the two ends hung down behind, and above all was the sombrero.

The women had sandals, short flannel skirts, shawls of bright colors, and handkerchiefs tied about their heads. Dolores liked to watch them all, coming and going, stopping at the stalls and filling their baskets, chatting, laughing, and passing on. Some of them looked happy, she thought. She liked to see the wine-seller, with his heavy boots of untanned leather, thick woolen jacket and rusty brown trousers, who drove his mules laden with skins of rich red wine (vino tinto) or pale val de penas, which the peasants called " leche de los ancianos " (old folks' milk), and above all she liked to see the titerero, who came sometimes to play his tricks in the Plaza.

But all that was over now, for terrible times had

come, and the country was full of the dreadful soldiers of the "frances." The father Rafael had gone to join Castanos' army, and every peasant boy who was old enough to wear the faja, or sash, and the navaja, or clasp-knife, the signs of his manhood, had gone too.

Dolores could no longer go to the Plaza to dance the boléro, for the Plaza was full of the frances soldiers.

Then the priest at the Church of San Antonio de Padua taught Dolores her catechism.

" Child, what art thou? "

" A Spaniard, by the grace of God."

" Who is our enemy? "

" The Emperor of the French."

" What is the Emperor Napoleon? "

" A wicked being, the source of all evils and the focus of all vices."

" How many natures has he? "

" Two: the human and the diabolical."

" How many Emperors of the French are there? "

" One actually, in three deceiving persons."

" What are they called? "

" Napoleon, Murat, and Manuel Godoy."

" Which is the most wicked? "

" They are all equally so."

" What are the French? "

" Apostate Christians, turned heretics."

" What punishment does a Spaniard deserve who fails in his duty? "

" The death and infamy of a traitor."

" Is it a sin to kill a Frenchman? "

" No, my father; heaven is gained by killing one of these heretical dogs."

Dolores learned it all carefully, but she didn't understand it all. This much, however, she did know, that it was harder now to get enough for the potaje, that the Matesca was always in a tremor of terror or rage, that the stick struck more often, that there was only one friend and that was Beppo the donkey.

One evening the Matesca ordered Dolores to go early in the morning with Beppo and the cart to Casitas, not far away, and bring back a bag of beans which old Pédro, the Matesca's brother, had promised to send her. So early in the morning, just as the gray dawn appeared upon the hills, even before the time that the whistle of the sereno used to blow in past days, Dolores started, driving Beppo in the little creaking cart. They passed out of the town and on to the high-road beyond. "Come, hurry, Beppo," said Dolores. Beppo could not go very fast, for he had not had much to eat for many days, but he trotted along as best he could, and Dolores sat in the creaking cart.

"Why, Beppo! There is a man lying in the road," said Dolores, and, as they came nearer, she said, "He is a dead frances."

The soldier was lying on his back, his uniform splashed with mud, and his thick dark hair clustering about his white forehead. Dolores stopped the cart and looked at him. "He is nice-looking," she said. "I am rather sorry he is dead. Come, Beppo." But as Beppo started he struck his hoof against the foot of the prostrate soldier, and the man groaned and opened his eyes. "Why, you are not dead after all!" said Dolores. "You are a wicked frances though, and so I ought to wish you dead. But somehow I don't," she added.

"Qui êtes-vous, mademoiselle?" asked the soldier feebly.

"Yo sé ninguno frances" (I know no French), said Dolores, and so the conversation stopped.

"He is a nice-looking frances," said Dolores to herself. "What would the Matesca say if I should help a frances? Beppo, would you help a frances if he were nice-looking like this one?" But Beppo didn't answer; he stood meekly, as was his wont, occasionally wiggling his long ears.

"Jusqu'où est-il à Alagon?" said the soldier, raising himself a little with one arm.

Dolores could only understand the one word "Alagon." "You want to go to Alagon?" she asked, pointing to the town. The soldier nodded. "Well," said Dolores, "I will take you to Alagon." She jumped down from the little cart and helped the soldier clamber into it. Then she rolled up her small shawl and slipped it under his head. Beppo started and the cart creaked slowly on while Dolores walked by the side. "I don't know what the Matesca would do," she said to herself, "if she knew I helped a frances."

They came to the stone fountain which stood near the gate of the town, and Dolores filled the tin cup with water and brought it to the soldier, saying, "Toma, para echar un traguito" (here is something to drink). He took it and smiled. "He is nice-looking," said Dolores.

She drove Beppo on to the Plaza de Fruta, where a detachment of French troops were quartered. Dolores had seen the soldiers many times in the town, and as they did not chase her with their bayonets as she had supposed they would do, she had rather lost her fear of them. She waited until the soldier was removed from the cart and then she drove away.

Pierre lay on his straw and thought of his situation. He was anxious to get back to Saragossa and see the Marshal, but then how could he suppose that the Marshal would credit his story? He fancied himself telling it all and Lannes saying sternly, "Young Pasquin, do you expect me to believe that my aide-de-camp Deteau attempted to kill you? The thing is absurd!" Then he thought of what Deteau had said regarding Marie and wondered if it were true. Ah, those were three wretched days he passed at Alagon.

His wound was not serious and he was soon able to be about again, but he was stiff and lame from the fall from his horse and lying all night on the damp ground. He was preparing to go back to the Marshal and tell his story as best he could, when the roll of drums was heard in the direction of Saragossa. The captain commanding the detachment stationed at Alagon ordered out his men, and Pierre hurried in the direction of the sound. As he came to the end of the narrow street at the outskirts of the town, he saw in the doorway of a tumble-down stone house the little Spanish girl whom he remembered so well and whom he had been hoping to see again. Pierre went up to her and held out a small gilt crucifix; it was all he had to give her. "Merci, mademoiselle," he said. She could not understand him, but she took the cross and smiled.

Along the road, with drums rolling, bugles sounding, arms flashing, sabres clanking and plumed officers on prancing steeds, came the 115th of the Line and the 13th cuirassiers.

"We are ordered back to France!" cried the Major

as he passed the captain commanding the detachment stationed at Alagon.

" À la France! à la France!   Vive l'Empereur!" the soldiers of the 115th shouted joyfully.

The band of the regiment struck up "Le Chant du Départ," Pierre fell in in the rear line, and they marched on, the colors flying, the bayonets of the infantry and the helmets of the cuirassiers glittering in the sunshine.

Standing in the doorway of her crumbling home and holding in her hand the small gilt crucifix, little Dolores La Zorillo watched them as long as they were in sight, saying softly, "Adios, Señor Frances."

CHAPTER VII

Aux Tuileries

J'ai trouvé la couronne de France par terre, et je l'ai ramassée avec la pointe de mon épée. —*Napoléon.*

IT was half-past six in the morning when Constant Véry, premier valct-de-chambre to His Majesty, dressed in his green and gold coat, white silk stockings and black knee breeches, entered the bedroom of the Emperor. He crossed the room, opened the tightly closed shutters and let in the light. The walls of the apartment were hung with heavy Lyons brocade. The gilded ceiling was painted with figures of Mars, Jupiter and Apollo, while the armorial bearings and cipher of the Emperor decorated the cornice.

Opposite the windows, upon a platform covered with velvet, stood the bed. A few chairs upholstered with Gobelin tapestry and a large chiffonnier with brass ornaments constituted the only furniture. This room had been formerly the bedchamber of Louis XVI.

"Ah, Constant!" said the Emperor, sitting up in bed, "open the windows that I may breathe the good air which God has made."

As soon as the apartment was aired, Napoleon jumped out of bed, and still keeping on his head the bandana in which he had slept, threw his dressing-gown about him, thrust his feet into an old pair of red slippers and sat down before the fire, saying to

Constant, " Call Ménéval." The private secretary entered.

" Where are my letters? " said the Emperor.

Ménéval handed them to him and Napoleon himself broke the seals and went rapidly through their contents.

" Here, Ménéval," said the Emperor, " Garnier wants to paint my portrait. Well, I give him leave, but I have no time to give him sittings. He shall paint me in my cabinet and you shall be there writing from my dictation. What is this? Canova wants to make another statue of me. Never! I will go through no more of those tedious sittings. The municipality of Paris beg leave to give a ball at the Hotel de Ville. Yes, let them give it, let it be magnificent. Josephine shall go, but as for me, I have no time to dance."

" This from the King of Prussia," said the Emperor, taking up another letter, " informs me that I am his very dear brother. Oh, I know that already; I shall continue to be so as long as I am lucky. I know the Berlin cabinet. The Queen is sovereign there. Marshal Victor writes me that Prince Augustus of Prussia is behaving badly again. That does not surprise me. He is a man of no intelligence. He spent his time in making love to Madame de Staël at Coppet. He could gain only bad principles there. He shall be informed that the first time he says anything I will lock him up in a fortress and send Madame de Staël to comfort him. What is this? Here is a poor woman, the wife of a soldier who fell at Friedland, who tells me that she is perishing from want. Look you, Ménéval, she is to have a pension of a thousand francs. Date it back two years and see that the arrears are given to her at once. And as for these," said Napoleon, scattering the other letters over the carpet, "there is my answer. Come, Ménéval, bring your papers." And he rose hastily and went into his bathroom.

"Well, what is the news?" inquired the Emperor, getting into his tub and turning on the hot water.

Ménéval unfolding his papers began with the "Moniteur." "His Imperial and Royal Majesty," read the secretary, "returned yesterday from Spain, where the glories of his arms have——"

"Bah!" said the Emperor. "Pass over all that. I know it already. They say only what they think will please me. Read the English papers. I am well cut up there, I warrant you."

"I do not find anything, Your Majesty."

"Nothing!" said the Emperor. "Well, there will be plenty to-morrow, then. It is an intermittent fever, but look carefully, Ménéval. Look for the 'Corsican Ogre' or 'Bonaparte the Usurper,' you will find something. Perhaps now I have shot Lannes in Spain as I shot Desaix at Marengo. Surely now I have poisoned some one or beaten Josephine. Look carefully, Ménéval."

"Here, sire," said Ménéval, "is a short article headed, 'Buonaparte and His Secretary.' 'The other evening Buonaparte was seated in his cabinet and had called in a young secretary named Ménéval in whom he had confidence. He told him to hold a light while he read. The secretary put the light so close to Buonaparte's head that it caught fire, and Buonaparte, thinking that an attack was being made on his life, seized a pistol which he always carries about him and fired point-blank at his secretary, killing him instantly. Buonaparte showed no remorse for the deed.'"

"Well, Ménéval," said the Emperor, "that is a fine obituary notice for you."

"'It is further reported,'" continued the secretary, "'that a few days ago Buonaparte got in a furious passion with Maret, his Secretary of State, rushed at him, knocked him down and dragged him about by the hair of his head, kicking him shamefully. Then he tried to hush the matter up by dictating to him a decree giving him a large forest estate. Such is Buonaparte.'"

"La vérité seule blesse," said the Emperor, laughing and again turning on the hot water.

The room was now so full of steam that Ménéval rose and opened the door.

"When are you going to be married, Ménéval?" inquired the Emperor, as he left the bath.

"I do not know, sire."

"Well, let it be soon, I will provide for you."

Napoleon slipped on a flannel waistcoat and dressing-gown of white dimity and tied his handkerchief around his head. Constant handed him a cup of orange-flower water on a gilt salver from his great traveling case, and the Emperor, sitting down by the fire, dictated two letters to Ménéval. Meanwhile the valets had prepared the dressing-room.

"Who are in the salon?" asked Napoleon as he finished.

"M. de Rémusat, M. Corvisart and MM. Fontaine and Barbier, sire," replied Constant.

"Admit them," said the Emperor, passing into his dressing room. There he found the Mameluke Roustan, who, dressed in his picturesque Oriental costume with his crimson and gold turban, was holding the shaving-mirror. Constant presented the basin and soap.

" Well, big quack," cried the Emperor as Corvisart entered, " how many people have you killed to-day? "

" As Your Majesty is my first patient," answered the physician, " I have killed none so far."

The Emperor laughed and covered one side of his face with the lather, splashing it all about him. He picked up his razor, the pearl handle of which was inlaid with gold, and shaved the side of his face rapidly from the top downward.

" Fontaine," said he, addressing the architect, " how is the Colonne Vendôme progressing? "

" Rapidly, sire, your statue is nearly ready to be raised to the top."

" If I had my way," said the Emperor, lathering the other side of his face, " that part would be left to posterity. The statues of a man put up in his lifetime are likely to be pulled down. Am I well shaved, Constant? "

" Yes, sire."

" Ah, you rogue," said the Emperor, pulling his ear, " there are still some hairs on the chin. Why do you say I am well shaved? " He quickly removed them and plunged his head into the great basin of his silver washing-stand.

" And what are you doing with the Arc de Triomphe on the Carrousel? " continued the Emperor, picking up a little pair of scissors and trimming his nails carefully. His hands were beautiful, and he took great care of them.

" It is nearly finished, sire," said M. Fontaine.

" Triumphal arches," said Napoleon, " would be

futile works and productive of no effect whatever and I should not have ordered them had I not thought that this was a means of encouraging architecture. I wish to stimulate sculpture in France by means of these triumphal arches for ten years. The Minister of the Interior is to erect another at the Étoile. One must be the Arch of Marengo and the other the Arch of Austerlitz. I shall have another built in some other part of Paris which will be the Arch of Peace and another the Arch of Religion."

The Emperor's scissors did not cut well and he threw them into the fire. Then he took off his flannel waistcoat while Constant poured eau de cologne upon his head and shoulders and two valets scrubbed him with stiff brushes. "Come, harder, harder," cried the Emperor, "brush as though you were rubbing an ass!"

He rapidly put on his flannels, his white silk stockings and his white kerseymere breeches.

"Barbier," said he to the librarian, "I have drawn up a scheme for a portable library to carry with me on campaign. There are many works on history, literature and science which do not exist in 12mo and 18mo editions. I mean to have such translated and reprinted and carry with me in boxes with compartments. Have you examined carefully the data I sent you from Marrac?"

"Yes, sire," replied Barbier.

At this moment Duroc, Grand Marshal of the Palace, entered unannounced, for he had the entrée at all hours.

"Monsieur le Maréchal," said the Emperor, "I want to go over the budget for the Imperial household with you this morning. Bring it to my cabinet. We must retrench on 1808. Three million five hundred thousand francs are too much. There is waste somewhere. How many pounds of sugar are consumed weekly by my household? "

" I do not know, sire."

" Well, you ought to know. I must know this morning. Three millions are all I shall allow for 1809. I am determined to save that five hundred thousand francs."

The Emperor had buckled on his sword-belt and put on his white kerseymere waistcoat, and was now putting on his green coat of the chasseurs à cheval of the Guard with its red collar and cuffs.

" Rémusat," said Napoleon, addressing the Grand Master of the Wardrobe, " what do I pay for my coats? "

" Two hundred and forty francs, Your Majesty."

" That is too much," said the Emperor, " that tailor Chevalier is continually raising his prices. He thinks no doubt that you are the officer of some great lord. Why should I pay more than others? Moreover," he added, " it is most unseemly that tradesmen should present their bills to me. Not long ago at St. Cloud, when I was in my calèche with the Empress at my side and in the midst of an immense concourse of people, I found myself called upon all of a sudden in the Eastern fashion, as if I had been the Sultan going to Mosque, by a man who had worked for my person and claimed a considerable sum, the payment of which had been long refused him. In future I will have nothing more to do with my wardrobe. Take care, M. de Rémusat, that you allow no debts to accumulate."

At a few minutes before nine the Chamberlain of the day, in his scarlet coat embroidered in silver, his white waistcoat and knee breeches, knocked at the door to announce the *lever*. The Emperor, who never carried watch or money, took from the hands of Constant his handkerchief, his eye-glass, his bonbonnier, his snuff-box, and finally his famous *petit chapeau*, and at nine o'clock precisely the doors were thrown open, the usher on duty announced " The Emperor," and he entered the salon where were assembled the great officers of the Crown and the officers of the household on duty. In front stood M. de Talleyrand, Grand Chamberlain, in his scarlet coat embroidered in silver; then M. de Ségur, Grand Master of Ceremonies, in violet; the Grand Huntsman and Lieutenant of the Hunt in green; M. Bausset, Prefect of the Palace, in purple; the Equerry in blue; Cardinal Fesch, Grand Almoner, in his ecclesiastical cassock; Daru, Intendant General, the Crown Treasurer, and M. Pasquier, Prefect of Police. The *lever* was short and formal. The Emperor passed about the circle, giving briefly to each one his orders. He said nothing to M. de Talleyrand. As he came to the Prefect of Police he inquired:

" How many bags of wheat are there now in the grain market? "

" About 20,000, sire," replied M. Pasquier.

" You ought to know exactly, sir," said the Emperor, who demanded exact answers. In future M. Pasquier, whose memory was somewhat defective, carried a note-book.

In a few moments the *lever* was ended, and by a slight bow the Emperor dismissed them, and then the Chamberlain of the day announced the Grandes Entrées. The persons who were entitled to this privi-

5

lege—the great officers of the Empire, the presidents
of the various bodies of State, the chief authorities of
Paris—had meanwhile alighted from their carriages at
the Pavillon de Flore, and entering the Palace, assembled in the salon de service. The Arch-Chancellor
Cambacères; Lebrun, Arch-Treasurer; Talleyrand,
Grand Chamberlain and Vice-Grand Elector; Regnier,
Minister of Justice; Clarke, Minister of War; Décres,
Minister of Naval Affairs; Gaudin, Minister of Finance; Mollien, Minister of the Public Treasury, senators, marshals, generals, the Princes of the Rhine Confederation, the Grand Duke of Baden, Prince William
of Prussia, the Prince of Mecklenburg-Strelitz, the
Archbishop of Regensburg, the Prince of Mecklenburg-Schwerin—all were waiting for the moment
which should admit them to the master.

The Grandes Entrées being summoned, the Chamberlain of the day admitted into the salon of the Emperor
all this glittering crowd in the order of their rank.
The Emperor, passing about the circle, spoke to everybody, questioned them, interrogated them, and talking
only business—administration, politics, war, the army,
finance—demanded exact answers to his precise and
minute inquiries. The generals returned from distant
missions were assailed with a volley of questions and
the Emperor soon gained the information he desired.
In half an hour the *lever* was ended and the throng
of dignitaries retired, but the Emperor retained the
Ministers of Marine and Finance, to whom he gave a
private audience in the same apartment, standing, as
was his wont, before the fireplace and occasionally
kicking the andirons with his heels.

At ten this audience was finished; the Emperor dismissed them by a bow and ordered his déjeuner. Dunan, Maitre d'Hôtel, assisted by his valets, brought in the small mahogany table upon which were placed the dishes with silver covers. His Majesty seated himself and ate rapidly, for with him breakfast was an affair of ten minutes. As he finished his coffee, the Prefect of the Palace approached.

"Sire," said he, "there is a dispatch from Spain."

"Admit him," replied the Emperor.

The door was opened, and the Baron Lejeune entered.

"From the Marshal Lannes?" inquired the Emperor, taking the letter.

"Yes, sire."

Napoleon tore the envelope with his finger. "You have been long on the way, sir," he said suddenly, looking up at Lejeune. "The surrender was on the 21st."

"Your Majesty, the Marshal's first dispatch to me at Tudela was intercepted," said the Baron. "I did not receive this until I had returned to Saragossa."

"To whom was the first dispatch entrusted?" inquired the Emperor.

"To a recruit by the name of Pasquin, I believe," answered Lejeune.

"A recruit!" said Napoleon in surprise, "were there no orderly officers?"

"I do not know, sire."

His Majesty made a sign that the interview was ended, and pushing his chair back quickly from the table, he rose and retired to his study. In his all-retentive memory the word *Pasquin* had become synonymous with *failure*.

CHAPTER VIII

THE IMPERIAL MAN OF BUSINESS

Now, by St. Paul, the work goes bravely on.
—CIBBER, *Richard III.*

How various his employments.
—COWPER, *The Task.*

THE Emperor's study was a room of no great dimensions and lighted by only one window, which looked out upon the Tuileries garden. Around the walls were high bookcases filled with volumes in plain bindings, each carefully catalogued, and stamped " Cabinet de l'Empereur." On one side between the cases stood a great regulator clock, and, opposite the fireplace, a long closet with glass doors which contained boxes for holding papers, and upon which was placed the only work of art the Emperor ever desired personally to have—a bronze equestrian statue of the great Frédéric, the sovereign whom he most admired, and whom he called the " great tactician." The paintings on the walls and ceiling remained as in the days of Louis XIV, and upon the dark canvases, almost black with age, might be seen Maria Theresa under the guise of Minerva.

In the centre of the room was a magnificent writing-desk covered with gilt bronze, and an arm-chair of antique shape, but the Emperor rarely used them except to give his signature. His habitual seat was on a small green-covered sofa near the fireplace, protected from the fire by a screen, and having near it a little table on which his letters were placed. One door of the apartment opened into a small back study, decorated, like the other, with paintings of the Louis XIV period, and here the Emperor sometimes gave audience to his ministers, for he rarely received people in his study, and strangers never.

Adjoining was the topographic cabinet, with its great tables and innumerable pigeon-holes in which were arranged in perfect order the maps—maps of the world, of Europe, of all parts of Europe, maps in detail and maps in relief—mounted on strong, thick linen and enclosed in cardboard cases covered with sheepskin. The chief of this department was the Baron Bacler d'Albe, who, assisted by two geometrical engineers, was constantly employed in Paris and on campaign in registering on the maps by means of colored pins the movements of the various army corps following the victorious eagles.

There was no luxury in these rooms; that was reserved for the State apartments. Here all was for work, and the necessary tools—maps, books, secretaries and engineers—were at the hand of the master.

When the Emperor entered he found M. de Méneval already at his desk in the recess of the window. The Emperor threw his hat and sword on a chair and sat down on the sofa by the fireplace, where for a few moments he ran over the letters placed on the small table. Then rising he said, " Let us begin, Méneval," and walking slowly to and fro across the room, sometimes twisting his right arm or pulling the cuff of his coat, he began his dictation.

First, a letter to the King of Bavaria, in which he informed him that he was about to assemble 150,000 French and Italians on the Po, 150,000 French on the Upper Danube, and that he counted on 100,000 Germans; to prevent war if there was yet time; to secure the prosperous issue of it should a conflict take place. Another, in the same general terms, to the King of Saxony, another to the King of Wurtemburg, another to the King of Westphalia, another to the Duke of Baden. He ordered them all to prepare themselves and demanded the assemblage of their troops around Munich, Dresden and Warsaw.

Then, to the King of Prussia, whom he informed that if he levied a single man beyond the 42,000 authorized by the Treaty of Tilsit, he would declare war against him; then to Murat, King of Naples, whom he ordered to distribute his army in two divisions, one between Naples and Reggio, the other between Naples and Rome; then to the Emperor Alexander, whom he informed of his return from Spain, of the armaments of Austria, and whom he called upon to fulfil the terms of agreement made at Erfurt; then to General Lauriston, whom he ordered to add 48 pieces of artillery to the Guard and to purchase 1800 horses in Alsace; then to Fouché, Minister of Police, whom he commanded to make a census of the old noble families living on their estates, enrol their sons and send them to the military school. " If they complain," he added " say that such is my good pleasure."

The Emperor continued to walk during his dictation, and as he became more interested he walked faster, while Méneval's pen ran rapidly over the paper.

" To the Marshal Lannes," said he abruptly, picking up Lannes' letter from the small table.

" Monsieur le Maréchal:—

" I have received your letter by the Baron Lejeune. The Minister of War will send you my instructions regarding the troops to be kept in Saragossa. It would have been of great advantage to me to have learned of the surrender sooner. In future send me no more recruits. Your Pasquin was a pasquin indeed. I am about to wage war with Austria. Come to Paris at once."

Then the Emperor sat down on his sofa and began to read the papers in the portfolio of the Minister of Justice. All the Ministers were required to send their portfolios to him; he read their papers, and wrote his answers on the margins. Ménéval, meanwhile, was busy writing out clean copies of the letters upon the thick, plain Imperial letter-paper and preparing them for the Emperor's signature.

After a time, the Grand Marshal entered, bringing the budget of the Imperial household for the ensuing year. The Emperor took it and began going over the items.

" Coffee costs me a great deal," said he, " let us see, there are 155 cups of coffee consumed daily, each cup costs 20 sous, coffee is 5 francs a pound and sugar 4 francs," and taking up a pen he began figuring on the margin. " That amounts yearly to more than 56,000 francs. We will have no more coffee in kind. I will give a money allowance. I shall save 30,000 francs." The Emperor went on over the other items, cutting here and retrenching there until Duroc declared that the Imperial household could not be maintained upon its present footing with so little. The Emperor laughed and pulled his ear, saying, " We shall see. Three million francs must do for 1809."

The Master of the Horse requested an audience and the Emperor went into the back cabinet to receive him. It was all about a certain coachman, Bonnat by name, who, having been twice discharged for drunkenness and taken back, had committed the offense a third time. " Yes," said the Emperor, " Bonnat is not worth much. However," he added, for he was slow to remove those who had been with him in the early days, " let him remain. He drove an ammunition-wagon at Marengo," and he went back to his study.

Méneval had prepared the letters for his signature, and the Emperor, sitting at his writing-desk, signed them rapidly; those to sovereigns in full, Napoleon; the others simply N. or Nap. It was half-past one. " It is time to go to the Council," said the Emperor, taking a pinch of snuff. Duroc handed him his hat and sword, and he went out into the salon, where he found the chamberlain of the day and the aide-de-camp on duty. Followed by them, he crossed the Hall of the Guards, and the Salle de Maréchaux, went down the grand staircase and up another which led to the Council Hall. The drums rolled, as he came up the staircase, and gave notice of his approach.

The Hall of the Council of State was very large. Its windows looked out upon the courtyard of the Palace, and on its ceiling was Gérard's famous picture of the battle of Austerlitz. At one end of the hall, on a dais, were three writing-tables; the Emperor's in the centre, the Arch-Chancellor's on the right, the Arch-Treasurer's on the left. By the windows were the tables of the Councillors of State and of the auditors, while at the other end of the apartment were the desks of the Masters of Requests.

Here were the men with whom the Emperor had worked upon the Civil Code, the Code of Procedure, the Code of Commerce, the Penal Code, the Code of Criminal Administration—the famous Tronchet, Portalis, Merlin, Ségur, Réal, d'Hauterive and Fourcroy; also the directors-general Duchâtel, Français, Bérenger, Pélet, Bérgon and Laumond. At the Council of State the former sous-lieutenant of La Fere, in spite of his strictly military education, displayed a legal erudition which astonished his hearers. He was prouder of the Code Napoléon than of Austerlitz or Jena, for, said he, " I shall go down to posterity with the Code in my hand."

The Council, which met at half-past twelve, had already been in session an hour when the Emperor entered. He sat down at his writing-desk and consulted the printed order of the day, which was placed there, and then, calling up a subject which interested him, invited discussion. He liked a free and general discussion and provoked young auditors to contradiction to make it so. At the Council he seemed to make good his statement, " I do not feel any limit to my power for work," and he kept everyone else up to the same pressure.

M. Fourcroy rose to report on the affairs of Holland; his report was long, and, as he read, the Emperor occasionally looked at him through his eye-glass, then he cut grooves in the arm of his chair or wrote mechanically upon a scrap of paper, " Mon Dieu, que je vous aime," seven or eight times over, and took large pinches of snuff, which he scattered on the floor about him. When the report was finished, he called for discussion, took part in it himself, and, with his analytical penetration, summed up clearly complicated questions.

The hours flew by, it was eight in the evening, and still the Council sat. The Emperor's dinner-hour was six, but he had forgotten all about it, and no one dared to remind him, for nothing interfered with the Council of State.

Since six o'clock, the Empress Josephine, dressed with that taste she knew so well how to display, to which she had accustomed the Emperor and which made him very critical of other women's toilets, had been waiting in her apartment. She always dined alone with the Emperor and was always ready, but she often had to wait. It did not make much difference to her, however, for she ate little, and was never annoyed if she dined at eight or at ten; but it was a source of great anxiety to the Prefect of the Palace and the maitre d'hôtel, who had to renew the boiling water in the dish-warmers and have a fresh fowl put on the spit every quarter of an hour. In spite of all their precautions the dishes generally suffered, but the Emperor never noticed it. Finally, at half-past eight, Napoleon dismissed the Council and entered the apartments of the Empress.

There was no dining-room at the Tuileries, and the Emperor dined one evening in the Empress's apartments and another in his own. Everything except the dessert was served at once, and the Emperor, sitting down to table abstractedly, ate the first dish that came to hand. He chatted with the Empress, admired her toilet, and then asked for M. Barbier, who had been summoned to read him the translation of a German paper.

The Prefect of the Palace approached. "Sire," said he, "there is a dispatch from Spain."

"Admit him," cried the Emperor, laying down his fork.

The orderly officer, booted, and splashed with mud from his hurried journey, entered and presented his dispatch. To these dispatch-bearers all doors flew open; they were received at all hours. "It is from Ney," said the Emperor to Josephine, "he is in pursuit of the English."

He rose from table. The dinner had lasted fifteen minutes, and, giving his hand to the Empress, Napoleon conducted her to his salon. There he took his coffee, which Josephine herself sweetened, or he would have forgotten it.

"Sire, you will come to-night to the ball at the Minister of Marine's?" said the Empress.

"Yes, I will come," said Napoleon, "but ten o'clock will be time enough. I am going to work at nine with the Minister of Finance."

He went back to his study, and at nine precisely, M. Gaudin was announced. He found the Emperor lying at full length on the floor upon an immense map of central Europe, in which he was sticking colored pins; near him was the Baron d'Albe. "There," said Napoleon, "I shall concentrate near Donauwerth, I shall beat them at Abensburg, or Ratisbon, and there lies the road to Vienna," and he pointed to the right bank of the Danube. "However, my good Gaudin," he added, "for all this we must have money, so let us get to work."

He seated himself on the sofa, d'Albe rolled up the map, and the Minister produced his papers.

"What is the amount of the budget for 1809?" inquired the Emperor.

"730 millions for general expenses and 40 millions for departmental; a total of 890 millions with the costs of collection," replied the Minister.

"In 1807 and 1808 the troops beyond the Rhine were paid from the army treasury," said the Emperor. "We must do the same in 1809."

"All the expenses of the army in Germany were paid down to the 31st of last December," said M. Gaudin, "and there should be in the army treasury about 300 millions; 20 millions from the war in Austria and 280 millions from the war in Prussia."

"But only forty millions of that will be available, and I have reduced Prussia's contribution 20 millions at the request of the Emperor Alexander," said Napoleon.

"The budget for 1809," remarked M. Gaudin, "has quite enough to do to pay the armies in Spain and Italy."

"True," said the Emperor, "there must not be a deficit in the budget, and it will take 77 millions to pay the troops in Germany for the year. Let us see where to get them." And the Emperor and his Minister began figuring.

Time passed and as the clock struck twelve there was a knock at the door. "Who is there?" called the Emperor. It was a page from the Empress. The ball was magnificent and all were impatiently awaiting the Emperor's arrival. "All in good time," cried Napoleon, "tell the Empress I am at work with the Minister of Finance. We are coming."

They continued their work, and an hour later there

was another knock at the door. It was again a page from the Empress. " We are coming," cried the Emperor, continuing his writing.

" What time is that, Gaudin? " he inquired finally as the clock struck.

" Three o'clock, sire."

" Ah, mon Dieu! it is too late for us to go to the ball; what do you think about it? "

" That is quite my view, sire."

" Then let us each go to bed," said the Emperor. " Well," he added, as M. Gaudin took his hat to depart, " many people think that we pass our lives in amusing ourselves, and, as the Orientals say, eating sweetmeats. Good night, Monsieur le Ministre."

CHAPTER IX

THE WIDOW PASQUIN

Smit with exceeding sorrow unto death.
—TENNYSON, *The Lover's Tale*.

IT was the third of March, and Henri Jodélle stood in his room reading a letter. He read it carefully, and his face grew grave as he did so. "I am sorry for the young Pasquin," said Henri. "He was not a bad fellow, and I rather liked the boy's pluck when he went off to the war. Now Deteau writes me that he has been killed at Saragossa. So *tout est fini*."

The garçon Gaspard put his head in at the door. "Père Henri," said he, "it is four o'clock. You wanted to go to the Trois Dauphins, didn't you?"

"Yes," answered Henri, taking up his cloak and hat. He went down into the café and out into the Place Grénette.

"Ah, good day, Henri," said old Frédéric Bonneville. "Have you any news from Spain?"

"Yes. Jean Deteau, the aide-de-camp to Marshal Lannes, you know, has written me a letter. Saragossa has surrendered, but a nasty fight those Spanish devils made of it. Sixty days they kept us at it. The Emperor should have been there. Things would have come to an end quickly then."

"Ajax is a good soldier," said old Bonneville.

"Of course he is," answered Henri, "but it takes

the Little Corporal to hurry matters. Look how
quickly he brought Madrid to terms. Ah, if I had
the two good legs I had once, I would go again
and have a hand at it myself. Where are you going,
Frédéric?"

"To the Café Jodélle."

"Well, go, and wait for me there. Gaspard will
give you a glass of wine. I am going to the Trois
Dauphins, but I'll be back at five o'clock. Adieu,
Frédéric."

Henri went on his way and entered the Rue Montorge. "I'll say nothing about the young Pasquin to
Marie to-day," he said to himself. "To-morrow will
be time enough. Now there is Widow Pasquin's
épicerie. I fancy she ought to know, so I will stop
and tell her."

He crossed the street and entered the shop. There
was no one in it, and Henri passed to the rear and
knocked at the door of the room in which Jeanne
Pasquin lived.

"Come in," said the Widow, and he entered.

The Widow Pasquin was sitting in her high-backed
chair before the little fireplace. The firelight played
over her white cap, heavy dark dress and curious
wooden shoes, and brought out more clearly the
wrinkles and lines of her sad face.

"Bon jour, mère Pasquin," said Henri. "I found
no one in your shop and so I knocked at your door."

"Come in, Henri Jodélle, and sit down by the fire,"
said the Widow. And when he had done so she asked,
"What can I do for you?"

Henri seemed a little embarrassed. "Well, mère
Pasquin," he said, "what news do you have from your
son Pierre?"

There was something in his tone which made the Widow grow pale and she looked at him nervously. " I heard from him at Saragossa," she answered. " He had been wounded, but was getting well fast. Tell me, père Henri, have you any news? "

Henri, with a soldier's bluntness, pulled Deteau's letter out of his pocket and handed it to her. She took it with trembling hands and read it hurriedly by the firelight. Then with a low cry, " Ah, mon Dieu! " she sank forward in her chair and buried her face in her hands.

The tears streamed from her eyes. " He is dead! " she cried. " My brave Pierre! my only boy! My God! My God! what will become of me! " And her wasted, trembling body shook with her sobs.

" This will never do," muttered Henri nervously, " I must cheer her up a bit." " Le diable! good mère Pasquin," he cried bluntly, " you son has had a gallant death. Why, if I had twenty sons I'd send them all to battle *pour la patrie!* Where can a brave man die better than on the field of honor under the banners of our glorious Emperor? "

" Stop, Henri Jodélle, stop! " cried the Widow, raising her feeble hand. " You little know, you hard, rough man, the grief that fills a mother's heart when she has lost her only boy! As for that man, that Napoleon whom you style ' glorious Emperor,' speak no more of him! Have I not given him my all; my Amand, my Robert, my Pierre! Go, Henri Jodélle, and torture me no more! "

Henri's face was a study as he walked along the Rue Montorge toward the Hotel des Trois Dauphins. " I didn't think she would take on like that," he said.

" When one's son goes to war one should be prepared to have him killed, and, after all, *quelle différence* if he but die gloriously on the field of honor."

In her little room the Widow Pasquin sat sobbing and moaning. The shades of evening came gradually on, and then darkness, and only the faint light of the fire illumined the sombre gloom of the room. The sobs became softer and finally ceased. It was night, and still the Widow Pasquin sat motionless in her high-backed chair. The light of the fire died away, and nothing remained but the dull gleam of the red embers; gradually that died too, and all was darkness. Then, on the lofty summits of the surrounding mountains, appeared the first rays of the morning, faintly at first, then brighter and brighter, and, at last, the sun rose, bringing light and life and joy; a new day had begun.

The bright rays shone into the little room, filling it with a blaze of light and glory, but the Widow Pasquin moved not; she still sat in her high-backed chair. The *homme du peuple* started to his daily toil, the *portière* took her broom and swept the doorways, the wretched *chiffonniers* went with their baskets in search of garbage, the pale-faced *soeur de charité*, with her white cap and cross and beads, began her errands of mercy, the *bouquétiere* arranged her flowers on the sidewalk, the torn and tattered *mendiants* tramped about looking for a few sous, the *marchand de coco*, with his long can strapped on his back, his tin cups and curious round hat, began to vend his wares, the *porteur d'eau* carried his water-pails hung over his shoulder, the *patissier* arranged his cakes for the boys going to school, the *facteur de la poste* delivered his letters, the *modiste* dusted the articles in her pretty shop, the gendarmes brought their prisoners before the *commissaire de police*, the *doulairière* commenced to tell her fortunes, the *maitresse de maison* sipped her coffee, the white-headed *jardinier de cimetière* raked his gravel walks, the *commissionnaires* ran about on people's errands, at the Trois Dauphins the *conducteur de diligence* waited for his horses to be put in. The life of the town had begun, and still the Widow Pasquin sat motionless in her high-backed chair.

Was she asleep, forgetting that she, too, must be about and doing? Ah, no! That in the chair was no longer Widow Pasquin: she had gone to join her Robert and père Amand.

When Henri came down into the room where he and his daughter took breakfast, he found Marie crying bitterly. Now, how can she have learned anything of this? thought Henri. "Do not cry, Marie," he said, "the young Pasquin was a plucky fellow and I am sorry that he is dead, but——"

"Why, father, he is not dead!" exclaimed Marie.

"What!" cried Henri. "Why, only yesterday I had a letter from Jean Deteau telling me so."

"And I have had a letter from Pierre this morning," answered Marie. "But, oh, father! dreadful things have happened! Jean tried to kill Pierre, and also told him that I was to marry an officer of dragoons. Ah, père Henri!" And Marie's eyes were full of tears.

Henri looked strangely puzzled. "Give me the letter," he said. He read it slowly, his eyes growing larger and larger and his face redder and redder as he did so. "Le grand diable!" he roared as he finished, striking his thigh with his hand. Then, seizing his hat, he hurried from the room, leaving Marie sad and bewildered.

Henri hastened along toward the Rue Montorge and his crutch thumped vigorously on the cobblestones. "The père Henri is in a great hurry this morning," said dame Bovard to her husband as he passed their door.

The shop of the Widow Pasquin was quiet, and Henri, passing through it, knocked at the door of her room. There was no response. He tried the door, it opened and he entered. Why, there she was before the fireplace! "Cheer up, mère Pasquin," he cried gaily, "your son——." And then he stopped and came slowly forward, looking at the pale face and closed eyes. He lifted one of the thin hands, put down his head and held his ear against the heart some minutes. Then he went softly out and closed the door.

As he came through the shop the *facteur de la poste* entered. "Here is a letter for the Widow Pasquin," he said.

"Good André," answered Henri slowly, "the Widow Pasquin will receive no more letters. She is dead."

"Well, that's a pity," answered André. "She's been looking badly for a good while, I've been thinking." And he hurried on.

Henri took up the letter and then drew from his pocket Pierre's letter to Marie and compared them. The handwriting was the same. He went back and quietly placed the letter in the mère Pasquin's hand, and as he came out and locked the door, there were tears in the eyes of stern old Henri Jodélle.

" Marie," said he, when he reached the café, " the mère Pasquin died last night. You must write to the young Pierre. Tell him I will attend to the funeral, and tell him—in the same letter, mind you—that if he proves himself a brave soldier and comes home safe and sound, he shall marry you. Tell him Henri Jodélle says that, and Henri Jodélle always keeps his word! "

" I owe that much to *la veuve* Pasquin," he muttered.

When he was alone he took Jean Deteau's letter from his pocket, tore it into small fragments and threw it into the fireplace, saying fiercely, " le grand diable! "

In the cemetery of Grenoble there stands a small gravestone, placed there by Henri Jodélle, and bearing this inscription:

La Veuve Pasquin,
Née à Vizille le 13 Avril 1758.
Morte à Grenoble le 3 Mars 1809.

CHAPTER X

The Night before Eckmühl

Tout soldat français porte dans sa giberne le bâton de
Maréchal de France.—Napoléon.

GREAT events were in progress, for it was now evident
that war with Austria was imminent, and this time
they were to fight on the battlegrounds of Europe
under the eyes of the Emperor himself.

Leaving Alagon, the 115th of the Line had marched
to Bayonne, and then northeast across France,
through Mont de Marsan, Cahors, Aurillac and St.
Etienne, to Lyons. This city, situated at the conflu-
ence of the Saône and the Rhone, is, by reason of its
industry and commerce, next to Paris in municipal
importance. Here the 115th went into quarters, and
they were kept constantly at work. It was drill, drill,
drill, from morning till night, in the Place Bellecour.
The Boudet and Molitor divisions were there, too, and
Pierre began to know some of those old soldiers who
had followed the victorious French eagles on so many
battlefields. At that time a division of the corps
d'armée consisted of four regiments of infantry of the
Line (forming two brigades), one regiment of light infantry and one regiment of chasseurs (forming the
vanguard), four regiments of cavalry, chasseurs and
cuirassiers, two companies of light artillery, eight
pieces of heavy artillery, twelve-pounders and eight-

inch howitzers, a park of reserve with the necessary ammunition for heavy and light artillery, and cartridges for infantry and cavalry. Then, too, there were butchers, bakers, sutlers and all the baggage-train.

What tremendous enthusiasm there was among the old soldiers of the Boudet and Molitor divisions! The 115th of the Line, who had been merged into the Boudet division, quickly caught the spirit and longed only for the day when the order should come to march. Finally the order came, and, on a bright March morning, the Boudet and Molitor divisions left Lyons and took the road to Strassburg.

The various Marshals of the Empire were not all at the Emperor's service for the present campaign. Ney, Soult, Victor, and Mortier were carrying on the war in Spain; Murat, recovering from his indisposition, caused mainly by his disappointment at being declared King of Naples instead of King of Spain, was not available. But the Emperor had three whom he valued most highly; Davout, Massena, and the brave Lannes, whom he had summoned after the fall of Saragossa. To each of these he had assigned fifty thousand men.

Davout, with the Morand, Friant and Gudin divisions and the splendid St. Sulpice cuirassiers, was stationed between Bayreuth and Ratisbon. Massena, with the Carra St. Cyr, Legrand, Boudet and Molitor divisions, light cavalry, Hessians and Badens, was to have his rendezvous at Ulm. The St. Hilaire division, the three divisions of General Oudinot and the cuirassiers of General Espagne were at Augsburg, awaiting Marshal Lannes, who had not yet arrived. At Munich, Landshut and Straubing were the Bavarians, Würtembergers and Saxons under Marshals Lefebvre, Augereau and Prince Bernadotte.   In reserve were the cavalry—dragoons, carabineers and cuirassiers of General Nansouty—and the Imperial Guard, twenty thousand strong, commanded by Marshal Bessières.   Prince Berthier was Major-General, M. Daru, Commissary-General, and over all was the Commander-in-Chief, the Emperor Napoleon, delaying in Paris until the last moment that he might better transmit his orders to his armies in Spain and Italy, keeping his eyes constantly fixed on the semaphore telegraph, and ready—at the first movement of the great Austrian army, 200,000 strong, commanded by the generalissimo, the Archduke Charles—to throw himself into his traveling carriage and take the field.

The Boudet and Molitor divisions had not proceeded far from Lyons when they received orders to turn toward Belfort and take the shortest road through the Black Forest to Ulm.   From Ulm they were hastened on to Augsburg, where Massena took command.

On the 10th of April, the Austrians crossed the Inn. The news was known in Paris on the evening of the 12th, and the same night Napoleon entered his carriage, and, driving furiously across France, reached Strassburg on the 15th, and Donauwerth on the 17th, outstripping his staff, aides-de-camp, and saddle-horses, and none too soon to repair the blunders of Prince Berthier, Major-General.   In four days from the time of the Emperor's arrival at Donauwerth the military situation underwent a remarkable change.   On the 17th the French forces were widely scattered, and the united Austrian army was advancing between them. By the 21st the French had united, repulsed the Austrian right, routed the Austrian centre and driven back the wings, stormed and captured Landshut, and sent the corps of Hiller and the Archduke Louis—the Austrian left—flying across the Isar. Then with all his united forces the French Emperor prepared to fall upon the Archduke Charles and the Austrian right and crush them at Eckmühl. And during these four days the Emperor Napoleon, galloping rapidly from one point to another, never taking off his coat or his boots, manœuvring in a country of great obscurity, dictating at all moments his orders, short, precise, clear—so clear that his lieutenants were never in doubt for an instant as to their meaning—had changed a seemingly desperate situation into one of triumph. Wherever galloped the white horse bearing the little man in the gray coat and the cocked hat, there flew the victory!

The evening of April 21st was cool and clear. The camp-fires of the great host burned brightly, casting their ever-shifting rays over the dark lines of huts, gleaming on the bright bayonets and military trappings, and throwing the shadows of the soldiers in great silhouettes upon the ground. Eight o'clock had come, soup had been served out, and the men, gathered about the fires, were making their evening meal.

Around one of these many centres of light and warmth was clustered a characteristic group. There was André Marceau, an old grenadier, whose face was disfigured by a deep red scar that extended from the bridge of his nose to the lower part of his jaw, and which was the relic of a sabre-cut received at Auerstädt. This was by no means André's first campaign, for he had fought in Italy, at Arcola and at Rivoli; in Austria, at Ulm and at Austerlitz; in Poland, at Pultusk and at Preussisch-Eylau.

There was Gustave Lébon, who had made the campaigns of Marengo, Austerlitz, Jena and Friedland. There was Gérard Etienne, who had seen service in Italy, Austria and Spain. There was Pierre Pasquin, who had been at the siege of Saragossa, and who was now, for the first time, seeing war on a large scale. And, greatest of all, there was old François Legrand, who wore proudly on his breast the Cross of the Legion of Honor, who had fought in Italy at Castiglione and at the passage of the Tagliamento, had been with General Bonaparte in Egypt at St. Jean d'Acre, the Pyramids and Aboukir, had served at Marengo, Austerlitz, and Jena, had entered Berlin in triumph, had faced the Russian cuirassiers in the cemetery at Eylau, and had witnessed the interview of the Emperors at Tilsit. A fierce old fellow was François Legrand, with his tremendous mustache and shaggy eyebrows, skilled with sword and pistol, and, from his proverbial insolence, nicknamed by his comrades, " le grand diable."

"We will have lively work to-morrow," said André Marceau, as he finished his soup and stuck his big pipe in his mouth.

"So much the better," said old Legrand. "This time let us make a finish of these white-coated Austrians. They'll wake up some fine morning and find us in Vienna. Trust the Little Corporal for that! He took us there fast enough in 1805. 'Come, hurry, boys,' said he, 'I fight with your legs now.' And we hurried too! The Viennese thought we were still fooling with Mack at Ulm, when, all at once, we marched into Vienna and said, ' Bon jour, Viennese!' Parbleu! but they were a surprised lot, those Viennese!"

" Ajax is coming to command," said Gustave Lébon. " Do you know what the Little Corporal said to Ajax one day at parade? 'Lannes,' said the Little Corporal, ' you never complain if the parade makes us late for dinner.' ' Devil a bit!' said Ajax. ' It's all the same to me whether I eat my soup hot or cold provided you make us work to warm up a good broth of those d——d English!'"

" You should have seen Ajax at Lodi," said Gérard Etienne, knocking the ashes out of his pipe. " He and the Little Corporal were the first men across the bridge. I was not far behind, and hot work it was too!"

" Vive le Maréchal Lannes!" cried old Marceau. " He was only a poor fellow like us once; and Ney and Murat too. Look at them now! Ajax is a Duke, Ney is a Prince, and Murat is a King! However, our time will come. Hasn't the Little Corporal said, ' Every French soldier carries in his knapsack the baton of a Marshal of France!'"

" Egypt was the place!" said François Legrand, throwing back his head and sticking out his feet nearer the fire. " Diable! but it was hot there! We came along to Cairo and saw the rascally Mamelukes waiting under the Pyramids all ready to chew us up. The Little Corporal rode along the ranks, reined in his horse, and said, ' Soldats, des hauts de ces pyramides quarante siècles vous contemplent!' Mon Dieu, but you should have seen us cut the throats of the d——d Mamelukes after that!"

"Do you remember the day we entered Berlin, Gus-tave?" asked André Marceau.

"Ventrebleu, but I do!" said Gustave. "That was a fine sight! All Davout's corps in new uniforms! How grand the Guard looked, and the Staff all blazing with gold and jewels! The Germans could hardly be-lieve that our little man with his old coat and one-sou cockade was master of it all."

"Well, they found out soon enough," said François Legrand. "The Little Corporal told them he would come if they didn't stop blowing so much about their grand Frédéric; but they wouldn't shut up and so he came. He always does what he says, the Little Cor-poral!"

"Indeed he does," said Gérard Etienne. "I'll never forget when I was drafted. You see there was no one to look after the mother but me, and I didn't know what she was going to do. So, thought I, I'll tell the Little Corporal and perhaps he'll help her. So I wrote out a petition. Have any of you fellows ever tried to write a petition? Maybe you can write better than me. Sacré, but it was hard work for me, and lots of pains I took with it! Well, the next *décadi* when we went to parade at the Tuileries, I carried the petition in my pocket. I was weak in the knees when I saw the big crowd around the Little Corporal that day! Two or three German Kings and a lot of aides-de-camp, all plumes and gold! 'Brace up, Gérard,' said I, 'or the poor mother will come to grief.' So I went out of the ranks. Mon Dieu! but you should have seen those aides-de-camp and German Kings look at me as if to say, *quelle effronterie!* What did I care for them! My business was with the Little Corporal, and I went straight up to him and held out my paper. He took it, and smiled and said, 'I will read it, mon enfant.' And he did too, and the mother got a pension of 1200 francs! Don't you suppose I'll die for the Little Corporal after that?"

"I have never seen the Emperor," said Pierre, who had been listening with close attention to the reminiscences of the old campaigners.

"Well, don't be fool enough to get killed until you have," said old Legrand. "You'll see him. He'll come riding along the ranks and look at you and order the charge, and you'll be ready enough to go wherever he says and do whatever he wants. Ah! it was a fine sight at Tilsit to see the Russian Emperor and the German King and all those Princes, Counts, and Barons, taking off their hats to the Little Corporal, and he the greatest of all."

"They were all born on thrones," said André Marceau, "but our Little Corporal was only a poor sous-lieutenant once, and that's the best of it. We've made him Emperor, and he'll make us all Marshals and Dukes as soon as we deserve it! Why, one day at Milan, I remember it as though it were yesterday, we were all in the great square. The Little Corporal was there on his horse, and up came a dragoon with a dispatch. The Little Corporal read it and gave him an answer and said, 'Hurry.' 'But,' said the dragoon, 'my horse fell dead from hard riding, and I have no other.' Well, what do you suppose the Little Corporal did? He got off his own horse and said, 'Take mine.' Mon Dieu, but that dragoon was amazed! You could have knocked him over with one finger! 'Perhaps you think he's too fine,' said the Little Corporal.

' Never mind, comrade, there is nothing too good for a French soldier!' "

" Vive l'Empereur! " shouted old François Legrand excitedly. The others took it up, and on the cool night air rang out, in tumultuous chorus many times repeated, the shout, " Vive l'Empereur! "

It was nine o'clock and the tattoo sounded for the soldiers to extinguish their fires, and soon the camp of Boudet division was wrapped in darkness and silence—a silence broken only by the stamping of the horses of the cuirassiers and the measured tread of the sentries on their beats. As Pierre lay on his straw, he reached out and felt the knapsack lying beside him, and thought again of what André Marceau had told them the Emperor said, " Tout soldat français porte dans sa giberne le bâton de Maréchal de France! " He wondered if there would be one in his, and, holding tightly to its straps, he fell asleep, to dream that he too had met " le petit caporal."

CHAPTER XI

PLACE AUX DAMES

Thy voice is heard thro' rolling drums,
   That beat to battle where he stands;
Thy face across his fancy comes,
   And gives the battle to his hands.
                    —TENNYSON, *The Princess*.

WHAT were the women of France doing while their husbands, brothers, sons, and lovers, high-hearted, eager for glory, proud of their country's greatness, marched onward toward Vienna? The women hoped and waited. Hoped that this campaign, like that of 1805, would be short and glorious; hoped that fortune would again grant France her favors; hoped that death once more would spare the dear ones upon whom their thoughts were centered; waited for the bulletins to tell them of hopes realized, or destroyed—those bulletins which brought joy or sorrow to so many homes!

At the Tuileries Palace the Empress Josephine forgot the multiplying demands of her toilet to scan eagerly the short, hieroglyphic notes that, from camp and battlefield, came to her from the Emperor. And throughout France, the wives of Dukes, Princes, Marshals, Generals, Majors, Barons, Captains, Corporals, Sergeants, Privates—the grand lady of the Imperial Court, who lived in her great hotel on the Avenue des Champs Élysées, and the humble peasant woman, who watched her children, planted her grain, and did her chores in rustic Dauphiné, or flowery Touraine—all watched, waited, and hoped. How many widows there were! One could see them everywhere. In the lofty aisles of Notre Dame, or before the little altar of the Church of St. Etienne du Mont, or in the grand cathedral of Tours, or at Amiens, kneeling in that Gothic marvel of Robert de Luzarche, where the arched and pinnacled façade, the flying buttresses, the wealth of sculpture, and the great rose windows—purpling and gilding with their rays the saints, apostles, martyrs, carved on every side with wondrous skill—set forth the Bible epic in a blaze of glory.

There was in the France of 1809 an anxiety, a discontent, which was new to the France of the Empire. Public opinion had, from the first, disapproved the Spanish war, and the stubborn national resistance encountered by the French in Spain—a resistance which could be summed up in the one word, Saragossa—could but deepen this disapproval.

The levy of 1809 had been called out, and also that of 1810 required in advance, while, in addition, the new levies upon the classes of 1806, 1807, 1808, which had supposed themselves free, caused dismay in many families. But for the present, although there were signs of discontent and disapprobation among high and low, France on the whole was hopeful, even cheerful. For France was marching, and at her head the greatest military captain of the world.

The Grand Army knew no doubts or fears; they left such things to diplomats, to merchants, to bankers, to courtiers, or to women. They looked straight ahead, eager to behold upon the crest of some hill the white coats of the enemy; to see in some valley the gleam of their camp-fires. In the morning, as they faced the Austrian cannon, or at evening, as they threw themselves upon the rain-soaked ground, they had but one cry, which ever and always expressed their thoughts, their hopes, and their devotion—"Vive l'Empereur!"

To Marie Jodélle it seemed the most natural thing in the world to see France marching thus to war. She could never remember any other state of affairs. When she came into the world in 1792, the throne of the Bourbons had fallen, the Revolution—"that many-headed monster thing"—had looked forth with bloody eyes upon the monarchies of Europe, the champions of "Royalty by right divine" had cried "To arms!" and the youth of France, keeping time to the "Marseillaise," were marching forth to battle for their new-found tricolor. When Marie was five years old, the père Henri came back from Italy, minus the leg he had lost at Castiglione. Then her mother died, and she had only the père Henri. He was a gruff old soldier—the père Henri—but he was a father good and kind. When she was older, she passed many an evening sitting on his knee before the fireplace in the Café Jodélle, listening with wide-open eyes, while he told her of the dangers and adventures through which he had passed. As he talked, she heard the rolling drums, sounding the charge at Valmy; she saw the brave Jourdan, sword in hand at Fleurus; she heard the "Allons enfants de la patrie" of the "Marseillaise"; and next, she saw upon the plains of Italy the young recruits of France, hungry, ragged, lacking everything but courage, to whom that little olive-tinted artillery officer came and said abruptly—" Forward, march!" And as they marched, above their heads flew trumpet-blowing victory!

That Frenchmen should be always fighting, since France had always enemies to combat, seemed, then, to her natural enough. Sometimes, however, she wished it were all over and that all this whirl and bustle, roar and thunder, would settle down to peace. She had been very sorry for the mère Pasquin when the news came that Robert was killed, and for the good dame Nevel, too, who lived near the Place St. André, and whose husband had fallen at Friedland. She was very sorry for them, very sorry, but she had the père Henri; he was all to her, then, and the père Henri was safe at home. But now—how was it now, when Pierre was marching, and each day might bring her news that would end forever her little dream of happiness, and that too just as the père Henri had given his consent?

There was one friend to whom Marie could always turn, and that was the garçon Gaspard. He was an orphan—the little Gaspard. His father had marched and fought at Henri Jodélle's side, and when, torn by the Austrian cannon, he lay dying in Italy, he had said, " Henri, don't forget Gaspard!" Henri had not forgotten. When he came home, Gaspard was brought to the Café Jodélle and lived there like one of the family. You might have searched Grenoble through and through, and looked in all the shops in the Rue Montorge and in the Grande Rue and in the Place St. André and across the river, and you would not have found a brighter, happier, handsomer little lad than the garçon Gaspard of the Café Jodélle. He

7

had large brown eyes, and he opened them wide and
looked at you straight in the face. You always liked
him when he did that. He was neat about his dress
too; his jacket and trousers were coarse and common
enough, but they were always clean, and how well he
looked in them! He looked well in anything, but
suppose he had had a fine uniform with a jacket
trimmed with gilt braid, a military cap, and shiny
boots? Well, if he had had all that, he would have
been one of the most gallant little chaps ever seen.
What a merry smile he had! He did not know much
as book-learning goes; he could read a little and write
some, too, in a curious round hand that was anything
but legible—but how quick he was! No matter how
many soldiers came into the Café Jodélle, Gaspard
could wait upon them all.

" Gaspard," said Marie one morning, " do you ever
worry? "

" Worry? What do you do when you worry? "
asked Gaspard.

" Well, you sit and think—think about some one
very dear to you, who is far away and exposed to all
sorts of dangers. You think about all the dangers,
and you wonder if you will ever see the dear one
again."

" No," said Gaspard, " I never have time for all
that. There is no one dear to me who is far away.
You and père Henri are here. Why should I worry
about any one else? If I ever did sit down in a
corner, old Frédéric Bonneville would come in and
shout, ' Gaspard, a glass of wine!' You can't worry
when you're running about, can you? "

" I suppose not," said Marie, " I always sit in my

room and look out on the Place Grénette. Oh, Gaspard, I wish the wars were over!"

"So do I," said Gaspard. "Then all the soldiers would come marching home through the town, the drums would go rat, tat, tat! and the fifes would blow. I like the fifes. Have you ever heard me play one? Jacques le Page taught me. He has a fine one. When I get large, I mean to have one, too."

"Gaspard," said Marie, "would you like to have me tell you a secret?"

"Oh, yes, I would like that," answered Gaspard.

"Well, then, the père Henri has said I shall marry Pierre. Isn't that fine?"

Gaspard's face grew grave. "No," said he, "it is not fine. When you marry Pierre, you will go far away to live. Me and père Henri will be left all alone at the café. There will be no one to take me on Sundays for a picnic to Vizille. No, that will not be fine at all!"

"But, Gaspard!" cried Marie, "I am not going far away. Pierre and I are going to live right here. Pierre will show you how to carry a gun, and Pierre knows how to play the fife and he will play it for you, and you can go with Pierre and me on picnics to Vizille."

"Oh, good! good!" cried Gaspard. "That will be nice! I would like that! Yes, you may marry Pierre."

Marie had a pretty room in the Café Jodélle. It was not a very large room, but it was very cosy. Her small writing-desk stood in one corner, and before the fireplace was a large, yellow-covered chair in which she often sat and looked out on the Place Grénette when she " worried." One morning, when she was sitting in the yellow-covered chair, Gaspard brought her a letter, and, as soon as she saw it, she gave Gaspard a kiss—she always did when he brought her that sort of a letter, and so Gaspard was sorry they did not come twice a day. Then Gaspard went down into the café, and Marie opened her letter, and this was what she read:

Straubing, Bavaria, April 25th, 1809.

Dear Marie,

I have seen him—the great Emperor! This is how it was. Three days ago the battle of Eckmühl was fought. We got up at four in the morning. Our division was écheloned toward Landshut and was to guard the road. About noon the order came to advance. Then we heard the cannon of Marshal Davout's corps. He had already engaged the enemy. Our corps came up. I never heard such a roar of cannon. I could see nothing much for the rise in the ground and the smoke. All our division was drawn up, and though we have marched many hundred leagues, we looked as well as on parade. If a fellow did not keep himself in trim, he would hear of it. Orderly officers galloped in all directions. A squadron of the cuirassiers of the Imperial Guard passed us at a trot. Never have I seen such men and horses! They must always conquer; one could see that in their faces. We gave them a cheer and their officer saluted us. Then they moved us up on to the higher ground. Smoke was thick on the plain, but we could see the Austrian fires. Marshal Davout was fighting on our right. The balls whizzed over our heads, some of the new ones ducked their heads, but the old ones stood up straight and paid no attention at all to them. I did not duck. We waited the order to advance. You may believe it is no fun standing still hour after hour when every one else is doing something. It was about four in the afternoon. We heard the roll of drums on our left and the soldiers of the Gudin division shouting "Vive l'Empereur!" He was coming! I was in the front rank on the right. Near me was François Legrand. I have told you of him before. How my heart beat—the Emperor was coming! Four chasseurs of the Guard with green coats and on beautiful black horses came first at a gallop, then the Emperor on a white horse, and with him the Major-General, and Marshal Massena. Crack! We all presented arms and shouted "Vive l'Empereur!" The Emperor saluted us. He stopped in front of our division, drew out his spy-glass, rose in his stirrups and looked to the right where Marshal Davout was fighting. The Emperor does not look like the picture you have in the Café Jodélle. He is stouter. He looks more like the picture we used to see in the window of Simon Loisell's book-shop on the Place St. André. The Emperor said something to the Major-General and got off his horse. The Major-General and the Marshal got off theirs. Roustan, the Mameluke, held the Emperor's horse. They brought a drum and spread a map on it. General Cervoni came up. Then the Marshal, General Cervoni, and the Emperor bent over the map. The Emperor was in the middle. While they were talking, a cannon-ball struck General Cervoni and carried him away. All our division groaned. The Emperor passed his hand across his eyes and then bent over his map. Two aides-de-camp came galloping up to the Emperor. He gave them some orders, and the aides-de-camp whirled and were off like a flash. The Emperor walked about and tapped his boots with his riding-whip. He looked impatient. "All does not go well," said François Legrand, "he is fretful." An aide-de-camp came from Marshal Davout to say that the Austrians were giving way. The Emperor sent for Marshal Bessières and ordered the charge of the cavalry of the Guard. Then he called for his horse. Night was coming on. Soon we saw the Austrians retreating up the high ground, and our cuirassiers galloping after them and overthrowing them at every step. We all clapped our hands and shouted, "Vivent les cuirassiers!" So ended the battle. We bivouacked where we were. I had no chance to engage. When I do, I hope better luck will come to me than came to General Cervoni. Anyway I will do the best I can. Last night I lay on the ground and looked up at the bright stars. One was very bright, and in it I seemed to see your face smiling down at me. I remembered the words you wrote me the père Henri said: "If he proves himself a brave soldier and comes home safe and sound, he shall marry you." I will try to prove a brave soldier, and as for the rest, that remains with the good God. I am so tired now that I cannot write any more. I will write soon again, if I can, though, perhaps, it may be a month. When I do, I will tell you how we took Ratisbon.

Your Pierre,
3rd Company, 115th of the Line, Grand Army.

Marie folded the letter, put it carefully away in her little writing-desk, and sitting down in the old, yellow-covered chair, looked thoughtfully into the fire.

CHAPTER XII

THE WALLS OF RATISBON

You know, we French stormed Ratisbon;
  A mile or so away,
On a little mound, Napoleon
  Stood on our storming day.
—ROBERT BROWNING, *Incident of the French Camp.*

"GOTT im Himmel! Vat vill become of mein garten?" cried Heinrich Hauptmann, when he first saw the French forces approaching the walls of Ratisbon. This town, called by the Germans Regensburg (from the small river Regen which here flows into the Danube), is one of the oldest cities in Central Europe. In 1809, it was surrounded on the south by a wall with towers at regular intervals, but the fortifications were old and poor, and the dry ditches outside the rampart were used as kitchen gardens by some of the thrifty inhabitants.

A stone bridge connected the town with the suburb upon the left bank of the Danube called Stadt-am-Hof, and by this bridge the Archduke determined to transport his army after the disastrous battle of Eckmühl. When the Marshal Davout evacuated the city to join the Emperor at Abensburg, he left, according to Napoleon's orders, the 65th of the Line, commanded by Colonel Coutard, to garrison the place and defend the bridge. To Ratisbon, then, came the Archduke Charles of Austria and his defeated army.

seeking by the stone highway over the Danube their only means of safety. The 65th fought bravely for some hours, but could not hold out against the mass of the Austrian forces, and Colonel Coutard surrendered the town. The Archduke led his troops across the river, leaving in Ratisbon a garrison of some 6000 men, whom, however, he could reinforce rapidly from the 60,000 soldiers that he had now assembled beyond the suburb of Stadt-am-Hof. Save for the means of retreat thus afforded him, the Archduke and his army would have been compelled to surrender.

But the Emperor could not march upon Vienna while the Austrians held Ratisbon, for, unless he took the town, the Archduke could again cross the Danube and attack him in the rear. Thus the capture of Ratisbon became the *sine quâ non* for the march to Vienna. To Ratisbon, therefore, came the corps of Davout, Lannes, and Massena, flushed with victory; to Ratisbon, therefore, rode the Emperor Napoleon.

Just outside the wall of the town, near the Straubing gate and built against the rampart, stood the house of Heinrich Hauptmann. Heinrich was a vender of garden truck, and in the ditches of the old fortification he had his small kitchen-garden, where he raised a varied assortment of beans, turnips, cabbages, horseradish, parsnips, and other delicacies which he sold in the Ratisbon market. Heinrich had been very loath to leave his little property. During Marshal Davout's occupation he had remained in his house, but when the Austrians, retreating from Eckmühl, attacked the place to wrest it from the 65th, Hauptmann was forced to retreat behind the ramparts, where he spent his time in cursing the " verderbt Oestreicher " (the wicked

Austrian) and the "schlecht Franzose" (the bad French). After the Austrians obtained possession of the town he went out again, but soon the approach of the great army of Napoleon compelled him once more to take refuge within the walls. In order to enter the city it was necessary for the French to descend into the deep ditch of the fortification, cross it under fire from the Austrians, and scale the rampart by means of ladders. The Emperor Napoleon, who had dismounted upon a hillock about a cannon-shot from the town, quickly perceived the house of Hauptmann near the Straubing gate and saw that it was built against the rampart. At once His Majesty ordered up several twelve-pounders and howitzers, and commanded their fire to be concentrated upon this house, that its ruins, falling into the ditch, might form an incline upon which the corps of Lannes could mount to assault the wall.

The cannonade began. Heinrich, who was in the Osten Casse near the Straubing gate, soon learned that something was going on in the direction of his cherished dwelling. Unable to restrain his anxiety, he managed to get up upon the rampart, and the situation was instantly revealed to him in all its stern reality, for at that moment a cannon-ball from one of the French twelve-pounders crashed into his house and tumbled part of it into the ditch. Heinrich nearly fell off the rampart from terror and rage.

"Tausend Teufel!" he yelled, "die französische Verbrecher! dey are shootin der damt balls right in mein house! Gott im Himmel! mein house vill be all von damt ruin!"

"Get down from here!" cried an Austrian soldier. "What do I care about you or your house!"

"Vat do you care about me or mein house?" roared Heinrich, bursting with rage, "Vell, dat's all right vat you care about me or mein house! Vat for you come in dis town und brought der schlecht französisch Kaiser Napoleon after you, who goes und troes his damt balls right in mein house, dat's vat I vant to know?"

But the soldier ruthlessly dragged Heinrich off the rampart, and as Heinrich continued to expostulate, he was informed that if he didn't " shut up " he would have his " head cracked "—a mode of procedure which did not leave much room for further argument.

Meanwhile the Morand and Boudet divisions had been ordered forward to within a short distance of the walls of Ratisbon and stationed in the rear of a large stone store-house that stood close to the promenade surrounding the town. Then Marshal Lannes, who had conducted this manœuvre, rode off to the little hill to receive the Emperor's final orders. The 115th of the Line were drawn up at the west side of the store-house, while in front of them were massed the 85th of the Line, which belonged to the Morand division. The twelve-pounders were thundering, the house of Hauptmann had already fallen, and the cannon-balls were now battering a breach in the rampart. François Legrand stamped his foot impatiently, and Pierre, who stood near him, wondered why the order did not come to advance. Suddenly they saw soldiers from the Friant, Gudin, Molitor, and Carra St. Cyr divisions, breaking ranks and running quickly toward the mound where the Emperor had taken his stand. The crowd grew larger and larger, and the Austrians, seeing that a part of the vast mass was within cannon-shot, turned their guns in that direction. The soldiers of the 115th and 85th wondered what it all meant. François Legrand grew pale, and Pierre heard him mutter, "l'Empereur est mort!" But all at once, as if in answer to his fearful exclamation, there came from the dark mass of troops about the mound a ringing shout, "Vive l'Empereur! Vive l'Empereur!"

"Hurrah!" shouted François Legrand.

"Hurrah!" cried Pierre and all the other grenadiers of the 115th and of the 85th, although they did not understand why they were cheering. Up dashed an orderly.

"The Emperor has been wounded!" he cried.

"Where?" shouted the soldiers.

"In the right foot, but it is nothing! He is having it dressed! He will come to review you presently! He is all right!" and the orderly gave his horse the spur.

"He's all right! He exposes himself as we do! Hurrah! Hurrah!" cried François Legrand.

"Vive l'Empereur!" roared the grenadiers of the 115th and 85th. They could see the dark mass breaking up and the soldiers running back to their respective regiments. And when a few moments later the Emperor, his pale face still slightly drawn with pain, galloped down the lines, throughout that vast host the banners floated, the shakos and bearskins waved in triumph on the bayonets, while thousands and thousands of voices swelled louder and louder the mighty shout, until it struck the ears of the inhabitants of Ratisbon like a thunder peal and drowned for an instant the salvos of the Austrian artillery—"Vive l'Empereur!"

Then the Marshal Lannes rode up to the 85th and
called for fifty volunteers to carry forward the ladders.
More than one hundred soldiers ran out of the ranks,
but the Marshal reduced the number to fifty, and they
started on the double in close column. Hardly were
they clear of the store-house when a hail of balls from
the Austrian sharpshooters struck them, and the
grenadiers to a man were hurled dead and dying on
the plain. And still the Austrian cannon thundered
on!

Again the Marshal called for volunteers from the
85th, and again numbers of soldiers ran forward with
alacrity. Another ladder company was formed, and
they dashed forward in column. But again the storm
of bullets struck them and left them crushed and
mangled on the sand. And still the Austrian cannon
thundered on!

Once more the Marshal called for volunteers, but
this time no one came forward. It was certain death,
they thought, to pass the protecting angle of the store-
house. Lannes lost all patience and sprang from his
horse. "Well, I will let you see that I was a grenadier before I was a Marshal, and am one still!" he
cried, and seizing a ladder, he would have started out.
But his aides-de-camp surrounded him, crying out that
they would be forever disgraced if they allowed him
to carry out his purpose. Marbot and DeViry grasped
the ladder out of the Marshal's hands and put
it upon their shoulders. The sight of a Marshal of
France disputing with his aides-de-camp as to which of
them should rush into the face of death was too much
for François Legrand, and although no volunteers
had as yet been called for from the 115th, he sprang

forward shouting, "I, too, will go!" "And I!" cried Pierre, following hard after François. "And I!" "And I!" "And I!" cried many of the grenadiers of the 115th and of the 85th.

The aide-de-camp Marbot took command of the detachment. "Two men to each ladder!" he cried, "we will run far apart, two and two. In that way we shall more easily escape the fire than in column. Some of us will get through alive. Dash into the ditch and plant the ladders against the rampart!"

"Good!" cried Lannes, "that plan will succeed! Off with you, boys, and Ratisbon is won!"

Out they dashed; the bullets whistled and the cannon thundered, but the men, running like the wind and far apart, were not an easy aim.

Pierre had seized a ladder with François, and as he rushed across the open space he heard François calling, "To the right! Pierre, to the right!" Down into the ditch they sprang and breathless climbed over the débris of Hauptmann's house. They were ahead of the others and might have been the first to scale the wall, but Pierre, running over the ruins in the ditch, tripped and fell his length, gashing his head on a rough stone. He was up in an instant, and wiping away, with the back of his hand, the blood that trickled down into his right eye, he helped François place the ladder against the parapet. At that moment they heard a tremendous cheer from the Grand Army, for further on Marbot and Labédoyère had reached the summit of the rampart, hand in hand.

Up the ladder ran François, calling, "Come on! young Pasquin, come on!" Pierre climbed after him, more grenadiers followed, and across the open space the 115th and 85th were hastening to the assault. The Austrians, seeing the French pouring over the rampart, ceased firing and drew back. One red-whiskered artillery-man seized a pistol and fired at François. The ball cut the plume on the grenadier's lofty cap, and the next moment François lowered his bayonet and, dashing forward, struck the Austrian full in the breast with such terrible force that the artillery-man fell over with a thud, the bayonet point buried itself in the floor of the rampart and the butt of the gun shook with the vibration. The Austrian was nailed like a fly to the floor.

"There! That will teach you who I am!" roared Legrand. He seized another musket, and he and Pierre and a dozen more of the grenadiers started down into the town, for Lannes had ordered them, if they were able to get into the city, to open the Straubing gate that the Morand division might enter. They rushed down into the Osten Casse and ran into the dark archway before the gate, then all at once stopped short, for massed in the gloom of the archway stood an Austrian battalion! They were facing the gate with their rear to the French, but their Major saw François and shouted, and the Austrians faced about. Another than François might have hesitated with twelve or fourteen men at his back and an Austrian battalion before him. But not François! The least hesitation would have been fatal. It was François' bravado that carried the day.

"Surrender!" he roared as though he had had a regiment behind him. "We have captured the town! Surrender!"

"We won't surrender!" shouted the Austrian soldiers. "You may go to hell first!"

"Après vous, Messieurs les Autrichiens!" cried Pierre.

The Austrian Major hesitated. In the gloom he could not tell rightly how many men he had to encounter; he could hear on all sides the shouts of the French. Still he hesitated. "Surrender, you fool!" shouted Legrand, seizing him by the throat, "Surrender! or I will run you through!"

And now the ringing blows of axes upon the outer side of the gate told the Austrian that in a moment he would be between two fires. "I surrender!" he cried.

"Ah, do you!" said Legrand, "I thought you would! You would have done so before had you known that I am François Legrand!"

The Major hurried his men out of the arch, and as the last Austrian passed him, Legrand rushed forward, seized a pick that lay near the further end of the arch, and dashing it down through the fastenings, split them asunder. The gates, bursting with pressure from without, flew open with such fury that they crashed against the sides of the arch as the Morand division, entering like a torrent, caught up François Legrand in their midst and carried him far down the Osten Casse, shouting in triumph, "Ratisbon is taken! Vive l'Empereur!"

The inhabitants of the town were all shut up in their houses with windows fastened and doors barred, and the Osten Casse was deserted. But, as the French advanced, there came running out of a low stone doorway a short, thick-set man who shook his fist in their faces and cried, "Französische Verbrecher! ver ist mein house? Vat for you shoot balls in mein house? Ach! you are dogs of Frenchmen! To der Teufel mit you und your damt Kaiser Napoleon!" And purple with rage he spit at the troops. Some muskets were raised, for the grenadiers were in no mood to receive such language, and it would have gone hard with Herr Hauptmann had not the Marshal Lannes, who led the division in person, rushed forward.

"Arrest him!" cried Lannes.

Heinrich kicked, struck and struggled, yelling, "Shoot! damt französische Verbrecher! Shoot your damt balls in me now you have spoilt mein house!" Two sturdy grenadiers of the Morand division soon had Heinrich bound hand and foot. They tied a handkerchief over his mouth and then Heinrich could only snort his rage.

A number of houses fired by French shells were blazing, and the sparks and bits of charred wood were flying over and into the Osten Casse, where were some thirty wagons abandoned by the Austrians. As the French were passing these, one of the Austrian prisoners cried to the Marshal, "We are all lost! These wagons are full of powder!" Lannes turned pale for an instant, then sprang forward. "Open ranks!" he cried. "Pile your guns against the houses! Push these wagons along from hand to hand until they are out under the arch! They are powder-wagons! Quick! Quick!"

How they worked, those brave grenadiers, with eyes set, straining every nerve as they pushed and pulled the heavy dark masses that rumbled along between their ranks. And the Marshal, how he worked too! Dashing his plumed hat to one side, he sprang forward and seized a wagon, crying, "Work fast, boys! Quick! Quick!" This sturdy Lannes!

This brave "Ajax!" This Marshal of France who was once a grenadier!

And François Legrand, how he worked too! The moment his great hands grasped the wheels of the heavy wagons they seemed to fly past him! And young Pierre Pasquin, with his bandaged head and bloody face—how he worked too! Let but one spark, whirled downward by the wind, set fire to one of those dark carriages, and the grenadiers of the 115th and of the 85th, a Marshal of France, and half of Ratisbon would be no more!

On, on they rolled, rumbling over the stones! One by one they passed the arch! One by one they were pushed outside the wall, and Ratisbon was saved! "Now for the bridge!" cried the Marshal. "Marbot, make for the bridge across the Danube!"

Marbot headed a detachment comprising some two hundred men of the 115th and they started. None of them had ever been in Ratisbon before, and soon, lost in a maze of little narrow streets, they did not know in which direction they were going—west, north, east, or south—but they pushed on. In adjoining streets they could hear the rattle of musketry fire as the troops of the Marshal drove back the Austrian skirmishers. They were passing through a short street at the end of which they could see the towers of St. Peter's Cathedral, when a door opened suddenly and a lady, charmingly dressed, ran toward them.

"I am French!" she cried. "Save me! Save me!"

"Who are you?" inquired the aide-de-camp.

"I am Mlle. Lelorge, modiste Parisienne. I have been shut up in my shop all day, for I feared the Austrians. Save me! Save me!"

"Of course you shall be saved," answered Marbot. "Now tell me—do you know where the stone bridge is across the Danube?"

"Yes, certainly."

"Well then, show us the way."

".Mon Dieu! with all this shooting going on? No! No! No! I am scared to death already! I wanted you to give me some soldiers to defend my shop. I shall run back at once!"

"Pardon me, but you won't!" rejoined the aide-de-camp. "You must show us the bridge first. Pasquin, take the lady by the arm! Now, forward, march!"

Poor Mlle. Lelorge! She screamed with all her might, but it was no use; Pierre marched her along.

"Where shall we go?" demanded Marbot as they reached the corner of the street.

"To the right! To the right!" cried Mlle. Lelorge. "I shall be killed! I know it! Stop holding me so tight! You hurt my arm! I shall be killed! I shall be killed!"

The musketry fire continued, and as they came nearer the river, the roar of cannon became deafening. Mlle. Lelorge sank on her knees and refused to budge. Pierre was perplexed.

"Sergeant Legrand," commanded Marbot, "take the lady's other arm and make her march!"

When François took hold of her, Mademoiselle was lifted in a twinkling several feet from the ground and on they went, Legrand's weathen-beaten face grave and impassive, while Mademoiselle kicked him with her heels and called him a "brute."

"Where shall I turn?" demanded Marbot.

"To the right! To the right!" screamed Mlle. Lelorge.

In a few moments they entered the square facing the bridge, at the further end of which was stationed an Austrian battalion that immediately opened fire. Close by the square was the little Chapel of the Virgin, and into it, by Marbot's orders, the grenadiers carried Mlle. Lelorge, who, trembling and thoroughly terrified, crouched down behind the Virgin's statue. "Legrand!" cried Marbot, as François and Pierre came out of the chapel, "Guard the lady!" Then the detachment advanced, firing and receiving the Austrian fire at every step. Suddenly, into the now deserted square, ran four Austrian troopers, driven back by Lannes' skirmishers. Seeing only one big French grenadier upon the steps of the little chapel, they dashed at him. Crack! crack! went Legrand's musket and two of the troopers pitched forward on their faces upon the stone pavement. The other two came on, shouting and cursing with their swords drawn. "Fools!" cried Legrand, "do you fancy you can get the best of a veteran of Eylau and Austerlitz? Au diable with you both!" He drew his short sword, and there they fought—cut! slash! parry! thrust! The swords rang sharp and clear, and the white steps of the Chapel of the Virgin were spotted with blood. And when, half an hour later, Marbot and the victorious detachment, having routed the Austrian battalion, surged back in triumph from the bridge, they found François Legrand smeared with blood, standing erect upon the steps of the little chapel, with four Austrian troopers dead at his feet—guarding the lady!

Thus it was that, on the 23rd of April, 1809, the

town of Ratisbon was captured by the French. On the same day the Emperor entered, and, as many houses were still burning in various quarters, he ordered his troops to assist the inhabitants in extinguishing the fires. As the Emperor, two of his aides-de-camp, and the Marshal Lannes, were visiting the northern quarter of the Osten Casse, His Majesty saw two grenadiers marching along with a stout German between them whose hands were tied behind his back.

" And what has he done?" inquired the Emperor.

" His head is turned, sire, by the loss of his house, which Your Majesty battered down near the Straubing gate," answered the Marshal.

" Halt!" cried the Emperor.

The grenadiers stopped in their tracks and their muskets clicked as they presented arms. The Emperor motioned to them to untie Heinrich's hands and summoned one of his aides-de-camp who knew German.

" What is your name?" inquired His Majesty.

" Heinrich Hauptmann, Herr Franzose General."

" And where do you live?"

" Ach! Gott im Himmel! I lif nowheres! Mein house is all von ruin!"

" And who has destroyed your house?"

" Who has destroyed mein house? Vhy who but your schlecht Franzose Kaiser, him you call der gross Napoleon! He has sent his damt balls right in mein house!"

" And you have lost all?"

" Have I lost all? Gott im Himmel! mein schönes garten is gone too!"

" Then the great Napoleon must give you one hundred little napoleons to build your house again," answered the Emperor. He motioned to his aide-de-camp, who opened a purse and poured the gold into the astounded Heinrich's hands. And thus came true that saying of the soldiers, that no foeman, however humble, could speak to His Imperial Majesty, the Emperor of the French, without receiving some reward.

Toward evening, after visiting the various quarters of the city, the Emperor went to see the brave regiments that had led in the assault, and when he came to the square where the 115th were bivouacked, he said to the Captain who saluted him: "Where is he who opened the gate and guarded the lady?"

"Legrand!" called the Captain, and the sturdy grenadier came forward.

"Ah! It is you!" cried the Emperor. "You are one of my old 'grumblers' of Italy!" And he pulled Legrand's mustache.

"I may be a grumbler, sire, but I march always."

"Why, so you do, and fight too!" said the Emperor. "Come, sit down here and tell me about your old father. Does he not live at Châlons-sur-Marne?"

"He does, sire," answered the grenadier.

And so upon the blackened timbers of a half-burned house in the Ratisbon Market they two sat down— the great, stalwart grenadier, with his towering plume and bearskin, and the short, gray-coated Emperor, kicking the débris with his boots and flicking the sand with his riding-whip. Old François Legrand and his good friend the Little Corporal! And the Emperor asked him many questions about himself and about his family.

"Why! it seems you were with me in Italy and

Egypt and at Austerlitz!   Well, what have you gotten
for it all? "

" I have the cross, sire," answered Legrand proudly.

" And you have no commission? "

" It will come some time or other," replied the
soldier.

" It has come," rejoined the Emperor.   He rose and
tapped the grenadier lightly with his riding-whip,
saying, " We'll march to-morrow to Vienna, *Captain*
Legrand! "

CHAPTER XIII

The Bold Duke Maximilian

He who fights and runs away
May live to fight another day.
—GOLDSMITH, *The Art of Poetry*.

ON the 10th of May, the French appeared before Vienna, that great city on the Danube, with its parks and palaces, its Prater and its moated Laxenburg—Vienna the Kaiserstadt, or Imperial City, whose boulevards—the Prater Strasse, the Karnthner Strasse, the Tabor Strasse, and the Graben—radiate from St. Stephen's Platz, where towers the great Cathedral of St. Stephen, upon whose roof of colored tiles a colossal mosaic of the Austrian eagle looks with one head toward Schönbrunn and with the other toward Aspern, Essling, and Deutsch-Wagram.

Twenty-seven days had passed since the Emperor set out from Paris; Tengen, Abensburg, Eckmühl had been fought; Landshut, Ratisbon, Ebersberg had been stormed; 60,000 Austrians had been killed or taken prisoners, more than one hundred cannon had been captured, the Archduke's army had been driven back into Bohemia, and for the second time the Viennese saw Napoleon at their gates.

The good people of Vienna were much astonished when they saw the French forces. "Don't be alarmed," the Archduke Maximilian had been telling them. "The French have been defeated. The Archduke Charles stays a long time in Bohemia, it is true, but it is a part of a series of skilful manœuvres that he is executing. The French may send a detachment to Vienna, but I will thrash them fast enough if they come! Don't worry!" And now here was the whole French army pouring down upon Vienna—Napoleon at their head!

The people ran through the streets howling with rage, and persons of quiet temperament got into their houses and locked the doors. When a French soldier bearing a flag of truce rode into the suburbs, the people grabbed him; Hans Loibel, the butcher's boy, who lived in Backer Strasse, ran him through, and the greasy mob put Hans upon the soldier's horse and trotted him about in triumph. "Down with the French!" they cried. "Where is our great Archduke Maximilian, who promised to blow them into little bits? Come out, Duke Maximilian, and keep your word!"

In an apartment of the Hofburg sat the Archduke Maximilian and his second in command, General O'Reilly.

"Well, they are here!" said the Archduke Maximilian.

"Indeed they are!" said General O'Reilly.

"We will show them a thing or two before we finish with them!" said the Archduke Maximilian.

"Indeed we will!" said General O'Reilly.

"What point shall we fortify against them?" asked the Archduke Maximilian.

"I don't know!" said General O'Reilly.

In the bright May sunshine the Emperor Napoleon

and the Marshal Massena rode round the fortifications
on the southern side of the city. Opposite Lusthaus
flows an arm of the river called the Danube canal,
beyond is the promenade of the Prater, and further
on the great Tabor bridge across the Danube. This
the Emperor determined to take, for then he could
prevent the Archduke Charles from marching to re-
lieve Vienna, could shut up the Archduke Maximilian
in the city and compel him to surrender. The Emperor and the Marshal rode near the bank of the
Danube canal, and the Emperor examined the position. " There are some boats over there at the left
bank," said he, " Massena, send some swimmers after
them."

The Marshal dispatched his aide-de-camp Sigaldi to
the Boudet division, which was stationed not far away
toward Kaiser-Ebersdorf. Soon twenty-five sturdy
fellows from the 115th came marching up. There
were André Marceau, Pierre Pasquin, Robert Despienne, Charles Roidot, Henri Vatel, and twenty more.

" Swim across and bring back those boats," said the
Marshal Massena.

They hurried down to the bank and stripped off
their clothes. Robert Despienne was in the water
first—Robert was always quick. Pierre was second,
old André Marceau was third, and the rest followed
together. They struck out vigorously, but the Austrians at the advanced posts had seen them and opened
fire. The balls splashed in the water about them.
Pierre was swimming hard after Robert Despienne,
whose black head was moving along before him. He
could hear André Marceau puffing not far away. A
musket-ball dropped into the water before him and

splashed it into his eyes. When he looked again, Robert's black head was gone. Poor Robert! a ball had gone through his eye and he sank like a log. "If they keep this up," said André Marceau, "we shall none of us get over." "Ah!" cried Charles Roidot, and down he sank. He had been shot in the neck. He left a wife and two little ones at Besançon. She had had great faith in the glory that was to come to Charles on this campaign—this was the end of all that.

"There are the boats!" cried André Marceau, spitting the water out of his mouth. They swam rapidly on and were soon among the low, black boats moored at the side of the canal. Not all of them were there, however, for six had perished on the way over. Pierre undid the fastenings of the first boat with which he came in contact, and climbing over the side, seized the oars. How hard he rowed!—his wet body glistening in the sun. The others did the same, and nineteen boats shot out into the stream. The Austrian fire began again. Pierre sat up straight and rowed with all his might. He remembered how the "old ones" had laughed when the "new ones" ducked at Eckmühl. "If the ball is going to hit you, it will hit you anyway," said Pierre, and on he went. But the Austrians dropped Henri Vatel and five or six more, and sent a ball that went through the port side of Pierre's boat just at water-line. He turned his foot and stuck his bare heel in the hole. That kept the water nearly all out, and on he went. There was the shore, and he gave a vigorous pull on the oars which sent the boat swashing on the sand. Then jumping out, he pulled it out of the water. He was the first to reach the shore.

André Marceau came in a few moments later, the others followed rapidly, and in a dozen minutes there were as many boats in line at the Marshal's service.

"That's not bad," said Massena, who with the aide-de-camp Sigaldi was standing on the bank. "Dress fast and be ready to take over some voltigeurs."

They could see a company of voltigeurs from the Boudet division coming up, and further on fifteen twelve-pounders advancing at a trot, for the Emperor was going to establish a battery on the side of the canal to demolish the Lusthaus and enfilade the avenue. Pierre slipped on his trousers and shirt and was about to put on his shoes, when the soldiers, who were dressing about him, sprang up, and, as they were—naked or half-dressed with shirts in their hands—stood at salute. Pierre jumped up and faced about saluting, holding his shoe in his left hand.

There on their restless and richly-trapped chargers were a dozen Imperial aides-de-camp in gorgeous uniforms covered with gold lace and jeweled decorations, and wearing busbys with large white or red plumes, while before them on his white horse sat the Emperor.

"You have done well," said His Majesty. "Which of you brought over the first boat?"

Pierre stepped forward, his shoe in his hand.

"What is your name?" inquired the Emperor.

"Pierre Pasquin, sire."

"Pasquin? Pasquin? I have heard that name before. Are you he who lost the dispatch sent to me from Saragossa?"

"It was stolen from me, sire."

"Stolen! How stolen? Were you not there to defend it?"

Pierre had never before seen Napoleon face to face. The tone of the Emperor's voice and the glance of the Emperor's eye so confused him, that it is doubtful if he could have answered anything which would have been intelligible; but at that moment the Austrian cannon beyond the Prater thundered. With a convulsive movement the Emperor wheeled his horse about and set off at a gallop in that direction, drawing out his spy-glass as he went, and followed furiously by his glittering staff.

Pierre's legs seemed to give way under him. He sank down and began to put on his shoes. That infernal episode at Saragossa! He could never set it right! If he could only explain to the Marshal Lannes perhaps something might be done, but, although he had seen the Marshal at Ratisbon, he had had no opportunity, and the Marshal had no doubt forgotten all about him by this time. Well, it was just as the poor mother had told him, " The Pasquins were not lucky." He put on his shoes and his coat. " Perhaps my turn will come some day," he said. " Anyway no one shall say that Pasquin does not do his duty, even if he is not lucky."

The battery established by the Emperor opened fire on the Lusthaus, the voltigeurs were transported across the river and captured the position; a bridge of boats was rapidly formed, and then the greater part of the Boudet division marched over and occupied the place. While this movement was being executed the Emperor placed, near the end of the faubourg of the Landstrauss, another battery of twenty howitzers which commenced to throw shells into the city, and many houses in the narrow streets were soon on fire.

" It seems that Bonaparte has captured the Lust-haus," said the Archduke Maximilian.

" That he has," said General O'Reilly.

" And he has placed a battery there, too," said the Archduke Maximilian.

" He has indeed," said General O'Reilly.

" Well, I'll drive him out of there!" said the Archduke Maximilian.

" If you can," said General O'Reilly.

So during the night of the 11th, the Archduke sent two battalions of grenadiers to seize the Lusthaus and break down the bridge of boats, but the Boudet volti-geurs, entrenched behind cut timbers in the Lusthaus, received them with a volley of musketry at short range, the artillery from the French batteries riddled their flanks, and the Austrians retreated beyond the Prater in disorder. The Emperor was accomplishing his purpose, and he would soon have the Tabor bridge.

" Now, there's one way left us," said the Archduke Maximilian.

" What is that?" asked General O'Reilly.

" I shall march out of Vienna; break down the Tabor bridge; go and find the Archduke Charles; come back and give these French a thrashing!" said the Archduke Maximilian.

" A good plan," said General O'Reilly.

" I shall leave you in command," said the Archduke Maximilian.

" I am honored very greatly," answered General O'Reilly.

" I must take the garrison with me, but I'll give you five hundred men of Hiller's corps and one battalion of the Landwehr," said the Archduke Maximilian.

" Thank you, sir," said General O'Reilly.

" Don't imagine I fear being taken prisoner! " said the Archduke Maximilian.

" Surely not," said General O'Reilly.

" Make a firm stand, and I'll return in triumph! " said the Archduke Maximilian.

" Certainly," said General O'Reilly.

On the morning of May 12th, therefore, the Archduke at the head of the garrison marched out of Vienna across the Tabor bridge, which he broke down behind him. " Stand firm! good people of Vienna! " cried the Archduke Maximilian. " Be united! Remember, I am before all else an Austrian! I shall soon return in triumph to deliver you and make the French repent their rashness! Meanwhile, obey General O'Reilly."

The cannonade was still continuing, and the French shells were flying into the city.

" Well, General," said Colonel Kahlenberg, " His Imperial Highness has gone. What shall we do to save Vienna? "

" Capitulate," said General O'Reilly.

CHAPTER XIV

THE STREET OF ESSLING

For courage mounteth with occasion.
—SHAKESPEARE, *King John.*

THUS Napoleon took possession of Vienna, and having firmly established himself in a manner to use to advantage the resources of that capital and to protect his means of communication, he turned his attention to the problem to be solved—namely, to transport across the river 1000 yards wide, an army of 150,000 men and 500 guns, in the face of an equal force, that upon the great plain of the Marchfeld he might fight a battle which should terminate the war. For this operation he chose that part of the Danube nearest to Vienna, where the river, wide rather than rapid and deep, was studded with islands, and by this division was made more manageable. Two leagues below Vienna opposite Enzersdorf is the island of Lobau, thickly wooded, a league long and a league and a half wide. To reach it one must cross the two arms of the great Danube, one 240 fathoms wide, the other 120, with a sand-bank between them; while a narrow branch of the river, 60 fathoms wide, separates the island from the left bank, where about the heights of Deutsch-Wagram, beyond the plain of the Marchfeld, the Archduke Charles was collecting his army corps.

It was a gigantic operation, this crossing of the

Danube; to hold in check the Austrian capital, to transport this mighty mass of men and guns and horses and ammunition across this broad impetuous river, to do battle on the plain beyond, with this river in the rear; but the situation left no alternative. Have not the eagles crossed the Alps, and shall they not cross the Danube, wide and swift-flowing though it be? To work then, soldiers of France! Collect the boats that you can find in Vienna; raise and repair those which the Austrians, foreseeing your need of them, have sunk in the river; search Vienna for cordage from one end to the other; cut and saw the timbers of the surrounding country to make planks, and, as there is no time to forge anchors from the iron-works of Styria, sink in the river heavy weights—guns found in the arsenals of Vienna and chests filled with cannon-balls. And as you march, and work, and run, and hammer, and saw, and lower, and hoist, and pull, and push, and dig, and carry—be sure of this; upon you all—from the white-plumed Marshal who gives commands, and the embroidered aide-de-camp who carries orders, to the humble pontonier who saws and hammers, and the never-flagging sentinel who paces through the thickets of Lobau—rests the " eye of the master! "

And so by the 20th of May all was ready; the Boudet and Molitor divisions passed over to the island of Lobau, and Lasalle's division of light cavalry followed with two artillery trains. They drove back and captured the few Austrian outposts on the island and crossed it to the narrow branch that lay between it and the left bank. In a few hours time the bridge of boats for this narrow arm of the river was prepared, and MM. Sainte-Croix and Baudru, having been rowed over with 200 voltigeurs, drove off the Austrian sharpshooters and fastened the cable which was to support the bridge. And after the bridge had been put in place, General Lasalle crossed with four regiments of cavalry. It was a fine sight to see them go over, so Pierre thought, for the 115th were drawn up near the bank, waiting their turn to cross, and Pierre could see clearly the bridge, the river, and the open plain beyond.

Lasalle came along on his beautiful black horse that tossed his head and curveted and picked up and set down his feet with springy precision. And Lasalle with his great cocked hat and big twisted mustache, clanking sword, prancing horse, and jingling bridle, looked, as he was, a swashbuckler par excellence. Don't fancy, however, that he was all waxed mustache and hussar uniform, sabretache, and nothing more. He was the best light cavalry officer in the army and had the keenest eye. Pierre remembered a story that André Marceau had told them one night about Lasalle, how the Emperor had given Lasalle 200,000 francs to pay his debts before he was married, and how Lasalle paid his debts with half and lost the other half at cards. " And when is your wedding, Lasalle? " said the Emperor when he saw him next.

" As soon as I have some money to begin housekeeping, sire," said Lasalle.

"What! Why, I gave you 200,000 francs last week! What have you done with them? "

" Paid my debts with half and lost the other half at cards."

And the Emperor, who would have scolded any

9

other general for such a statement, laughed, pulled Lasalle's ear and gave him another 200,000 francs. So much for having a keen eye! thought Pierre.

When General Lasalle reached the opposite bank, he drew his sword, gave that beautiful horse the spur and made him go bounding off over the green Marchfeld, which was a pretty sight to see. After him trotted the lancers, with their long pennants fluttering, and then came the hussars and chasseurs clattering over the bridge—the vanguard of Napoleon's great army had passed the Danube! Then the Boudet division was marched over and the other divisions followed, and they advanced through the grain fields to the village of Essling. Pierre trudged along and looked at the fields and the little houses of Essling spread out on the plain. Over to the left he could see the church tower of Aspern. The sun became hot, and the insects buzzed about among the growing corn and garden truck of the Essling farmers. Pierre did not feel very joyous that morning. He seemed so small and insignificant among that great host massed in and around Vienna; and sometimes he wondered how he had ever come to imagine that any honor would come to him. He had been up nearly all night, working about the bridge and crossing to the island of Lobau; then, two days before, he had lost a shoe and had had to borrow one from André Marceau. It was too tight and had rubbed his heel so that he could hardly walk. And when they were crossing from the island of Lobau, his tooth—that wretched back tooth in his lower right jaw—had begun to ache, and now it was making his head crack. His knapsack weighed a ton, he thought, and his gun at least half a ton; the sun's

rays grew hotter, and the dust rolled up thick and
slowly settled in his ears and eyes. Things looked
peaceful enough about this little town of Essling.
There would probably be little done there that day;
and suppose there were fighting—what chance for
him, an insignificant soldier? Look at all those
plumed officers, gold-laced aides-de-camp, jingling
hussar captains, and majestic marshals! The world
stood at salute when they went by! He was only a
poor chap who was "not lucky," who had a sore heel
and the toothache—could he ever hope to be like
them? Ah! what was it that André Marceau, by the
camp-fire before Eckmühl, had told them the Emperor
said?—"Every French soldier carries in his knapsack
the baton of a Marshal of France!" Every French
soldier? Yes, *every* French soldier! It would—it
must prove true! It was the Imperial word!

The Boudet division was stationed in Essling, where
an enclosure with a large house of hewn stone formed
a citadel. The Molitor division was marched to Aspern, and between Aspern and Essling were placed the
cavalry and artillery, while across the bridges and the
island of Lobau more troops—infantry, cavalry, and
artillery—were being hastened forward to reinforce
those corps already in Aspern-Essling. So the hours
of the morning passed quietly enough for the 115th of
the Line in Essling, but about noon, far in the distance
across the Marchfeld, they saw the advance guard of
the army of the Archduke Charles. Nearer and
nearer they came in a vast semicircle toward Aspern-
Essling, until their white uniforms and glittering arms
were seen clearly beyond the green corn-fields. The
Marshal Berthier, who had the best eye of any man

in the army for measuring extent of ground and numbers of men, calculated, from his post in the church tower at Aspern, that they were 90,000 strong and sent this word to the Emperor. As yet only six divisions— the infantry divisions of Molitor, Boudet, and Legrand, and the cavalry divisions of Lasalle, Marulaz, and Espagne—in all about 23,000 men, had crossed the river. But the Emperor determined to hold Aspern-Essling, to recover which would cost too much; and he hurried forward the passage of the army from the right bank. So the Imperial aide-de-camp, César de Laville, came riding up to the Boudet division and said to General Boudet, " The Emperor orders you to hold Essling!"

Villages of Aspern-Essling, on you the sun shines brightly, about you the waving corn-fields and the quiet kitchen-gardens grow peacefully, and in your white-walled streets the fluttering standards and the many-colored uniforms glitter resplendent. But before another sun shall rise your gardens will be trampled in the mire, your walls be torn with shot and shell, your towers fall, your houses burst with flame, your streets run red with blood! 'Tis two o'clock! Your hour has come! The cannon on the Marchfeld thunders! Napoleon Bonaparte and the Archduke Charles of Hapsburg have let loose on you " the dogs of war!"

The Austrians directed their main attack on Aspern, which was furiously assailed by the corps of Hiller, Hohenzollern, and Lieutenant-General Bellegarde. Prince Lichtenstein and the Austrian cavalry charged the cavalry of Lannes posted between Aspern-Essling, while the corps of Rosenberg advanced against the latter place. Thus all the afternoon the conflict raged. Again and again the Austrian grenadiers charged through the streets of Aspern. Again and again the French drove them back. Twice the corps of Rosenberg advanced through the streets of Essling, and twice the soldiers of the Boudet division drove them back. Prince Lichtenstein's white-coated horsemen and Lasalle's fur-jacketed hussars met in full career, and reared, and pranced, and cut, and slashed, and whirled away to the trumpet-blast. Aspern was on fire in many places, and Essling smoked, blackened and dismantled—and all the time across the bridges of the Danube and the island of Lobau came the French army—horse, man, and gun—advancing to the seat of war. So the French held their own, and when night came, and the firing, charging, stabbing, trampling ceased, Napoleon had transported 60,000 men across the Danube, ready for the battle of the morrow. If with 30,000 men and fifty guns he had held this great mass of Austrians in check, would he not beat them on the morrow, now that he had transported 150 guns and 60,000 men? Beat them? Yes— if ammunition did not fail and the Danube bridge held firm!

Night came. Pierre was on guard duty on the embankment before Essling, and with his gun on his shoulder he paced along the smooth, narrow path. Around him was the broad, dark Marchfeld, and in the distance the Austrian fires. Behind him was Essling, dark and silent, its weary defenders stretched in sleep about the bivouacs in the streets or in the houses. To his left was Aspern, its smoking ruins still sending forth in some places a dull red glow.

Over the dark Marchfeld glittered here and there, like busy fireflies, the lights of the ambulance corps picking up the wounded, and ever and anon upon the still night air was heard the far-distant blast of a cavalry bugle or an adjacent groan. And the moon came up and shed her quiet light over the green Marchfeld, making the lights of the ambulance corps grow dim, covering the battered walls of Essling with hazy romance, and drawing from the stacks of arms in Essling's streets a glancing gleam. Shine on, silver Diana, you are queen to-night! Your reign is peace! The first beams of the morning will announce the chariot of the Sun and crimson-crested Mars!

As Pierre paced thus in the moonlight, he saw a man, wrapped in a long dark cloak, advancing along the embankment. His head was somewhat bent and his high cocked hat concealed his face. " Halt! " said Pierre. The man raised his head abruptly, and at the same instant Pierre recognized—the Marshal Lannes. He saluted and waited for the Marshal to speak. " Is all quiet?" said Lannes. " All is quiet, Monsieur le Maréchal," answered Pierre. The Marshal saluted him and was about to pass on, when Pierre, whose heart was beating thump! thump! said suddenly, " Monsieur le Maréchal! "

" Well? "

" Do you remember, Monsieur le Maréchal, at Saragossa a soldier named Pasquin whom you sent to Tudela with a letter for the Emperor? "

" Yes, well? "

" That letter was never delivered, Monsieur le Maréchal."

" I know it, and what of this soldier? "

"He is here before you, Monsieur le Maréchal."

Lannes stepped quickly forward and looked closely at Pierre. "And why did you not hand my letter to the Baron Lejeune?" inquired the Marshal sternly. Then on the embankment, in the quiet night, Pierre told him the story; how he and Jean had ridden out of Saragossa, and what had happened on the rising ground near Alagon, and how, when life seemed dark indeed, there came a bright angel in a little creaking cart. And the Marshal heard the story in silence, wrapped in his cloak, looking out over the dark Marchfeld. When Pierre had finished, quick as a flash the Marshal whirled about, looked him in the eyes and asked roughly, "Boy, are you telling me the truth?" And Pierre looked back at him steadily and said, "I am telling you the truth, Monsieur le Maréchal."

"Yes, so you are," said Lannes.

"And what has become of Jean Deteau, Monsieur le Maréchal?"

"Deteau? He was transferred to Marshal Soult's staff. He is still in Spain. Well, justice shall be done, young man, when we get back to Paris. Now we have work. To-morrow strike your blows for France!"

"Yes, Monsieur le Maréchal, for France and for the Emperor!"

The Marshal passed on, and Pierre was left alone upon the embankment. At four in the morning the French and Austrian sharpshooters began to exchange shots, and Napoleon, on horseback at the tile-yard between Aspern-Essling, gave his orders to his Marshals. Massena with the Molitor, Legrand, and Carra

St. Cyr divisions was to hold Aspern, and Lannes with the Boudet, St. Hilaire, and Oudinot divisions was to hold Essling, while between the towns were the French cavalry and artillery, and in reserve toward the Danube was the Imperial Guard.

The battle began furiously, and while Massena held Aspern with stubborn tenacity and Boudet held Essling with cool firmness, Lannes, with 20,000 infantry and 6000 cavalry, advanced into the plain against the Austrian centre. The Austrians, assailed throughout their whole line, began to fall back. Vainly the Archduke Charles strove to rally his wavering centre; vainly he seized the flag of Bach's division and led it forward in person, giving to his soldiers the inspiring example of an Imperial Prince of Hapsburg advancing under fire. The Austrian centre still fell slowly back, when all at once the French halted, and their eagles, a moment before flying victoriously, fluttered in the midst of the Marchfeld with smoke and fire on every side. For an Imperial aide-de-camp had brought to Marshal Lannes the Emperor's orders to suspend his forward movement and fall back gradually to the line of Aspern-Essling, sparing his ammunition. The great bridge across the Danube, owing to the swelling of the flood and the timbers and burning buildings which the Austrians floated down the stream, had broken just as Davout's artillery regiments and wagons were preparing to cross, and now the Emperor of the French, with 60,000 men, was cut off from his main army on the right bank and from all his ammunition! The Danube in his rear and 90,000 Austrians before him! It was nine in the morning on the 22d of May, and not until night could the French

hope to retreat over the single bridge uniting the left
bank to the island of Lobau.   The corps of Marshal
Lannes fell back, and all along their line the Austrians
advanced with renewed vigor.   In and about Aspern-
Essling the battle began again more furiously than
ever.   To the left of Essling, Rosenberg brought up
fifty guns, and they began—roar and thunder, thunder
and roar!   Crash! crash! the roofs of the houses of
Essling, along the street leading to the citadel, fell
into, and beside the houses.   Bricks, stones, and
mortar lay in heaps, and walls fell in, and houses
blazed, and timbers were hurled through the air, and
smoke and dust were on every side.   The soldiers of
the 115th barricaded themselves with wagons, ploughs,
beams and stones, and when the Hungarian grenadiers
came charging up the street, they gave them a volley
that sent them charging back again.   A shell fell near
François Legrand and burst, knocking François
down.   But François got up, covered with dirt, and
waved his sword and cried, "Your Captain is not
hurt! You may depend upon him! Aim straighter
next time, Austrian fools!"

Again the Austrians charged and again were
beaten back.   A cannon-ball struck a whole file and
knocked them on top of Captain Legrand, and under
the pile of wounded, bleeding men, they heard François shouting, "Close up the ranks!"   Pierre helped
to drag him out and cried, "Captain, the hilt of your
sabre is gone!"   "No matter," said François, "the
battle is not over yet."

Now the cannon thundered faster and faster.   The
balls came and rolled over three men at a time, and
sent the grenadiers' caps spinning twenty feet in the

air, but as soon as one file was down, there came from François the stern command, "Close the ranks!" The file next Pierre was cut down, and something struck him on the arm. He dropped his gun, thinking that his arm was cut off, for it had no feeling in it. And then he saw a piece of flesh sticking to his wrist, a piece of flesh of one of his brave comrades which had been dashed against him with such violence that it had adhered to his wrist! André Marceau came up and shook his arm, and the piece of flesh fell off. How glad Pierre was to find that his arm was only stunned, and that he could use his fingers! "Leave your gun and take your sabre," said André Marceau. "I have none," said Pierre, "a ball carried it away." So he took his gun in his left hand. Then a ball from an Austrian twelve-pounder crashed into the roof of the granary and sent the stones flying, and Charles Varterre ducked his head. "You must not duck your head!" shouted François Legrand, slapping him on the knapsack with his sabre. "I won't!" cried Charles, and up he stood. Again the Austrians came in solid column, spitting flame. "Forward!" cried Legrand. And over the débris in the street and the dead bodies of their comrades they rushed and met with a crash, and for a few moments there was shouting, swearing, sabring, bayoneting, and pandemonium supreme. Pierre received a cut from a bayonet over his left eye, as he parried the thrust of an Austrian grenadier. Then the Austrians fell back, and Pierre saw François Legrand surrounded by three of them, who had seized him and were shouting, "Surrender!" Pierre ran up and, pointing his gun with his left hand, he made it play see-saw with his right, and plunged his bayonet into the bellies of first one and then another of the Austrian grenadiers. The third was thrown down by François, who ran his sword into his throat. Pierre was wet with sweat, and covered with dirt and bits of mortar, and his face was red with blood from the cut in his forehead, and his bayonet and the barrel of his gun were smeared with blood and entrails. And so the fight went on. Again the Austrians charged; Pierre saw an Austrian captain leading, and, taking a cartridge, he made the sign of the cross for good luck, rammed it in his gun, fired, and hit the Austrian in the face. And so the fight went on.

Now the Austrians brought up more artillery. They must drive the French out of this little town of Essling; they must get to the bridge, and if they did, it would be all up with the French army, it would be all up with the Emperor Napoleon. It was well toward evening now. Essling was broken and battered from one end to the other; the houses were on fire, and there were barricades of stone, great timbers, dismantled guns, abandoned knapsacks and cartridge-boxes, dead horses, dead Austrians, dead Frenchmen, bloody corpses torn and mangled, bloody walls and smoking ruins everywhere. When for the sixth time the Austrians advanced, and the brave Boudet cried, "Charge!" there were few left to respond to his call; and at last they were driven back into the granary and surrounded. As they fell back, François Legrand saw an Austrian battalion coming up through one of the narrow streets amid the smoke and flame. If they could pass this street, they could pass the granary, they could penetrate Essling, they could reach the bridge, they could— "Forward!" shouted François, and the 3rd company of the 115th ran after him to the head of the narrow street. They seized a wagon, threw it over, and when the Austrians were within range, gave them a volley. The Austrians returned their fire furiously, and they fired again, and the Austrians returned it, and they fired again, and as they were shot down, their comrades piled their dead bodies beside the wagon and fought behind them as from a rampart. Soldiers of the Boudet division, do you know the work cut out for you? It is this—conquer or die! Yes, they knew it, and as they saw the Austrian cannon preparing to fire, they said to one another, " That one is for me! " " All right, I will get behind you. That is a good place. Keep quiet."

So night settled down, but enveloped by smoke they fought by the light of burning houses, and, when they fired, the Austrians fell, and when the Austrians fired, they fell, and the wall of bodies grew higher and higher. And after a time there were left behind that wagon and that wall of bleeding corpses, only three— François Legrand, Pierre Pasquin, André Marceau— and they were black with dirt, and singed with fire, and red with blood from crown to heel. And alone against that host they loaded their muskets and cried, " For France!" and fired, and, when they fired, three Austrians fell. Ah! not since the days of the Eternal City, when the Spurius Lartius on his right and Herminius on his left, Horatius held the bridge against Lars Porsena, had the world seen braver work than this. And when some hours later General Mouton, at the head of the fusileers of the Imperial Guard, came charging into Essling, bringing relief, respite, and rescue—amid the blazing houses, the falling timbers, and the crash of arms, still came from those three the all-conquering shout, " Vive l'Empereur!"

CHAPTER XV

In the Island of Lobau

What though the field be lost?
All is not lost; the unconquerable will
And courage never to submit or yield.
—MILTON, *Paradise Lost.*

FOR thirty hours the battle had raged in and about Aspern-Essling, and then the Archduke Charles, despairing of driving the French into the river, and finding that he was running short of ammunition, gradually withdrew his forces and sullenly waited for day.

Near the bank of the small arm of the Danube, under a great fir-tree on the island of Lobau, the Emperor Napoleon paced to and fro, while at a little distance stood the Marshals Bessières and Massena and the Prince of Neufchâtel, wrapped in their cloaks. The night was dark, and across the narrow bridge that united the island to the left bank passed and repassed the ambulance corps, carrying the wounded. No word was spoken by those four. The Marshals stood in silence, and the Emperor walked in silence, occasionally striking his boots with his riding-whip, or opening his snuff-box and, without making use of it, snapping the lid mechanically again. What a day it had been! Thousands and tens of thousands of the best soldiers of France lay dead and dying in those villages of Aspern-Essling, sacrificed by stern necessity to save the balance of the army and repair the fault of having with a presumption born of years of triumph, crossed, on a single bridge, the widest river in Europe, in the face of all the power of the Austrian Empire.

St. Hilaire, the veteran of Italy, would lead the charge no more; and Lannes, the old comrade of the early days, struck by the cannon-ball at Essling, was soon to close his glorious career of arms and perish, " a giant," when giants were most needed to extricate the army from its perilous position. In the heart of the Austrian Empire, France and her victorious Emperor had received a check, and let it once be thought that check had impaired their prestige, and Germany, affrighted by Ratisbon and Eckmühl, would recover courage, Austria would awake to new vigor, Holland would lift up her head, Spain would shout more fiercely her guerilla war-cry, England would scatter firebrands on every side, and from the Baltic to Gibraltar one shout would reverberate through Europe—" On to Paris! "

So in silence the Emperor paced the bank, and the Marshals awaited his pleasure. Soon the splash of oars was heard, and a boat rowed by four voltigeurs was seen nearing the shore; it contained the Marshal Davoût. When the Marshal had landed he joined the Emperor, and together they went to the great fir-tree, where the Emperor sat down on a log. Marshal Davoût sat on one side of him and Marshal Massena upon the other, while Bessières and the Prince of Neufchâtel stood wrapped in their cloaks. It was a council of war.

" Well," said the Emperor to the Prince of Neufchâtel, " what is your opinion? "

"Sire, I do not see what we can do but cross to the right bank as best we can.   After the terrible losses we have experienced to-day we certainly cannot remain longer on the left bank.   It seems to me that our only hope lies in getting back into Vienna."

"And what do you think?" said the Emperor, turning to Marshal Bessières.

"I am of the same opinion as the Prince of Neufchâtel, sire."

"Are you of the same opinion, Massena?" inquired the Emperor.

"I think, sire, that it would be extremely dangerous for us to attempt to maintain our position in Lobau. Our losses to-day have been something——"

"I know," said the Emperor quietly.

Davoût said nothing, but his face was very sad. "Gentlemen," said the Emperor, "the day has been a severe one, but it cannot be considered a defeat, since we remain masters of the field of battle.   It is doing a great deal to retire safe after such a conflict; sustained with a huge river at our back and our bridges destroyed.   Our loss in killed and wounded is great, greater than any we have before suffered in our long wars, but that of the enemy must have been a third greater.   There is a retrograde movement, proper and necessary, to recross the small arm of the Danube and wait there for the water to subside and the bridge to be rebuilt.   This movement can be performed to-night without losing a single wounded man, a single horse, or a single gun; above all, without losing honor.   But there is another retrograde movement, dishonoring and disastrous, to repass not only the small arm but also the great arm of the Danube, scrambling over this as best we can with boats that can carry only sound men, abandoning our wounded, our cannon, and our horses, and also the island of Lobau, which is the true ground for ultimately effecting a passage. If we act thus and present ourselves thus to the Viennese, they will overwhelm us with scorn and soon summon the Archduke Charles to expel us from the capital. In that case it is not a retreat to Vienna for which we must prepare, but a retreat to Strassburg. Prince Eugene, now on the march to Vienna, will find the enemy there and perish in the trap. Our allies, made treacherous by weakness, will turn against us. The fortune of the Empire will be at an end! The grandeur of France will be destroyed! Davoût and Massena, Lannes is dying, but you live, you will save the army!"

The impulsive Massena jumped up and seized the Emperor's hand.

"You are a man of courage, sire, and worthy to command us!" he cried.

"No! we must not fly like cravens who have been beaten! Fortune has not been kind to us, but we are victorious, nevertheless, for the enemy, who ought to have driven us into the Danube, have fallen before our positions. Let us cross only the small arm of the river, and I pledge my word to drown in it every Austrian who shall attempt to cross it in pursuit of us!"

And Davoût said in his quiet way, "I will defend Vienna from any attack by way of Presburg, or Krems, during the renovation of the bridges."

"Your Majesty is right," said the Prince of Neufchâtel. So the council broke up. The Marshal Massena returned to Aspern to superintend the passage of the army to the island of Lobau, while Napoleon and the Prince of Neufchâtel entered a boat to cross the main branch of the river to the right bank.

It was twelve at night, and the darkness dense and black, and the great flood rolled along the timbers and débris, which the Austrians above Aspern kept sending down the stream.

Row steadily, boatmen, be not dismayed by the darkness of the night or the surging of the Danube! You will reach the shore in safety—you bear " Caesar and his fortunes! "

CHAPTER XVI

THE DUKE OF MONTEBELLO

> The glories of our blood and state
> Are shadows, not substantial things;
> There is no armor against fate;
> Death lays his icy hands on kings.
> —SHIRLEY, *Contention of Ajax and Ulysses.*

FATIGUE clips the laurels of victory. After his exertion at Essling, Pierre was greatly depressed; nature demanded her due. But although he lacked rest, he did not lack misfortune. He was frying a piece of bacon with André Marceau when François Legrand came running toward them. "Here's a biscuit for you, François," said André. François reached the fire and stopped. He paid no attention to André's biscuit; he swore. Now, there are different degrees of swearing. There is the oath habitual, the oath circumstantial, the oath terrible, and the oath artistic. François' swearing combined the last two. He cursed the Austrians alive and dead; he cursed them in monosyllables and in sentences; he consigned them individually and collectively to the depths of hell, while against the gunners of Enzersdorf in particular he hurled a whirlwind of blasphemy. Pierre and André looked in surprise.

"What's happened?" said Pierre.

"'Ajax' is killed!" cried François, and he sobbed.

"The devil!" cried André Marceau. Then he swore; but he was no past-master in profanity, so his attempt seemed tame after what had preceded.

Pierre's heart was chilled—it meant so much to him. Ajax! did he not say on the Essling embankment. "Justice shall be done, young man, when we get back to Paris"? Who would see now that justice was done? Ajax, his friend, was gone!

In one point, however, François was mistaken, as Pierre learned later. The Marshal Lannes was not dead, but dying. He had been struck down at the close of the day of the fight at Aspern-Essling, when, sitting down to await the carrying out of orders he had given, a three-pound shot from a gun at Enzersdorf had crashed into his knees, smashing the kneepan of the one, and tearing the sinews of the other. He had been carried to the tête-de-pont of the bridge, where Dr. Larrey, against the advice of Dr. Yvan, had amputated one of his legs. There the Emperor had found him, and knelt by the stretcher to embrace his old comrade, whose blood stained his kerseymere waistcoat. Then across the island of Lobau he had been brought to Kaiser-Ebersdorf, and, when he was unable to drink the muddy water of the Danube, Marbot had filtered it through one of the Marshal's shirts and thus relieved his thirst. And now in a house at Ebersdorf, with one leg gone and the other swathed in bloody bandages, the Marshal Duke of Montebello lay dying —dying when France had need of him!

A brave man, this Marshal Duke of Montebello! We, who have seen him in the breach at Saragossa and before the walls of Ratisbon, have seen little of his history. Let us look more closely at his brave career.

Jean was his name, and he was born in the Gascon town, Lectoure, in April, 1769, and so was four months older than his Emperor and friend. His father was a dyer, and the young Lannes learned his trade, and learned, too, from his elder brother, reading, writing, and arithmetic. Then came the Revolution, and under the banner of "Liberté, Égalité, Fraternité," shouting "Ça ira!" and "Allons enfants de la patrie!" monarch-terrifying, throne-shaking, people-rescuing, young France began to march!

And Lannes marched, too, enrolling in the volunteers of Gers, and soon his comrades named him sous-lieutenant. Why? Because they found him zealous, brave, hard-working, and of ready wit. He served in the Pyrenees with Augereau and was made a colonel, and then was sent to Italy, where soon a greater than Augereau came to take command. Firm friends they were, the thin, sallow Bonaparte and the dashing Gascon colonel, and side by side they fought across the bridge at Lodi, in the marshes of Arcole, and on the plain at Rivoli. And then in Egypt, where, amid Mamelukes, pyramids, and Pharaohs, they traced at St. Jean d'Acre the footprints of Richard the Lion-hearted. Then through the 18th Brumaire, when victory crowned the victor, and France, emerging from chaos, raised aloft before astounded Europe her talisman of triumph—Bonaparte, First Consul! So over the Alps to Montebello and Marengo, and on, ever on, till the 2nd of December, 1804, when the son of the Gascony dyer, become Marshal of France and Duke of Montebello, advanced with the Imperial procession into Notre Dame and heard the white-robed Pius VII exclaim, "Send down, O Lord, the treasures of thy grace upon thy servant Napoleon, whom, in spite of our unworthiness, we consecrate this day as Emperor, in thy name!"

And now, in the house at Ebersdorf, the Marshal Duke of Montebello lay dying—dying when France had need of him!

"Marbot," said the Marshal, "is the army getting across in safety to Lobau?"

"Yes, Monsieur," replied the aide-de-camp.

"Oh! there is so much to be done and here I am, useless! My poor grenadiers—how they fought at Essling! What a slaughter!"

And the Marshal groaned. The aide-de-camp came up to the bed and straightened the pillow.

"Marbot," said the Marshal, "I must get out of this. Now I want you to write to Mesler. I have heard that he made an artificial leg for Count Palfy and that the Count can walk and ride as well as ever. Ask Mesler to come and measure me for a leg."

But the Marshal Duke of Montebello was to walk and ride no more. In a short time a raging fever set in, the wounded man became delirious and tossed upon his rough bed. "Bring up the guns!" he cried. "Where are the guns? And Massena, how long will he hold Aspern?"

Then the surgeons came and held a consultation.

"Well?" cried the Marshal, "am I going to recover? Are you going to save me?"

"Alas! I fear not, Monsieur le Maréchal," answered Dr. Yvan, and the tears gathered in his eyes.

The Marshal tossed wildly. "What!" he cried, "not save a Marshal of France and a Duke of Montebello! Then the Emperor shall hang you!"

The fever grew, and the Marshal became more delirious, thinking all the while that he was on the field of battle, holding the Austrians in check at Aspern-Essling.

Whenever he could, Pierre came to the house in Ebersdorf; he questioned the sentinels; he hung about the door, endeavoring to obtain news; he looked up at the windows of the room where the Marshal lay—those sad windows with green shutters. Must Ajax die now—now, when they all needed him so much—now, when he needed him so much—now, when justice was to be done in Paris? He heard muskets, presenting arms; turning, he saw Napoleon and Prince Berthier advancing rapidly toward the house. They were on foot. Although it was May, the weather was cool, and the Emperor wore his gray greatcoat buttoned, concealing his uniform. His gloves were white and his face was equally colorless, but his eyes gleamed like meteors. Pierre saluted. The Emperor raised his hand to his hat, and entered the house, and Berthier, glittering gold on every seam, followed him. Then Pierre had a thought—a foolish, childish, improbable, impossible idea—but the thought grew, and became a hope, and chained him there with his gaze riveted on the windows of the Marshal's room. And this was the thought, that perhaps the Marshal might think of him and speak of him to the Emperor, and so justice might be done in Kaiser-Ebersdorf instead of Paris.

Poor boy!—he was only a boy—and this was so large in his world-horizon; yet many men, touched by time's silver wand, have had hopes equally chimerical, and upon them have staked fame or fortune.

As Napoleon advanced to the bed, the aide-de-camp said sadly, " He no longer recognizes any one, sire."

" Lannes," said the Emperor, " do you know me? "

"They are coming!" cried the Marshal. "Bring the guns to Essling! Boudet must hold his own! He must! I say, he must!"

"Lannes!" cried the Emperor, "do you not recognize me? It is Bonaparte! It is your friend!"

"Be off with you!" shouted the Marshal. "Take my commands to Bessières. Tell him the Emperor has put him under my orders! Tell him I order him to charge home! Do you hear! But for me the Marshal Bessières would fiddle about all day! Why don't you go? Obey! or the Emperor shall hang you!"

So he raved and tossed, while Yvan and Marbot tried in vain to soothe him, and the Emperor went sadly away. But in the night the fever weakened and his delirium ceased. "Ah! Marbot," said the Marshal, "you are here? How kind you are, Marbot." And he took his aide-de-camp's hand. "Marbot," he continued, "when you go back to France you will see my wife and my poor children and my old father. Tell them I thought always of them. Tell him his son died for France." Then he rested his head on the aide-de-camp's shoulder and seemed to fall asleep. The room was quiet enough now, and after an hour there was a low sigh, and that was all. It was daybreak on the 31st of May, 1809.

Not long after the Emperor came, and the aide-de-camp met him at the door. "Sire," said he, "it is all over. The atmosphere of the room is already infected. I advise Your Majesty not to enter." But the Emperor brushed him aside, and, entering, he went up to the bed and embraced the dead body. And while the tears stood in his eyes he said, "What a loss for France and for me!"

Then the Prince of Neufchâtel came and gently tried

to draw the Emperor away, but the Emperor waved him aside. He remained for an hour, and at last when the Prince of Neufchâtel said, " Sire, General Bertrand and the engineer officers are waiting for you—you have yourself fixed the time," the Emperor rose and passed out into the open air.

It was soon known throughout the army that " Ajax " was no more. Then the grenadiers came and stood outside that doorway—old, grizzled veterans who in Italy and Egypt and Germany and Poland and Austria had followed the plume of him who lay within. And they stood outside that doorway and cried. The tears streaked their weatherbeaten faces, and, rolling down, were lost in their rough mustaches and beards. And among those weeping veterans were André Marceau and François Legrand and Gustave Lébon. They wept for the loss to France and to themselves, for they had marched behind him. There was also another who stood there and wept, who wept for the loss to France, and who thought of the mission to Tudela and of the midnight talk on the embankment before Essling, and wept for the loss to himself.

House of Kaiser-Ebersdorf, we do not know your past, what Austrian peasants have been born, or married, or have died within your walls. Near you are palaces and churches, buildings which surpass you in architectural beauty, in decoration and in embellishment; but from this day, May 31st, 1809, you outlive them all; for History, recording the deeds of heroes, stamps you with the seal of fame, when before your doors she sees the weeping grenadiers, and within your humble walls the mutilated corpse—all that was mortal of that sturdy Lannes, that brave " Ajax," that Marshal of France who was once a grenadier!

CHAPTER XVII

THE DANUBE

Attempt the end, and never stand to doubt,
Nothing's so hard but search will find it out.
—HERRICK, *Seeke and Finde.*

IT was now the month of June, 1809, and this is how the Emperor of the French and the Archduke Charles of Austria passed it. He, for the first time in his life, had stood before Napoleon and had not been defeated, and for some days he enjoyed this unwonted sensation and received congratulations upon his victory. Since he was so satisfied with the battle of Aspern-Essling, it would seem natural that he should endeavor to use all his resources to make the coming conflict even more disastrous to the French—to construct works which should render Wagram and Neusiedel unassailable, to call Kollowrath's corps from Lintz to Wagram, and Archduke John from Presburg, and Archduke Ferdinand from Poland. This would have added 50,000 men to his forces, and if the French, crossing from Lobau, had found Wagram and Neusiedel impregnable, defended by 80,000 men, and 120,000 ready to attack them in flank—what then? This the Archduke Charles of Austria might have done. This he did not do. Archduke Charles of Austria, you are a brave soldier, but your name is not enrolled with Condé, Turenne, Marlborough, or

Prince Eugene, much less with Caesar, Frederick, Hannibal, and Napoleon.

The French Emperor was busy. He had materials for building bridges prepared everywhere. Vienna was full of timber. He ordered it to Ebersdorf, and employed Vienna workmen, paying them with Austrian paper money seized in the Imperial coffers. He ordered all the ready-trained conscripts in France to be put *en route* for Strassburg; he ordered Prince Eugene and General Macdonald to come from Italy; he determined to connect Lobau with the right bank by a bridge on piles, for the bridge of boats had again been broken, and he employed in this work all the engineer soldiers and carpenters. Sixty wooden piles were placed in the river, and the bridge, laid upon them, was above the highest flood-mark and furnished a broad way for cavalry and artillery. The old bridge of boats below was strengthened and served for the infantry, so that all arms could pass at once. A great weir was made at the sides of the bridge, planted obliquely in the river, and seamen of the guard in boats, moving about above the weir, hooked all floating masses and drew them to the shore. He built also a vast tête-de-pont in the island of Lobau to defend the island and bridge in case of retreat. Over the marshy parts of the island he had causeways raised so that the troops could manœuvre in any weather. He built a powder magazine on the island, erected ovens, laid in stores of flour, collected cattle from Hungary, and wine from the convents on the Danube and in Vienna. He made roads through the island of Lobau and lighted them at night with lamps. He gave a play to the Imperial Guard in the theatre at

Schönbrunn and invited the ladies of Vienna. And
every week the Imperial auditors brought the reports
from the ministers in Paris, and he went over their
papers, and he sent orders to his armies in Spain and
France and Holland, and he wrote to his wife, and he
protected his lines of communication, and he watched
his foe, and his flanks, and his rear, and every morning he galloped from Schönbrunn to Lobau and went
about the island, over the bridges and under the
bridges, visited the wounded, examined the ovens,
tasted the soldiers' wine, watched the carpenters, inspected the tête-de-pont, climbed his pine-tree and
surveyed all the operations, came down and hurried
on the works, and every evening he galloped back to
Schönbrunn. Yes, the French Emperor was busy!
And the 115th were busy, too, drilling and working on
the fortifications, and during the month they had two
additions to their number, one of whom brought them
no credit and remained only a short time with them,
but the other brought them honor and remained with
them always. This is the way it was. One morning
the Emperor received news that an Austrian spy was
in the island of Lobau. His Majesty came at a
gallop from Schönbrunn, ordered all the works
stopped, and every man on the island—soldiers, officers, butchers, bakers, canteen-men, and pontoniers—
to be drawn up on parade—thirty thousand of them in
all. Then the Emperor said, " A spy has come among
us. Every man look at his neighbor to left and to
right." There was silence while every man did as he
was told. Pierre looked to his right, and there was
André Marceau looking at him—good! Then he
looked to his left—why! this was not Illar! This was

a strange fellow with an ugly eye, and there was Illar further on and looking surprised too! So Pierre and Illar cried out, "Here is a man we don't know!" He was arrested quickly enough after that, and a lovely spy he proved, for he was a Frenchman who had gambled away his property and gone to Austria to escape his creditors, and there offered himself as a spy. He used to come over at night in a boat and work among the French soldiers during the day, and make sketches of their works, and then go by night to the Austrians. He wept a good deal when he found himself caught, something after the fashion of Sinon before Troy, and they were thinking a little of pardoning him, when he offered obligingly to go over and spy on the Austrians and come back and tell the French. After that the Emperor concluded that he would hardly be a valuable addition to the Grand Army and had him shot, and every one was satisfied. So much for the one who brought no credit and left suddenly. Now for the one who brought honor and remained always.

Pierre was finishing his supper one night, when, by the light of the fire, he saw a dog. He was an old dog, his ear was cut, he was dirty and ugly, and he had only the stump of a tail. He looked at Pierre and wagged the stump, and Pierre said "Good dog," and gave him some bread and a little bone. And after that he stayed always with the 115th and followed the flag, for he remained faithful to a corps as long as he was well treated. He had been with the St. Sulpice cuirassiers before, but a colonel of that regiment had struck him with the flat of his sabre, and that was enough for him. His name was Corps-de-garde, he had received a bayonet thrust at Marengo, and had

had a paw broken by a shot at Austerlitz, and he was
the " bravest dog of the Empire!"

So passed the month of June, and by the beginning
of July all was ready and the French army, 150,000
strong, was massed in the island of Lobau. Colonel
Sainte-Croix was sent over and captured Enzersdorf,
the carefully prepared bridges were swung into place
across the small arm of the river, and during the night,
while the rain fell, the thunder crashed, and the light-
ning gleamed in bright flashes, the French army—
artillery, cavalry, and infantry—went steadily over
them—tramp! tramp! tramp!

The sun rose brightly on the morning of the 6th of
July, and there on the plain of the Marchfeld was the
great host, 150,000 men and 600 guns. The pennons
fluttered, the arms gleamed, the heavy artillery came
up with rumbling wheels and clanking harness, the
orderly officers pranced in all directions, the gold-
embroidered hussars galloped into position, the crested
and shining-cuirassed cavalry advanced proudly into
the plain, the trumpets sounded, the drums beat, and
the bands played the air they all knew well:

> On va leur percer le flanc,
> Ran, ran, ran, rantanplan, tirelire,
> Rantanplan tirelire en plan,
> On va leur percer le flanc,
> Que nous allons rire!
> Ran, tan, plan, tirelire,
> Que nous allons rire!

On a gently sloping eminence that overlooked the
Marchfeld stood the Emperor surrounded by his Marshals, and near-by was Roustan, the Imperial Mame-

luke, holding the white Euphrates. And His Majesty looked over his great army, and over the rolling Danube with its island of Lobau bristling with fortifications. And then he looked toward Aspern-Essling and Deutsch-Wagram where stretched the long lines of the army of the Archduke Charles, and, as he mounted his horse, he softly hummed:

Malbrouck s'en va-t'en guerre.

CHAPTER XVIII

WAGRAM

Battle's magnificently stern array!
—BYRON, *Childe Harold*.

THE French army was drawn up in three lines. On the left, Massena with the Boudet, Molitor, Legrand, and Carra St. Cyr divisions; in the centre, Bernadotte with the Saxons and the divisions of Oudinot; on the right, Davoût with the divisions of Friant, Gudin, and Morand. In the second line, the Viceroy, Prince Eugene, the divisions of Marmont and six regiments of foot-guards in reserve. In the third line, four divisions of light horse, three of dragoons, three of cuirassiers, the cavalry of the Saxons and the cavalry of the Guard. Opposite the French lines from Neusiedel to Wagram, and continuing in a semicircle from Gerarsdorf to the Danube, stretched the Austrian army. On its right, the corps of Klenau and the Prince de Reuss; in its centre Bellegarde and the Archduke Charles; on its left, Rosenberg and Hohenzollern, with Nordmann's advance-guard. Over the corn-fields of the Marchfeld shone the summer sun of the 6th of July, and, as far as the eye could see, from distant Neusiedel—the village of the Square Tower—extending in great curves by Aderklaa, Wagram, Gerarsdorf, and Aspern-Essling, were floating banners, shining helmets, fluttering pennons, uniforms white, blue, and scarlet, crest

on crest of tossing plumes, line on line of flashing
sabres, row on row of gleaming bayonets, league on
league of black-mouthed guns! All the ladies of
Vienna had mounted to the roofs and towers of the city
to witness the spectacle, and they had seen many brilliant dramas in the Hofburg and at Schönbrunn, but
never one like this. Imperial France and Imperial
Austria battling *à corps perdu*—face to face! While
high above Deutsch-Wagram, on a snow-white cloud
gilded by the first rays of the morning sun, stood
Victory, holding in her uplifted hand a laurel-wreath—
waiting to crown the victor!

The first gun was fired, the curtain was up, and the
great Imperial drama had begun!

The Austrians began the attack on Aderklaa, while
Prince Rosenberg, descending with the left wing from
the heights of Neusiedel, advanced against Davoût at
Grosshofen and Glinzendorf, and soon the artillery fire
was general all along the lines. The Emperor came
up to his threatened right wing with Nansouty's cuirassiers and some batteries of light artillery, which, taking the Austrians in the flank, compelled them to recross the Russbach and fall back toward Neusiedel.
Then the Austrian cavalry charged the French centre
and drove back Bernadotte and the Saxons in confusion. And Bernadotte, galloping back into the plain
to head off his men and restore order, met the Emperor, who had hastened up from the right wing. The
Emperor had learned of Bernadotte's remark after the
fight at Aspern-Essling, when the Marshal Prince of
Ponte Corvo had declared that if he were commanding
the French army he would, by a scientific manœuvre,
have forced the Archduke Charles of Austria to sur-

render. When, then, in hot pursuit of his flying troops, he encountered the Emperor, His Majesty remarked coldly, " Is that your scientific manœuvre by which you were going to make the Archduke lay down his arms? " Bernadotte attempted to reply, but the Emperor continued, " I remove you, sir, from the command of the army corps which you handle so badly. Withdraw at once. A bungler like you is no good to me." Then, riding among the Saxons, Napoleon restored order and sent them against the Austrian line.

Meanwhile the Austrians were pushing forward their right wing against the Boudet division, hoping to break the French left and reach the island of Lobau and the bridges over the Danube. The Austrian cavalry charged, a mass of shouting, swearing, plumed, white-coated, galloping horsemen. On they came, plunging and rearing, and Pierre thought he was in a whirlwind. He fired as fast as he could, jumped aside as an Austrian trooper's horse came by, stumbled and fell into a low ditch that ran transversely toward the Danube. There was a little water in the ditch, and also a part of a broken wagon-wheel, which he struck as he fell. He lay there and saw the Austrian cavalry pass over him—a cloud of legs, boots, spurs and scabbards, horses' tails and horses' bellies. In spite of all their efforts the Boudet division were driven back, and, through their glasses, the members of the Imperial staff could see the ladies of Vienna, on the housetops of the city, waving their handkerchiefs in triumph as the Austrian right wing advanced.

Pierre climbed slowly out of the ditch and looked around him. The Austrian cavalry were wheeling

11

about on the plain, preparing to charge the French left wing again, while the batteries, which the Emperor's forethought had placed about the island of Lobau, had opened fire and were raking the Austrian ranks. As he stood for a moment uncertain in what manner to rejoin the 115th, there came bounding through the long grass a dirty, bloody dog that jumped with joy when he saw Pierre, and barked, and started to run, and came back, and whined, and stood impatient. " Go on, Corps-de-garde, I'il follow you," said Pierre. Corps-de-garde gave a joyous yelp and started over the Marchfeld toward Essling. But, before he had gone far, he ran in among the trampled corn, and Pierre heard him barking loudly. Pierre hurried after him, and there on his back lay Colonel Hulot, colonel of the 115th, with a sabre-cut across his forehead, bleeding, but alive. Corps-de-garde was snuffing him and wagging his stump of a tail. With his handker-chief, which he found was wet from the water in the ditch, Pierre wiped the colonel's face, and tied the bloody rag about his head, while Corps-de-garde looked on approvingly. He had dropped his gun on the ground, and he now raised the wounded man in his arms and got him partly on his shoulder, and, staggering at first, for the colonel was a heavy load, he started toward the French lines, intending to get across the plain as best he might and, if there were no other way, to go again into the ditch. Then it suddenly occurred to him that by turning to the right and going to the river he could follow it until he reached the island of Lobau, while the corn, in that direction not much trampled, and the bushes would screen him largely from the plain. So he turned toward the river, while Corps-de-garde, wearing an air of importance, trotted before him. The ground was rough, and twice Pierre was compelled to set down the wounded man. He hated to do it, for the colonel groaned each time, but there was no other way. Each time, however, he raised him firmly again, and the second time he got him well up on his shoulder, and on they went.

The guns on the fortifications at Lobau were going in earnest now, and making such a racket that Pierre's head buzzed, when, all at once, the corn before him on the left parted, and he saw an Austrian trooper, sabre in hand. "Surrender!" said the Austrian. But that was all he said, for, before Pierre could set down his burden and draw his short sword—since he had left his gun where he had found the colonel—there was a growl, a bound, and a spring, and Corps-de-garde had fastened his teeth in the trooper's throat, and shaking himself violently, was tearing out the Austrian's windpipe. The trooper threw up his arms and fell, but Corps-de-garde never let go his hold until the Austrian lay still and mangled. And so, while the guns of Lobau thundered over them, and the Austrian cavalry charged again upon the French left, and the Viennese waved their handkerchiefs in premature rejoicing, Pierre, carrying his wounded colonel, toiled painfully along the bank of the Danube, while before him marched the ever-alert Corps-de-garde, the " bravest dog of the Empire!" At last he reached the first bridge to the Island of Lobau, and placed Colonel Hulot in the hands of the army surgeons.

The battle was raging furiously at Aderklaa, now, where the Austrians, encouraged by the repulse of

Bernadotte, were striving to break the French lines, and had already driven back slowly Massena's 18,000 men by sending against them the corps of Klenau, Kollowrath, and Lichtenstein, 50,000 strong.

The Marshal Massena, the "Enfant chéri de la victoire," injured by a fall from his horse, commanded from an open four-horse carriage in which he lay bandaged, and upon which the Austrians, imagining that it contained some person of importance, poured their fire, until the ground about the Marshal's carriage was covered with the wounded and the dead. The Carra St. Cyr division, driven back from Aderklaa, threw Massena's troops into some confusion, but the Emperor, coming up at that moment, got into the Marshal's carriage, and His Majesty's presence at once restored order. And now through Aderklaa the Aspre grenadiers were advancing victoriously, led by the Archduke Charles. The Emperor looked at them through his glass and went on quietly talking to Massena and outlining the manœuvres he desired him to execute. He ordered the Marshal Duke of Rivoli, with the Molitor and Legrand divisions formed in close columns, to wheel to the right and advance to the Danube to the aid of Boudet, already hard pressed by the Austrian cavalry. Massena drove off to carry out these orders, while the Emperor mounted his horse and dispatched an aide-de-camp for General Macdonald and the army of Italy; a second for the fusileers and mounted grenadiers of the Guard; a third for the cuirassiers of General Nansouty; a fourth for Lauriston with sixty guns from the Guard; a fifth for Drouot with forty guns from the French and Bavarian artillery. For it was His Majesty's intention to shake the Aus-

trian centre with the fire of a hundred guns, and then
to pierce it with the infantry of Macdonald and the
cavalry of Nansouty.

The right wing of the French was driving back the
left wing of the Austrians; the right wing of the Austrians was driving back the left wing of the French,
and about the ground quitted by Massena, slowly up
and down before the line of the Carra St. Cyr division,
waiting for the artillery he had ordered, rode the
Emperor on the white Euphrates, while behind him on
a coal-black stallion came the aide-de-camp Savary.

The Austrian cannon were firing as fast as musketry
now, and the white Euphrates, with his neck arched
and his red nostrils expanded, quivered a little at each
detonation, and snorted, and shook the foam from his
bits. Let us not forget them, those sturdy white
Arabians—Marengo, Ali, Bishop, Soliman, Euphrates
—that upon so many battlefields bore, amid the shells
and cannon-smoke, the fate of France!

Thus they rode, and every moment came from the
officers of the Carra St. Cyr division the short words
of command, "Serrez les rangs!" as many a brave
man pitched forward on his face, struck by the Austrian balls. But no ball struck the aide-de-camp
Savary, no ball struck the white Euphrates, no ball
struck the green-coated little Emperor!

So for an hour backward and forward before the line
rode the Emperor, his eyes fixed ever upon that far-
distant point across the Marchfeld where were stationed his artillery reserves, while with his hand he
patted the neck of his horse. There they came at last,
making the earth tremble—sixty guns belonging to the
Guard, and forty from the French and Bavarian

artillery. They were wheeled into line—a long dark
line of deep-booming, roar-fulminating, death-belching
mouths—and then they fired, and the Austrian cannon
answered with a will, and the most terrific cannonade
of the Empire began in multisonous thunder.

Firing continually upon the double line of the Austrian centre, the French guns pierced it with balls and
dismounted the Austrian artillery. But the Austrian
centre still stood firm, and then the Imperial tactician
prepared his *coup de grâce* and ordered General Macdonald and the Army of Italy to charge. So into the
plain of the Marchfeld, with the Broussier and Seras
divisions in single file, Lamarque's divisions on the
wings, and, behind all, twenty-four squadrons of Nansouty's cuirassiers, advances Macdonald. Into them,
in front, and on the left, and on the right, the Austrians pour their fire. The first ranks melt away, but
over their bodies, leaving behind them a long dark
trail of dead and dying, the gallant corps goes on.
And now at full speed come the horsemen of the
Prince John de Lichtenstein, swift-galloping, bent to
retrieve the fortunes of Imperial Austria. Macdonald
meets them with three lines of fire, and the proudly-
charging cuirassiers dash all in vain against his bayonets. Have they not done enough, these grenadiers
of Italy, as they stand there far on the Marchfeld
among their heaps of dead, the horsemen of de Lichtenstein retreating, and a sea of fire all about them?
Ah, no! Their mission is yet unfulfilled. The Austrian centre still stands firm. While life shall last,
march on! And so, over the blazing Marchfeld and the
wrecks of the Austrian cavalry, over the débris of all
those brave soldiers who have perished there since

morning, closing their rent, torn, and bloody ranks, bearing above them their eagle, and fixing their eyes on the iron Macdonald, while upon them from every side is poured a hail of shot and shell, they go to the very heights of Deutsch-Wagram, where, through the smoke and the flame they can see the white coats of Imperial Austria. Shall they pause here? No! No! The Austrian centre still stands firm! While life shall last, march on!

See! See! upon the right, beyond the towers of Neusiedel appear the fires of Davoût; Friant, Gudin, and Morand are driving back the Austrian left. And on the left, Massena, with Boudet, Legrand, and Molitor, is crushing out the Austrian right. While in the centre, far in advance, in the very heart of the Austrian position, surrounded by the torn and bleeding remnants of his regiments, under the tattered shreds of a tricolor, floats the white plume of Macdonald. The Emperor lowered his spy-glass, and turned to the Prince of Neufchâtel, saying, "The battle is won!"

CHAPTER XIX

A MARSHAL OF FRANCE

Great is the glory, for the strife is hard.
—WORDSWORTH, *To Haydon*.

"'Tis o'er! and France, foredoom'd to sway
Where'er her flashing eagle shone,
Hears the proud victor named that day
In victory's shout—'Napoleon!'"

ON the following morning the Emperor, surrounded by his staff, rode over the battlefield to superintend, according to his custom, the removal of the wounded. Then he rode to the bivouac of Macdonald's corps, and, when he saw the General Macdonald, he held out his hand and said, "You have behaved valiantly and have rendered me the greatest services. On the battlefield of your glory, where I owe you so large a part of yesterday's success, I make you a Marshal of France."

"Sire," answered the Marshal Macdonald, "since you are satisfied with us, let the rewards and recompenses be apportioned and distributed among my army corps, beginning with Generals Lamarque, Broussier and others, who so ably seconded me."

"Anything you please," replied the Emperor, "I have nothing to refuse you."

So it was. And the Marshal Berthier, Prince of Neufchâtel, the Duke of Bassano, Secretary of State, the Marshal Massena, the Viceroy Prince Eugene, generals, colonels and Imperial aides-de-camp came and grasped the hands of Macdonald and embraced him. And some of these had, and would have, passed coldly by the *General* Macdonald, but they threw their arms about the neck of Macdonald, Marshal of France.

So the rewards were distributed. Macdonald was made Marshal, Oudinot was made Marshal, Marmont was made Marshal, Massena was made Prince of Essling, Berthier was made Prince of Wagram, privates became corporals, lieutenants became captains, captains became chefs-de-bataillon, Boudet rose in rank, André Marceau got the cross, hundreds of others got this and hundreds of others got that, and Pierre—got nothing! Well, it was just as the poor mother had said, "The Pasquins were not lucky."

And after the summer had passed in diplomatic fencing, the Treaty of Vienna was signed, and, in October, Napoleon and his army bade adieu to the capital of Imperial Austria and took the road to France.

CHAPTER XX

THE STUDY OF THE EMPEROR

This hath been
Your faithful servant; I dare lay mine honour
He will remain so.
—SHAKESPEARE, *Cymbeline*.

THEY had a triumphal march through Bavaria, Würtemberg and the states of the Rhine Confederation. The people in all the little towns turned out, hung flags, erected arches and gave them as warm a welcome as the French could have done. And their Majesties of Bavaria and of Würtemberg could well afford to encourage such demonstrations, for both had been gainers by the Treaty of Vienna in territory and in population. So they reached Strassburg, where the Boudet division took the route through Luneville and Nancy. The Marshal Massena was with them, and when they reached Luneville, about five o'clock in the morning and sooner than they were expected, all the people came out in a hurry in somewhat abbreviated costumes. The red-faced sub-prefect stood by the door of the Marshal's carriage with his coat under his arm, his waistcoat unbuttoned, his feet in his slippers, and his hat on his head. He was too busy to take it off, for he was trying to get his sword in place, fasten his necktie, and think of his speech of welcome. Pierre laughed when he saw him in this predicament—it was the first time he had laughed for quite a while—but the Marshal spared the industrious prefect the trouble of remembering his brilliant harangue, by ordering the postillions to drive on.

For some months the Boudet division was stationed at Metz, where life went slowly enough. Not that there was not plenty to do—drill and guard duty and work of various kinds—but they did the same things over and over every day. Finally, on the 5th of January, the division was ordered to Paris and went into barracks there. It was near the end of the month of January, either the 30th or the 31st. The rain had been falling hard all day, and the stone-paved courtyard of the barrack was glistening and slippery, while the gutters were running full of water. Pierre had been on guard duty for three hours, and he had three hours more. It was not cheerful work, pacing up and down that wet courtyard, but he had become used to things that were not cheerful. In fact, the whole winter, gay enough for others, had seemed gloomy to him. Yet he often reasoned with himself that it should not be so. If he had failed to gain honor as a reward of his labors, no matter—he had done his duty and had fought for France.

One thing he had tried to do and that was to send cheerful letters to Marie. He had constantly alluded to the hope he had that soon he could pay a visit to Grenoble, if only for a day or two. But he thought when he wrote it that his return would be rather different from what he had anticipated when he set out. To go away a simple private and come back one! Why, it was like wearing a tag on your coat front—"The Pasquins are not lucky."

So he paced up and down in the wet, his gun on his shoulder. It was growing dark now, for darkness comes early in the January afternoons, when he saw an officer wrapped in a dark blue cloak crossing the courtyard toward him. When the officer reached him, Pierre faced about and presented arms, and then he recognized—Colonel Hulot.

" Is your name Pasquin? " inquired the Colonel.

" Yes, sir," said Pierre.

" Well, beau garçon," said the Colonel, " I've come to thank you for pulling me out of a damned unpleasant situation at Wagram. You put my props under me again, or I shouldn't be here to-day."

" And how did you know, sir, that it was I who helped you? " said Pierre.

" Aie! That I found out from the surgeons. Michel knew you and told me you had brought me in. I have heard other things about you, too, young man."

" I hope they were good things," said Pierre.

" Good things! Sacré! They were fine things! " cried the Colonel. " I reached here only yesterday. That cursed wound of mine laid me up and kept me boxed like a setting hen. But I've been talking to Captain François Legrand. You know him, eh? " And the Colonel slapped Pierre on the shoulder.

" Yes, I know him well, sir," said Pierre.

" Yes, I think you do! " cried the Colonel, " and he knows you too. He has told me a few things. C'est touché. Young man, you've struck your blows for France. And you've saved my life, and you're a friend of mine. And Hulot don't forget his friends. General Boudet shall know of what you did at Essling and at Ratisbon. His Majesty shall know of it, and then you'll see."

" I thank you, sir, for all your interest in me," said Pierre.

" Interest! " cried the Colonel, " Don't you see it's due to you that Hulot isn't lying six feet deep in that worm-eaten Austrian Empire? And if Hulot's services are worth anything to France—and I rather fancy they are!—they've got to reward you handsomely. If they give you nothing, they as much as say, Well, Hulot is not worth anything to us. Parbleu! but I like that. Hulot who fought at Marengo and chased the pot-bellied Prussians at Jena and the beggarly Spaniards at Somo Sierra!—Hulot worth nothing! That's the way I'll put it. Rather cleverly put, don't you think, eh? "

" Yes, sir, very cleverly put," said Pierre.

" Well, you leave it to me, beau garçon, I'll find Boudet and fix it up, never fear." And the Colonel threw his cloak about him and tramped over the court-yard into the barrack.

Pierre paced up and down again, and strange to say, although the rain had not stopped, he thought it was a jolly good evening—just the evening for a nice cool walk in the courtyard. And when the guard was changed, he was astonished that three hours had passed so soon. Curious, wasn't it? That night General Boudet came to the barrack and sent for Pierre and asked him many questions. And as they talked the General referred to Saragossa and asked what Pierre had done there. So Pierre related to him the story of his mission to Tudela just as he had told it to the Marshal Lannes. Then came a surprise, for General

Boudet drew out of his pocket a case and produced a paper which he handed to Pierre. It was the copy of a letter from the Marshal Duke of Montebello to the Minister of War. The letter was full of matters pertaining to military affairs, but under the Marshal's signature were these words, written hurriedly: "Private Pasquin (115th of the Line) has explained satisfactorily his conduct at Saragossa." The letter was dated at Essling the 22nd of May, 1809. Evidently it had been ready to send off, and when the Marshal returned from his midnight tour of inspection, he had added the postscript.

"That was given me this afternoon at the Ministry of War that I might look into the matter," said General Boudet, "and I think I have done so."

And Pierre looked at the letter and at General Boudet, and when his eyes fell again on that bold signature, Lannes, and he thought of the brave dead Marshal, who, amid all the whirl and turmoil at Aspern-Essling, had thought to put at the end of his letter those few lines so full of meaning for himself, the tears came to his eyes.

Two days later, on the evening of the 1st of February, the Grand Marshal Duroc, going to the Emperor's study to carry to him the list of, and particulars concerning, those soldiers of Italy and Egypt who were to be among the troops reviewed by His Majesty on the morrow, met General Boudet and Colonel Hulot leaving the Emperor's salon.

At two o'clock in the morning the Emperor, who had gone to bed at eleven, woke up, rang for his valet-de-chambre, and putting on his dressing-gown, his drawers with feet, and his slippers, tied his hand-kerchief about his head, and went into his study. Then, turning up the lamp upon his large writing-desk, he sat down in his chair and began going over his papers. It was a common custom of his—for he seldom slept more than four hours—to go at two or three o'clock into his study and work till dawn. The Emperor picked up the list which Marshal Duroc had brought him and read it over. He often had such lists prepared before a review, containing the names of old veterans in any particular corps, their position in their company—as first rank, third from the left—also any facts concerning their families. Then at parade the Emperor, passing that company, would stop sud-denly with all the air of an impromptu, and, glancing at the man previously designated, exclaim " You here! Why! I saw you at Aboukir. And your father, is he well?" Thus throughout the army the conviction grew that they were all personally known to the Em-peror. It was true that he knew and remembered a prodigious number of them, but, in the manner above referred to, the Imperial actor gave them the impres-sion that he knew them all.

So the Emperor read his list, and when he had finished, he took a pen and added a name—Pierre Pasquin—and under it he drew a line. Then he ex-amined the reports of his ministers, making notes on the margins, or read the returns on the situations of his armies—to him the most enjoyable books in his library. He reckoned up his soldiers man by man, company by company, division by division; he fol-lowed them along the roads of Europe; he learned exactly the positions of all their corps, where they were marching, where they were halting, when they would arrive.

Thus in the silent hours he worked. And without was the dark façade of the Tuileries Palace, the deep dense gloom of the Tuileries garden, the blackness of the Place de la Concorde, and Paris wrapped in night. But in the dark façade of that Tuileries Palace shone the light from the Emperor's study, and the rays from that light in the Emperor's study kept watch over it all.

CHAPTER XXI

THE CROSS OF THE LEGION OF HONOR

Sound, sound the clarion, fill the fife!
To all the sensual world proclaim,
One crowded hour of glorious life
Is worth an age without a name.
—SCOTT, *Old Mortality*.

A REVIEW-DAY under the Empire! Would you see it?
Look on Bellangé's canvas in the gallery at Versailles,
or follow with me now the gaily-dressed Parisians
wending their way along the Quay of the Tuileries
toward the great archway of the Louvre that opens
upon the Place du Carrousel. In this bright Sunday
sunshine of the 2nd of February, 1810, all Paris is
in the streets, and along the Rue de Rivoli and the
Rue St. Antoine, converging from the Place de la
Concorde and the Place de la Bastille, come regiments
of infantry, squadrons of cavalry, loud-rumbling artillery trains, and all the pomp of war.

To the clear-toned blasts of blaring trumpets and the
sounding strains of martial music, with the clank of
arms, the clatter of hoofs, the roll of wheels, and the
gleam of polished steel, they come—pouring into the
Place du Carrousel and into the great courtyard
of the Tuileries Palace where Napoleon, the world-
conqueror, reviews his army. There are the Boudet
and Legrand divisions, the St. Sulpice cuirassiers, the
12

divisions of Oudinot, Mortier and Carra St. Cyr, and, last of all, the great Imperial Guard. How proudly they march! their breasts decked with the insignia of their valor, their faces scarred with their " quarterings of nobility," their eagle-topped standards bearing the record of their glory. How proudly they march! For them there is no god but Mars, and Napoleon is his prophet.

What a setting for the martial scene! The long façade of the Tuileries, with its massive dome, above which floats the tricolor, the great palaces of the Louvre on either hand, and, in the centre of the vast open square, the majestic Rome-reflecting monument of Austerlitz of Jena and of Friedland, upon whose summit stand the famous horses of St. Mark, brought by General Bonaparte from Italy to grace his Arch of Triumph on the Place du Carrousel.

Tell us, bronze horses of St. Mark, you who were made by the cunning hand of Lysippus for the great Alexander, and, high on the triumphal arches of this world, have seen pass beneath your feet the Macedonian phalanx, the armies of Constantine with their motto " In hoc signo vinces," the legions of Rome, the spoils of Gaul, and laurel-crowned Caesar—have you yet seen a conqueror like this? But the horses of St. Mark return no answer, they are silent. All else is activity. Aides-de-camp galloped in all directions, while, under the command of the Colonel-General of the Guard, the infantry regiments took up their position in the palace courtyard; the cavalry and artillery on the Place du Carrousel. As soon as the various corps were in position, the flag and standard-bearers, coming out of the ranks, assembled before the

Pavillon de l'Horloge, the main entrance to the Tuileries Palace, and, conducted by an officer, went up the staircase to the salon of the Emperor. There the chamberlain announced them, and, having made a trophy of the flags and standards, they returned in the same order, and as they marched out of the palace doorway, the drums beat, and the officers saluted the colors. By this time all the palace windows were filled with people—the court and the *corps diplomatique*—while against the railings that separated the courtyard from the Place du Carrousel was packed an eager, show-loving, glory-worshiping crowd. Before the palace door stood Roustan, the Mameluke, holding the white Euphrates, while behind him, held by servants in the green and gold livery of the Imperial household, were a dozen other horses belonging to members of the Emperor's staff, and, most conspicuous among them, the gorgeously-bedecked *cheval de bataille* of the King of Naples.

As the clock of the Tuileries Palace struck the hour of one, the noise of boot-heels, spurs and trailing scabbards was heard upon the staircase, and a moment later, wearing his green coat of the mounted chasseurs, his white knee-breeches, and his famous cocked hat, the Emperor appeared in the doorway, while behind him came his staff,

> " Glittering in golden coats, like images;
> As full of spirit as the month of May."

And instantly the drums rolled, the arms flashed, the banners waved, the people shouted, and the proud Imperial trumpets clamored—crash!

The Emperor mounted his horse and rode at a gallop along the ranks, and after him rode his staff—four Colonels-General of the Guard; Duroc, Grand Marshal of the Palace; the Prince of Neufchâtel, Vice-Constable; the Grand Equerry Caulaincourt, the Minister of War, the Governor of Paris, and Joachim Murat, the King of Naples. A showy man, this King of Naples, with his stalwart figure, large blue eyes and long black hair, his Polish coat covered with gold, his gilded belt holding the scabbard of his diamond-hilted sabre, his trousers of aramanthine purple embroidered in gold, and his hat with its wind-blown crest of heron's plumes. His war-horse, too, no less magnificent, with sky-blue housings worked in gold. Hungarian saddle and flashing stirrups. And what did the veterans of the Grand Army think of this Imperial popinjay, Murat, the King of Naples? They thought well of him, for they had seen those blue eyes burn with fire, that long hair flying in the wind, that Polish jacket black with powder, that mighty war-horse streaked with foam, that diamond-hilted sabre red with blood. And, as at Jena, Eylau, Friedland, they saw the charging squadrons pressing hard after that heron's plume, that led them ever where the fight was fiercest, that led them ever on to triumph, they thought well of him, for they saw him as he was—Murat, the phenix-knight of chivalry, the king of cavaliers!

After riding along the ranks at a rapid gallop, the Emperor returned to the palace entrance, dismounted, and began the manœuvres. An officer of the Guard, who possessed a strong voice, stood near to repeat his commands. The Emperor put the Boudet and

Legrand divisions through the manual of arms, then, taking the Legrand division, His Majesty said to the commanding officer, "Order them to form a square by divisions as you march, and do so with the fewest manœuvres." So the order was given: "Form a square on the second division as you are marching; first division by the left flank and by right file; quick time! third division by the right flank and by left file; quick time! fourth division by the left flank and by left file; quick time! second division, slow time!" But the Emperor did not like the way it was done, and they had to do it a second, a third, and a fourth time. Then His Majesty inspected each regiment man by man, having all the knapsacks opened before him, and, when he was satisfied that all was right, the Legrand division marched out into the Place du Carrousel.

The Boudet division now marched forward, and were put through the manœuvres, the knapsacks opened, and the regiments inspected. Then, with his staff following him, the Emperor walked down the line and stopped before the 115th. It was very still in the great Tuileries courtyard now, filled as it was with row on row of silent statues holding guns with long bright bayonets. The Emperor made a sign, and the Captain François Legrand called "Pasquin!" and Pierre, whose heart thumped so loudly that he thought it must be heard by every one, stepped forward two paces and presented arms.

"Sergeant Pasquin," said the Emperor (and he placed special emphasis on the word Sergeant), "your deeds are known to me. You were the fourth across the walls at Ratisbon, you were the first to bring the

boat across the Danube, you fought against great
odds at Essling, you saved your colonel on the field
of Wagram. I now give you the cross. You have
deserved it." As he spoke the Emperor detached the
Legion of Honor from his breast and held it against
the breast of the grenadier, while Marshal Duroc, who
was watching him closely, quickly pinned it there.

"Moreover," added His Majesty, "I appoint you to
the Guard," and he passed on down the line and
mounted his horse before the Pavillon de l'Horloge.

And then, in the Tuileries courtyard, within the
shadow of the Arch of Triumph, Colonel Hulot
stooped and fastened a red ribbon about the neck of
Corps-de-garde. He was only a dog, but God made
him, and he was the "bravest dog of the Empire."

The bands of the regiments took their station before
the Pavillon de l'Horloge and the march past began.
But of all that host, that with flying banners and
resounding shouts marched, to the stirring notes of
the "Veillons au Salut de l'Empire," past their Imperial War-Lord and out under the Arch of Triumph
into the Place du Carrousel, none carried his head
higher, none moved with lighter step, than the cross-
decked Pierre Pasquin of the Garde Impériale.

That evening after the parade was over and the
115th had broken ranks, Pierre was surrounded by
his comrades. They all wanted to grasp his hand and
they all wanted to slap him on the back. "Parbleu!"
cried François Legrand, "don't tell me I can't keep
a secret. I knew this morning you were to get something."

"Mon Dieu!" cried André Marceau, embracing
Pierre, "to think of it! A sergeant!—the cross!—and
the Guard!"

"None too much," said Colonel Hulot, elbowing his way through the crowd. "He saved me—Hulot— a man that France cannot afford to lose. If I had had my way he'd have been lieutenant."

Pierre thought the handshakings and embracings would never end, but finally he got away from all the crowd and walked alone to the barrack, and as he entered it, the sentinel in the doorway presented arms. Pierre looked about to see if there were an officer near. But no, he was alone.

"Is it to me that you are presenting arms?" he asked.

"Yes," said the sentinel, "we are ordered to present arms before all those decorated with the cross of the Legion of Honor."

Pierre went into the barrack, lit his candle, placed it on the table, took his pen and paper and began to write. When he had finished his letter it was very late, and he had forgotten his supper, but that was no matter, for the letter was to Marie, and it was beautifully written, and these were the words with which it ended—"It was the finest day of my life!"

CHAPTER XXII

MARIE

In peace, Love tunes the shepherd's reed;
In war, he mounts the warrior's steed;
In halls, in gay attire is seen;
In hamlets, dances on the green.
Love rules the court, the camp, the grove,
And men below, and saints above;
For love is heaven, and heaven is love.
—SCOTT, *Lay of the Last Minstrel.*

THE little dining-room in the Café Jodélle had never presented so festive an appearance as on the 1st of March, 1810. Pierre had obtained leave of absence and had come down from Paris a few days before. Leave of absence was not so hard to get now since there was peace, and a fellow wanted to be married, and beside the great Emperor himself was going to be married before long.

What a welcome they had given him at the Café Jodélle! Henri could hardly believe that this big strapping fellow with the lofty bearskin cap was the boy of the Rue Montorge whom he had known in the past. And Marie—this exceeded all she had ever hoped. The cross! The rank of sergeant! The Imperial Guard! The brave soldier home again safe and sound! It was almost too good to be true, yet true it was, and there he stood before her eyes. How the boys crowded round him! Gaspard brought a lot of

them every day, and they stood about with their large
eyes popping out of their heads in silent wonder. And
the old fellows too—Frédéric Bonneville and Philippe
Courteau—they all wanted to take the cross in their
hands, and would insist upon hearing over and over
again the story of the walls of Ratisbon, the march
down the Danube, and the great fight upon the plain
at Wagram.   But Pierre broke away from them whenever he could and went to find Marie, and one morning they walked to the little house in the Rue Montorge—it was Pierre's house now, and Henri had kept
it in good repair—and they sat for a while in the room
where the mère Pasquin had died. Afterward they
walked to the cemetery and stood beside the small
gravestone.   And then a curious thing happened,
for the grenadier of the Imperial Guard knelt down
and read the inscription, and then, leaning on the
gravestone, he buried his face in his hands and remained there a long time.   Marie stood beside him,
crying softly to herself.   And after a while the grenadier got up and brushed his hand across his eyes.
Marie took his arm, and they went homeward. " If
mother were here now, I should be very, very happy,"
said Pierre the grenadier.

How gay the dining-room in the Café Jodélle appeared on the evening of the 1st of March, with the
candles on the table and in the two bright brackets
on the walls! How fine the table looked with the
best white cloth and the silver dish which once belonged to Marie's mother! Aunt Zirélle had loaned
them a couple of silver dishes also, and that made a
grand show. As for the feast—Henri had surpassed
himself. There was a *purée* of chestnuts and a maca-

roni soup, a *brochet à la Chambord*, beef garnished with vegetables and cauliflowers *au gratin;* for *entreés, filets* of duck *au fumet de gibier;* mutton cutlets *à la Soubise*, a fricassee *à la chevalière;* and for *entremets* a jelly of oranges, *gaufres à l'allemande* and coffee cream *à la française*, also bottles of sealed wine. Surely it was a *festin pour le roi*—a feast for a king.

What a merry company they were! At the head of the table sat Henri, who had put on once more his old regimentals of Italy. The coat was badly faded and the braid was worn, but the coat had an imposing look for all that and seemed to say, " I too have seen the Austrian fire!" On Henri's right sat Marie in a pink dress—such a pretty dress, thought Pierre, much prettier than the dresses he had seen on the gay Parisiennes in the Tuileries garden. And next to Marie sat Pierre in his blue coat with white lapels, his knee-breeches, his vest and gaiters of white basine, and his shoes with silver buckles—the uniform of the Imperial Guard. Then came Gaspard in a new coat made expressly for the great occasion, with bright buttons in which Gaspard could see his face; and then Jacques le Page. On Henri's left sat Philippe Courteau, who kept the Hotel des Trois Dauphins—a great big fellow who had followed the tricolor upon the sands of Egypt and lost an eye at St. Jean d'Acre. He wore a black patch over his eye, but he was a fine-looking man in spite of that. He also had an old coat with a rent through one arm made by a Mameluke sabre on the plain at Cairo, and it too seemed to say, " Look at me! I am better than all your fine new coats, for I have been at the front amid the cannon-smoke, under the eyes of the great general."

Then came old Frédéric Bonneville, and next to him the good dame Bovard and her stout husband Robert Bovard, and at the end of the table Henri's sister, the Widow Zirélle. A fascinating person was the Widow Zirélle! She had already buried three husbands and was now looking for a fourth. Her first was Gustave Pepin. He was a round, fat, good-natured, moon-faced, little man who kept a pie-shop near the Rue Montorge. She could never complain of Gustave Pepin. He was a good husband and not a bit jealous. Sometimes on Sundays he put on his best clothes and took her for excursions to Voreppe or Buisserade. Some days, when he wanted to sit at home and smoke his pipe, he allowed her to go with his good friend Loredan Devienne. One night he went across the river to a spread at the house of his friend Caboul Lorette, and coming back over the bridge, he fell in, and that was the end of him. She thought she would cry her eyes out when she heard of it; she wanted to drown herself too; but she rallied and married Devienne six months afterward. Dear! dear! what a man Devienne was after all! What a temper he had! Why! the wretch actually commanded her one day to pull off his boots. It was as bad as Lauzun and the Duchess de Montpensier. And was he jealous? My! My! If she as much as smiled at any cavalier who came into the shop, Devienne turned green. His jealousy finished him, though, and that was a good thing, for one day she kissed her hand to the young Sainte-Perme and Devienne challenged him and Sainte-Perme ran him through, and so she was a widow again. Then she married old Zirélle. He was twenty years older than she, and had the gout so badly that he rarely left the house, but sat all day in a high-backed chair and grunted. Now, why did she marry him? Why did the Maintenon marry Scarron? Why did la grande Mademoiselle marry Lauzun? Why do some women do anything? They never give reasons. People did say, however, that he left her a house in the Grand Rue and two thousand francs in the bank when he died. Now she was perfectly happy, for here was stout Robert Bovard on her right with whom she could flirt. And if she enjoyed anything it was flirting with a married man, and right under his wife's nose too. How she managed her fan! Even La Pompadour couldn't have beaten her at that.

"I thought grenadiers' coats were all covered with gold braid, Pierre," said Gaspard.

"Not in the Guards," answered Pierre. "We have plain coats. The Emperor wears a coat like this on Sundays and at fêtes."

"I would rather have a coat like that than all the gold-embroidered uniforms of Murat," said Henri Jodélle.

"Won't you tell us again, Pierre, what the Emperor said when he gave you the cross?" asked Frédéric Bonneville.

So Pierre related once more the scene in the Tuileries courtyard.

"They didn't have crosses in my day," said Philippe Courteau, "the Little Corporal hadn't established them, but they had sabres of honor. When you come to the Trois Dauphins, Pierre, I'll show you mine."

"I should like to see it very much," said Pierre.

"That was a lively scrimmage you had at Essling," continued Philippe, "but I'll bet it wasn't anything to the one we had at Cairo. Those Mamelukes are very devils at riding. They used to rush up and rear their horses right on our bayonets and sabre us if they could, though they might as well have tried to chop down the pyramids as one of our squares with the Little Corporal in the middle of it."

"Robert! Robert! Give me some wine," said dame Bovard, who was beginning to be annoyed at the industry displayed by the stout Robert in helping his fair neighbor the Widow Zirélle.

"Mon cher Robert," laughed the Widow Zirélle, "will you not give me some *gaufres* and coffee cream? Ah, merci, you are most kind, Robert, you are most attentive."

"Robert! Robert! do you hear me?" demanded dame Bovard, pulling his sleeve. "Give me some wine."

"Ah! How can I serve two at once!" cried Robert, as he passed her the coffee cream.

"No!" cried dame Bovard, "attend to me, Robert. I want some wine. Do you hear?" And the good dame made her meaning more plain by giving him a sharp pinch in the arm. And so they kept on until stout Robert was soon muttering under his breath, "Les femmes au diable!"

"Come, a song! a song!" cried Henri Jodélle, who perceived that all was not peace at the other end of the table. "We'll begin with Frédéric, and each shall sing a song in turn."

"I don't know any song," said Frédéric.

"Oh, yes, you do," cried Jacques le Page. "You know the 'Marquis de Carabas.' That's a jolly song.

We'll all join in the chorus and rap with our knives on the table. Begin! begin!"

So old Frédéric got up and sang with his gruff voice the "Marquis de Carabas."

> "Hear me, ye vassals all,
> Castellans, villeins, great and small:
> Through me, through me alone
> The King was set upon his throne.
> If he should neglect
> All the deep respect
> Which I claim, to pay,
> Then the deuce I'll play.
> Chapeau bas! Chapeau bas!
> Hail to the Marquis of Carabas!"

"Bien! bien! Frédéric," they cried, "another verse."

"That's all I know," said Frédéric.

"Well, Philippe, it is your turn now," said Henri Jodélle.

"I know only one song," said Phillippe, "'le bon roi Dagobert.'"

"And a good song too," cried Henri.

Philippe pushed his chair back from the table, and rising, straightened himself to his full height and roared out his favorite song:

> "The good King Dagobert, so stout,
> When fighting, flung his blows about.
> Good Saint Eloi
> Said: O mon roi
> I fear they will
> Your Highness kill.
> Then said the king: They may, said he,
> So clap yourself in front of me."

"Bravo! Philippe," cried Henri Jodélle.

"The good King Dagobert the great,
   When he had tippled, walked not straight.
      Good Saint Eloi
      Said: O mon roi,
      Your footsteps slide
      From side to side.
   Pooh! Monsieur, said the King, said he,
   When you get drunk you walk like me."

"Très-bien! très-bien! Philippe," they all cried. Philippe waved his hand to them and sat down.

"And now," cried Henri Jodélle, rising from his chair, "a toast. Join me all. Good luck and happiness to Marie and Pierre."

Up they rose, and little Gaspard stood on his chair from very joy, and they held their glasses high, and they all cried together, "Good luck and happiness to Marie and Pierre!"

"Now, Pierre, a song from you," said Henri.

"Here! here!" cried Philippe Courteau and Frédéric Bonneville. "You have sung no song yet, Henri. You cannot pass yourself in that manner. It is your turn now."

"Ha! ha!" laughed Henri. "You have caught me, have you? I know no songs."

"Ah, père Henri," said Marie, "you know the song the Emperor sings, 'si le roi m'eut donne, Paris sa grande ville.'"

"Yes, I know that one," said Henri. "Well, you shall have it." And old Henri in his faded uniform sang in his deep bass voice:

   "If the King had given to me
      Paris his great town,
   And if I were forced to flee
      And leave my love alone,

To King Henry I would say:
' Take your Paris back, I pray;
Better I love my love, O gay,
Better I love my love! ' "

" Bravo! bravo! Henri," cried Philippe Courteau.
" That is a good song, and all the better because the
Emperor sings it.   Now we will have the song from
Pierre."

" What shall I sing? " asked Pierre.

" Sing the ' Partant pour la Syrie ' of la reine Hortense," said old Frédéric Bonneville.

And so Pierre began:

" Partant pour la Syrie,
    Le jeune et beau Dunois
    Venait prier Marie
    De bénir ses exploits.
' Faites, reine immortelle,'
    Lui dit-il en partant,
' Que j'aime la plus belle;
    Et sois le plus vaillant.' "

" Il trace sur la pierre
    Le serment de l'honneur,
    Et va suivre à la guerre
    Le comte, son seigneur.
    Au noble voeu fidèle,
    Il dit, en combattant,
' Amour à la plus belle!
    Honneur au plus vaillant! ' "

" ' Je te dois la victoire,
    Dunois,' dit le seigneur,
' Puisque tu fais ma gloire,
    Je ferai ton bonheur.
    De ma fille Isabelle
    Sois l'époux à l'instant,
    Car elle est la plus belle,
    Et toi le plus vaillant.' "

> " A l'autel de Marie,
>   Ils contractent, tous deux
>   Cette union chérie,
>   Qui seule rend heureux.
>   Chacun dans la chapelle
>   Disait, en les voyant,
> ' Amour à la plus belle!
>   Honneur au plus vaillant!' "

And when, on the following morning, Marie in her simple white gown and Pierre in his splendid uniform of the Garde Impériale stood up before Father Morot in the little Chapel of St. Laurent, old Henri Jodélle, Frédéric Bonneville, Philippe Courteau, Jacques le Page and all the rest, cried—

> " Amour à la plus belle!
>   Honneur au plus vaillant! "

CHAPTER XXIII

THE MISSION OF THE PRINCE OF WAGRAM

Hail to thee, lady! and the grace of heaven,
Before, behind thee, and on every hand,
Enwheel thee round.
—SHAKESPEARE, *Othello*.

THEY spent the honeymoon in Grenoble in the simplest, happiest way. Once they dined with dame Bovard, and that day was memorable, because on their way home they met Monsieur Montfort, the rich banker, and he stopped and talked to them, hat in hand. When they walked on, Pierre felt that he would like to run again to the Rue Montorge and cry to the dear mother, "Monsieur Montfort, the rich banker who lives in the Place Grénette, has talked to me, hat in hand. What do you think of that?" He was only a boy, after all. Once they walked to the fortress called La Bastille, from the old feudal castle which stood there many, many years before. The bright March sun was sinking and the gray walls glowed gloriously in the ruddy light. They went up to the battlements. At their feet, Grenoble with its ramparts and canals lay spread out as though on a plain; the straight road to Vizille stretched in front, and the winding valley of the Isère ended in the barricades of Mont Blanc.

"Isn't it beautiful, Pierre?" said Marie.

"Yes," said Pierre.

He put his arm about her and drew her closely to him. She nestled her head, and they stood, looking out over the city—the city of their youth, the city of their love. Pierre drew himself up proudly, for Grenoble, glowing in the ruby rays, appeared to be doing him honor; the murmuring city seemed to say, "He has won his fight; he has won his cross; he has won his bride. Hurrah for the brave soldier!"

A great thrill of pride and joy swept over him. He felt as he fancied the Little Corporal did when he placed on his head the crown which had cost him so much thought and effort. Pierre had no crown to give the wife at his side, but he stooped and kissed her.

Honeymoons, however, like all else in this everchanging world, must end, and on the 15th of March, Pierre was summoned to Paris to attend another wedding—a wedding amid Imperial pomp, a wedding amid the acclamations of two nations, a wedding amid a wondering world. For the Emperor Napoleon, having been divorced, whom will he marry? That was the great question agitating the minds of the French statesmen—aye and the statesmen of all Europe, too—in the early days of 1810. Come forth, then, eligible princesses of Russia, Austria and Saxony; let us consider you to see which of you is worthy to sit upon the Gallic throne and give sons to France. For it is a son that the Emperor desires, who, bearing the title King of Rome, may one day consolidate his work, inheriting his diadem of France, his iron crown of Lombardy, and his Empire of Charlemagne *redivivus*.

Behold then in the early days of 1810, the Emperor Napoleon, the King of Holland, the Viceroy of Italy, the Cardinal Fesch, the great dignitaries, the ministers, and the presidents of the Senate and of the Corps Législatif, assembled in solemn council in the Tuileries Palace to decide this matter.

Saxony having been set to one side, there remained but Russia and Austria—a grandduchess and an archduchess—and all the momentous possibilities that a choice of either of them implied. The pros and cons were discussed at length. Fouché, and especially the Arch-chancellor Cambacérès, favored the Russian grandduchess, and each in turn expressed his views, some saying much, some little, and finally it was M. de Talleyrand's turn. Hear, then, Prince Machiavelli de Talleyrand-Périgord as he rose nonchalantly from his place at the council board, snuff-box in hand. "Suppose," said he, "that the Emperor Napoleon marries the grandduchess and that we are in a year's time from now assembled in this room and at the same table; the door is thrown open, the arrival of a messenger is announced and this messenger brings the news of the death of the Emperor Alexander. As a result of this death the whole situation undergoes a complete change. No longer are we sure of a Russian alliance; the influence of Austria, Prussia and England becomes paramount at St. Petersburg and all the advantageous results of the marriage are a thing of the past. Let us assume the contrary hypothesis. The Emperor marries an archduchess; when after a year's time news comes of the death of the Emperor Francis it is nothing more than a case of family mourning. The political interests of both countries are bound up together and do not undergo any modification, and the Austrian cabinet continues to be as anxious to preserve intact the alliance as does the French one. This consideration is so potent a one in my estimation that it does not suffer me to hesitate as to the advice which I am not called upon to give."

All the world knows to what decision the council came and whether it was a Russian grandduchess or an Austrian archduchess whom Napoleon married.

"I am somewhat surprised, Monseigneur," said M. Pasquier two days later to the Arch-chancellor Cambacères, "that your opinion did not prevail."

"That need not surprise you," answered Cambacères, "when a man has only *one* good reason to advance and when it is impossible to utter that, it is natural that he should be beaten."

"What do you mean?" inquired M. Pasquier.

"Oh, no matter," replied the Arch-chancellor.

"But I assure you I am most anxious to know."

"You give me your word that you will keep it a secret?"

"I give you my word."

"Well," said Cambacères, "you will see that my reason is so good that a single sentence will be enough to make it understood. I am morally certain that ere two years have gone by we shall be engaged in a war with the power whose daughter the Emperor will not have married. Now a war with Austria does not give one the slightest anxiety, but I dread a war with Russia, for its consequences are not to be calculated."

Merrily rang the bells of old Vienna on the 5th of March, 1810; gaily the people thronged the avenues, brightly the garlands floated from the house-fronts, pompously the imperial carriages rolled out of the Hofburg, for on this day the Marshal Berthier made his solemn entry to ask, for his all-powerful friend and sovereign, the hand of Marie Louise. Less than a year before Prince Berthier had stood at Napoleon's side before Vienna while the French shells crashed into the city; less than a year before he had gained his title, Prince of Wagram, upon the plain beyond the Danube while the Austrian army of the Archduke Charles fell back before the guns of Lauriston and the bayonets of Macdonald. But now the court and people rushed to greet him, for he rode no longer thundering in the Imperial train among the bayonets of the Old Guard, but came bearing palms of peace and hopes of friendship with Cupid *victor* as postillion. The happy Viennese could hardly be restrained from taking out the horses and drawing into their Imperial Kaiserstadt the carriage of the Marshal Prince of Wagram.

" My child," said the Emperor Francis, " you are to go to France and marry Napoleon. The interests of Austria demand it. The glory of the House of Hapsburg requires it."

" Yes, papa," said the Archduchess Marie Louise.

Four years later, in the palace at Rambouillet, the Austrian Emperor said to the wife of Napoleon and the mother of the King of Rome: " My daughter, you are to go back to Vienna. The interests of Austria demand it. The glory of the House of Hapsburg requires it."

" Yes, papa," said the Empress Marie Louise.

Ah! but why look ahead? Ring the bells merrily, hang the windows with gay tapestries, rear the great pavilion at Braunau, fire the guns of Munich, raise the triumphal arches of Strassburg, light the illuminations of Luneville and Nancy, cover the walls of the Imperial apartments at Compiègne with gorgeous cashmeres. For Marie Louise, the daughter of the Caesars, taken from her quiet Schönbrunn boudoir, her birds, her embroidery and her spaniels, is *en route* to wed the Man of the People, whom genius and glory—Rivoli, Marengo, Austerlitz, Jena, Friedland, Wagram—have made the Jupiter Tonans of the world's Olympus; is *en route* to mount the proudest throne since the days of Alexander, of Caesar, or of Charlemagne, and find Europe at her feet.

Loudly the poets—Tissot, Sauzon, Cazélle, Arnault, Émenard, Rougemont, Brugnière—sang their peans. Was not the Fourth Dynasty founded now all-gloriously, all-immovably? Did not the *Étoile Napoléonienne* shed light on all the world? Sing, then, melodious poets, strike the golden lyre, spring on white-winged Pegasus and, soaring to the blue, ethereal realm where glitters that bright Star Napoleonic, chant a glorious epic! *Vincit amor omnia!* France and Austria united by the hand of Marie Louise!

"Who will be *dame d'honneur* to the new Empress?" cried all the great court ladies, and the Mortemarts, Montmorencies, Bouillés, Vintimilles, Canisys, Rovigos, Duchâtels and Lauristons bestirred themselves, and all the court feminine was in a flutter of agitation. But one little lady sat apart from it all, mourning in her widow's weeds. And the day came when the Imperial decree was published, and in it the Emperor said to all the world, " I'll not have a Mortemart, a Montmorency, a Bouillé, or a Vintimille. The rank of *dame d'honneur*, first lady in waiting to the

Empress, the highest court favor I have to bestow, I give to the Duchess de Montebello, the widow of my sturdy Lannes, my brave 'Ajax,' my Marshal of France who was once a grenadier."

And now the Emperor, awaiting impatiently at Compiègne the arrival of his Austrian bride, received news that she was approaching Soissons, would in fact arrive at Compiègne upon the morrow, the 28th of March. Upon the morrow? Why not to-day? Why be held any longer by that tedious, people-impressing, sensation-producing ceremonial against which he had already railed?

" Constant! a carriage without livery and my gray greatcoat of Wagram," cried the Emperor, and with Murat, the King of Naples, he set out at a gallop in the pouring rain for Soissons. And when the cortège of the Archduchess came clattering over the stones and pulled up at the post-house to change horses, he flung open the door of her carriage, sprang in all wet and muddy from his hurried journey and threw his arms about her neck, while the Queen of Naples thus announced him, " Madame, it is the Emperor."

There was a splendid supper awaiting the Archduchess and her suite at Soissons. The lights glittered and the tables loaded with savory viands sent forth tempting odors. Hungry ladies and gentlemen of the Imperial cortège, do you fancy that you will taste these good things to-night? If so, you greatly err. Fresh horses have been put in, the postillions are in the saddles, and the indisputable word is uttered, " En avant! To Compiègne! "

So they went at a gallop from Soissons to Compiègne, through the mud and rain and cheering crowds

of people, up the grand avenue by torchlight to the
very palace gates. Now, ladies and gentlemen, you
may rest and eat what the palace *chefs* at eleven
o'clock at night can find for you. The Imperial
Lochinvar has won his bride!

On the 31st of March the court set out for Saint
Cloud, and on the following day, Sunday, the 1st of
April, 1810, in the grand Apollo Gallery adorned by
Mignard's brilliant frescoes, in the presence of Louis
Napoleon, King of Holland, Jérôme Napoleon, King
of Westphalia, Joachim Murat, King of Naples,
Eugene, Viceroy of Italy, the Prince Borghese, the
Grand Duke of Würtzburg, the Grand Duke of
Baden, Hortense, Queen of Holland, Julia, Queen of
Spain, Catherine, Queen of Westphalia, Caroline,
Queen of Naples, Augusta, Vice-Queen of Italy,
Elisa, Grand Duchess of Tuscany, Pauline, Princess
Borghese, Stephanie, Grand Duchess of Baden, the
Imperial Mother, Madame Mère, the Prince Arch-
treasurer, the Prince Vice-Grand Elector, and the
Prince Vice-Constable, the Arch-chancellor of the Em-
pire, the Prince Cambacères, rose before a richly-cov-
ered table upon which lay the marriage contract and
said, "In the name of the Emperor." And as he
spoke, Napoleon and Marie Louise rose from their
places and stood waiting the Arch-chancellor's word.

It was a far cry from that Sunday the 1st of April,
1810, to the day when at the military school of Brienne
the little Corsican boy had led the attack upon the fort
of snow, and, with "Homer in his pocket and his
sword by his side, hoped to carve his way through the
world." Strange things had come to pass since then.
Until now in the Apollo Gallery of that beautiful Pal-

ace of Saint Cloud, once the palace of Louis the Grand
Monarque, now the palace of Napoleon, Emperor of
the French, surrounded by all those Kings and Queens
whom he had placed on thrones and whom he held
there by his victorious sword, he stood, waiting to say
the word which should unite him to the great Imperial
House of Hapsburg and found a dynasty Napoleonic,
with all Europe looking on.

" Sire," said the Arch-chancellor Cambacères, " does
Your Imperial and Royal Majesty declare that he takes
in marriage Her Imperial and Royal Highness Marie
Louise, Archduchess of Austria, here present? "

And the Emperor answered, " I declare that I take
in marriage Her Imperial and Royal Highness Marie
Louise, Archduchess of Austria, here present."

" Madame," said the Arch-chancellor, " does Your
Imperial and Royal Highness declare that she takes in
marriage His Imperial and Royal Majesty Napoleon,
Emperor of the French, here present? "

And the Archduchess answered, " I declare that I
take in marriage His Imperial and Royal Majesty,
Napoleon, Emperor of the French, here present."

" Then in the name of the Emperor and of the law,"
said the Arch-chancellor, " I declare that His Imperial
and Royal Majesty Napoleon, Emperor of the French
and King of Italy, and Her Imperial and Royal Highness Marie Louise, Archduchess of Austria, are united
in marriage."   And the thunders of the artillery in the
palace park and at the Invalides in Paris shook the
windows of the Apollo Gallery in the Palace of Saint
Cloud.

At eight o'clock on the following morning, the day
of the public entry, every window on the line of march

from Saint Cloud to the Tuileries was filled with men and women. The people from all the surrounding country had flocked to Paris, and from the iron railings of the courtyard of Saint Cloud, through the Bois de Boulogne and the Avenue des Champs Élysées, a vast concourse of humanity, joyous and expectant, stretched to the doors of the Tuileries Palace. Flags, bunting, portraits and monograms of the Emperor and of the Empress abounded, and the Imperial eagles flapped their wings on every side. All night the carpenters and decorators had been busy putting the finishing touches to the great temporary structure erected upon the rising foundations of the Arc de Triomphe, which bore in large letters, " To Napoleon and Marie Louise, the City of Paris." At the top of the arch were twelve medallions, and on one of these which contained a portrait of the Empress was this inscription, " She announces happy days to the world."

It was nine o'clock when the procession left Saint Cloud. First came the cavalry of the Imperial Guard, lancers, chasseurs, and dragoons; then the carriage of the Empress, empty and drawn by eight gray horses; then the gilded coronation coach with its crown and eagles, in which were the Emperor and the Empress, and by the side of which rode the Marshals of the Empire. Then thirty gilded carriages containing the court, and finally detachments of cavalry from all the army corps.

And so while the cannon of the Invalides sounded, and the bells of the city churches tolled and the people shouted again and again the Imperial name, the glittering pageant advanced majestically through the Bois de Boulogne and the Maillot gate, down the Avenue des

Champs Élysées and across the Place de la Concorde
—that Place de la Concorde where seventeen years
before another Austrian Archduchess from the summit
of her scaffold had looked for the last time on earth
toward the dome of the Tuileries Palace.   Shout, people of Paris!   The wars and revolutions are over.
The Dynasty Napoleonic is founded forever.   France
and Austria are united.   As a pledge of their sincerity
behold your Empress, a daughter of the Caesars—
" She announces happy days to the world! "

In the great gallery of the Louvre that stretched
from the Old Louvre to the Chapel at the end of the
Tuileries Pavilion, on the side next to the Pont Royal,
were three rows of benches crowded with the great
ladies of Paris.   At regular intervals in this long gallery were placed ninety-six canteens of refreshments,
served by fifty non-commissioned officers of the Imperial Guard commanded by General Dorsenne.   Pierre
was stationed at the third canteen from the great door
that led to the Imperial Chapel, and he had forty-eight
ladies to serve.   And wonderful ladies they were with
their dresses cut so low in the front and back that
Pierre was almost embarrassed when he went to offer
them refreshments.   Some were young and some were
old, some were beautiful and some were ugly, some
had clear white skins and some were yellow and
wrinkled like parchment, but they were all gorgeous
in necklaces, bracelets and tiaras of rubies, diamonds
and pearls.   The men in their short breeches and
splendidly-embroidered coats with diamond-shaped
steel buttons, stood behind the ladies, and Pierre felt
that he had never known what clothes were until that
moment.

When the shouts in the Tuileries courtyard announced that the Imperial couple had arrived, everyone in the grand gallery rose, and soon Pierre saw the pompous procession, framed by the gilded paintings of the Louvre and the long lines of jeweled and embroidered *dames de cour*, advancing slowly to the Chapel. The Empress Marie Louise, with her splendid diamond diadem and her train borne by the Queens of Holland, Spain, Naples, and Westphalia, created a profound impression, and the Emperor Napoleon appeared happy and serene. But, as they reached the door that led into the Chapel, Pierre saw the Queen of Holland lift her handkerchief to her eyes. And when all that imposing array of Kings and Queens, Grand Dukes and Grand Duchesses, had passed by, General Dorsenne collected the grenadiers and marched them into the Chapel, where, in the solemn silence while all the assembly remained standing, Pierre saw Napoleon and Marie Louise kneeling on cushions decorated with the golden bees, receiving the benediction of the Church.

That night Paris was on fire with illuminations; the Garde-Meuble, the Temple of Glory, the Tuileries Palace, the Corps Législatif, the Bridge Louis XV, the Avenue des Champs Élysées, houses, palaces, and churches even to their lofty towers, glittered with light. There were transparencies representing peace, and genii carrying bucklers, and magistrates, warriors and people presenting crowns to the Emperor and the Empress, and the Seine and the Danube surrounded by children; there were orange-trees of flame, and garlands of colored lamps, and columns of dazzling brightness, and tripods of fire, while over all and above all, from the dome of Sainte Geneviève, scintillating like a diamond, blazed a great Imperial star.

Ah! shout, good people of Paris. Fire your guns and light your illuminations. Your great War-Lord has sheathed his sword. The Lion is in love, and Marie Louise is *Venus Victrix*. "She announces happy days to the world!"

What did Pierre think of this Austrian marriage? We only know that when, a year later, the hundred guns of the Invalides had announced the birth of a King of Rome, and from all parts of the Empire deputations were thronging the Tuileries Palace, bearing their congratulations to the second Charlemagne, Pierre received a letter from Grenoble, which said, "Pierre, you have a little daughter. What shall we name her?"

And Pierre sent back this answer: "Let us call her *Josephine.*"

CHAPTER XXIV

At the Royal Palace, Dresden

His sceptre shows the force of temporal power,
The attribute to awe and majesty,
Wherein doth sit the dread and fear of kings.
—SHAKESPEARE, *The Merchant of Venice.*

"PIERRE," said François Legrand, coming one morning into the barracks at Courbevoie, "get yourself a fur pelisse. We're going to Russia."

Pierre dropped the belt which he was cleaning and looked up. "The devil we are!" said he. "How do you know that?"

"Jovyac told me. His brother is an agent of Fouché's; so he knows all state secrets."

"Well, what are we going to Russia for?" inquired Pierre.

"What for?" exclaimed François. "To give them a d——d good licking, of course. What else should we go for?"

"Oh, we'll lick them fast enough," said Pierre, picking up the belt, *"Cela va sans dire;* but there's politics mixed up with it, isn't there?"

"Pish!" cried François, contemptuously, "who cares for politics? March and fight, that's my politics. Good politics, too. Look what it's done for the Little Corporal. Sacré! I haven't smelled powder for two years. This lazy life is killing me."

François meant what he said. War is the soldier's trade. In times of peace he is restless, for he has no opportunity to practice his profession. Peace, so dear to the heart of the civilian, means to him only the dull routine of barrack life. He longs for the camp, the combat and the crash of arms.

Soldier of the Empire, your wish shall be gratified. Your great War-Lord marches with Western Europe in his train; and in that far-distant Russia, where your martial imagination beholds victory waiting to crown her favorite son, you shall see the Kremlin's dome— and *more!*

There have been triumphal marches, but the march of the Imperial Guard from Paris to Dresden was one perpetual ovation. In every town they passed beneath arches erected in their honor; in every town they advanced between lines of cheering people. The peasant girls ran forward and threw flowers to them, or fastened roses in their lofty bearskin caps; and the men cried, "See! it is the Imperial Guard." "How proudly they march!" "They have never been beaten." "They can never be beaten." "They are the Emperor's pride." Then from the throngs came the shout repeated over and over again, "Vive la Garde Impériale!"

Add to it all the music of a hundred bands, and no wonder the veterans held their heads high. Pierre was drunk with glory, while François Legrand declared he had never seen anything like it before, and he had seen much.

Thus honored and acclaimed, the grenadiers reached Dresden on the 28th of May, 1812, and swept with a swinging stride into the crowded Zwinger. The bands of the regiments played the warlike strain, and the marching veterans sung their triumph-song:

Vive l'Empereur!
It is our battle-cry.
With it we gaily face the foe;
With it we gladly die.
We love it like a wife or child,
And glory, its reward.
We're heroes of a hundred fights,
The great Imperial Guard.

En avant! En avant!
The conqueror goes to war;
The cannons loudly roar,
The eagles proudly soar.
En avant! En avant!
The conqueror goes to war.
Behold advance the flag of France,
Triumphant tricolore!

Vive l'Empereur!
It is our battle-cheer.
With it we summon courage;
With it, inspire fear.
It burnishes for daring deeds,
Made glorious by the sword,
The cuirass of Napoleon,
The great Imperial Guard.

En avant! En avant!
The conqueror goes to war;
The cannons loudly roar,
The eagles proudly soar.
En avant! En avant!
The conqueror goes to war.
Behold advance the flag of France,
Triumphant tricolore!

The crowds took up the refrain and followed the grenadiers. Dresden was a gallant sight that day,

for Dresden was *en fête*. Through the beautiful
Zwinger of Augustus II and across the great Theater
Platz rolled long lines of gilded carriages, drawn by
splendid horses, crowded on the steps with laced
and powdered footmen and bearing the grand lords
of Germany to the Royal Palace. About the palace
gates was gathered a dense mass of people, pushing
and jostling each other in their eagerness to catch
a glimpse of the Dukes, Princes and high dignitaries
who passed by them in rapid succession.

One after another the carriages dashed into the
palace courtyard and drew up before the main entrance, and, as their occupants ascended the marble
staircase, the Royal Guards presented arms. In the
grand gallery were assembled the Prince of Saxe-
Weimar, the Grand Duke of Würtzburg, the Grand
Duke of Baden, the Prince of Saxe-Coburg, the
Prince of Nassau, the Grand Duke of Hesse-Darmstadt, the Archbishop of Regensburg, the Prince of
Mecklenburg-Strelitz, M. de Metternich the Austrian
Ambassador, the Prince Primate of the Rhine Confederation, the Prince of Mecklenburg-Schwerin, and
with them a great throng of Barons, Generals, Counts
and diplomats.

The King of Saxony had never held so brilliant a
levée. And as that numerous assembly, gathered in
groups, was engaged in animated conversation, the
folding doors at one end of the apartment were
thrown open and the voice of an usher resounded
through the gallery, "His Majesty the King of
Würtemburg, His Majesty the King of Bavaria."

They too had come, then, to grace the King of
Saxony's levée. They mingled among the crowd of

courtiers, and the conversation went on. The King of Saxony had grown great indeed when his brothers of Würtemburg and of Bavaria paid him such an honor. Again the doors were opened, and again the voice of the usher resounded through the gallery, "His Majesty the King of Naples, His Majesty the King of Westphalia."

But the conversation did not stop, and the Kings of Naples and of Westphalia, like their brothers of Bavaria and of Würtemburg, mingled among the crowd. They too had come to grace the King of Saxony's levée. Again the doors were opened, and again the usher's voice resounded through the gallery, "His Majesty the King of Saxony." The Saxon King had never held so brilliant a levée.

The King of Saxony entered slowly, and the Kings of Würtemburg and of Bavaria advanced to meet him. But the conversation did not stop. The court circle was not formed. It was evidently not to honor the King of Saxony that all those sovereign Princes had assembled. Whom then had all those sovereign Princes come to honor in the Saxon capital, if not the Saxon King?

Again the doors were opened, and again the usher's voice resounded through the gallery, "His Majesty the King of Prussia and His Royal Highness the Crown Prince."

It was the King of Prussia, then, that all those Princes, Dukes, and Barons had come from all parts of Germany to.honor.

As the King of Prussia entered, the King of Saxony, M. de Hardenburg, and the Prince of Mecklenburg-Schwerin came forward. But the conversation did not stop, and the Kings of Bavaria, of Würtemburg, of Naples, and of Westphalia, hardly noticed the Prussian monarch. He too, then, was a courtier. Suddenly the roll of drums was heard upon the staircase, the folding doors were thrown open, and the usher announced with becoming grandiloquence, "His Imperial Majesty the Emperor of Austria!"

Ah! he surely was the person for whom that brilliant assembly waited in the Royal Palace, Dresden.

The King of Saxony, the King of Bavaria, M. de Metternich, and the Prince of Saxe-Weimar hurried forward to meet the Austrian Emperor. But the conversation did not stop. The court circle was not formed. Nor did the Emperor of Austria appear to expect it, for he quietly drew M. de Metternich into a corner and began to talk earnestly with him. And now, as the palace clock struck nine, the folding doors at the other end of the grand gallery—those doors which until then had remained fast closed, those doors toward which had been directed the glance of many a King, sovereign Prince, Grand Duke and Grand Elector—were opened, and instantly the conversation stopped.

Upon the threshold appeared an Imperial chamberlain with his white waistcoat, knee-breeches, and silver embroidered coat of scarlet silk, and, looking at the assembled sovereigns, he said slowly, "*Messieurs, l'Empereur vous accorde les grandes entrées.*"

Through the doorway passed the Emperor of Austria, the King of Prussia, the King of Saxony, the King of Bavaria, the King of Würtemberg, the King of Naples, the King of Westphalia, the Grand

Duke of Baden, the Grand Duke of Würtzburg, the Prince of Saxe-Coburg, the Grand Duke of Hesse-Darmstadt, the Prince of Mecklenburg-Schwerin, and all that crowd of Barons, diplomats and Grand Electors. At the further end of the apartment into which they entered, dressed in his plain uniform of the *chasseurs à cheval*, with one hand thrust into his waistcoat and holding in the other his famous little hat, stood Napoleon. He it was who held the grand levée. He had passed some days in the capital of his friend the King of Saxony, and from all parts of Europe his vassal and allied sovereigns had come to do him homage, and on the morrow he was to set out to place himself at the head of five hundred thousand men and begin his march to Moscow. He came forward, and the long lines of glittering Kings, Princes, Dukes and Barons assumed an attitude of respectful attention.

"And how is Your Majesty this morning?" said he, smiling and addressing the Emperor of Austria.

"Quite well, sire, my son," answered Francis, "I have very gratifying news for you."

"What is it?" asked the Emperor, with a look of interest.

"I trust it will give Your Majesty as much pleasure as it has given me," said the Emperor of Austria. "I have discovered that the Bonapartes were formerly sovereigns at Treviso. There can be no doubt about the matter. I have caused the authentic titles to be procured and presented to me. I have already told Marie Louise and she is enchanted at the news."

While the Emperor of Austria was speaking, Napoleon's face had lost its interested look, his eyes wandered about the room and a faint smile appeared upon his mouth.

"My dear father-in-law," said he, "it is really very good of you to take this trouble on my account, but I assure you I have no need of ancestors. I am the Rudolph of Hapsburg of my family. My title of nobility dates from the battle of Montenotte."

"Sire, my brother," said the King of Prussia, dropping the tassels of his sword which he had been nervously fingering and coming a step or two nearer Napoleon, "my son is anxious to learn the art of war. I am sure he can learn it nowhere better than under your conquering eagles. Will Your Majesty do me the honor to take him as aide-de-camp in the Russian campaign?"

"My staff is very numerous now," replied the Emperor. "He is rather young, but I will think of it."

"Let me repeat to Your Majesty my assurances of inviolable attachment to the system which unites us," continued the King of Prussia.

"Yes, I feel confident that I can rely upon you," rejoined Napoleon. "How are matters in Berlin?"

"Never better, sire. I must tell Your Majesty about the new coat I have designed for my guards. It has fourteen buttons on the front and is lined with blue and red."

"It will be a splendid coat, no doubt," said Napoleon, looking at his snuff-box.

"I have fourteen buttons on the coats of my guards too," said the Emperor of Austria.

"No, sire, my brother, your guards have only twelve buttons on their coats," said the King of Prussia.

"I am sure there are fourteen," answered Francis.

"Father-in-law," said Napoleon, "Your Majesty cannot dispute the King of Prussia. He is *au fait* in the matter of buttons. He knows the cut and color of every uniform in Europe. I found that out at Tilsit." His Prussian Majesty appeared much flattered.

"You must come with me and make a tour of the shops," said the Emperor Francis to the Prussian King. "I always like to rummage about among the shops when time hangs heavy on my hands."

"Your Majesty might visit the fortifications," remarked Napoleon. "The fortifications of a country are always useful and never injurious when they are well understood. If Vienna had been fortified in 1805, the battle of Ulm would not have decided the issue of the war. Had Berlin been fortified in 1806, the army beaten at Jena would have rallied there and been joined by the Russian army."

The King of Prussia looked blankly at the floor, but the Austrian Emperor grew red and quickly changed the subject.

"What does Your Majesty think of Charles XII, who like Your Majesty contemplated a march to Moscow?" he inquired.

"Charles XII set out from his camp at Alstadt near Leipzig in September, 1707," said Napoleon. "He was in condition to have brought together 80,000 of the best troops in the world. In January, 1708, he arrived at Grodno, where he wintered. In June he crossed the forest of Minsk and presented himself before Borisov, defeated 20,000 Russians who were strongly entrenched behind marshes, passed the

Borysthenes at Mohilov and vanquished a corps of Muscovites near Smolensko. He was now advanced to the confines of Lithuania. Until this time all his movements were conformable to rule. He was master of Poland and Riga and distant only ten days' march from Moscow, and it is probable he would have reached that capital had he not quitted the highroad thither and directed his steps toward the Ukraine in order to form a junction with Mazeppa, who brought him only 6000 men. Had Charles XII wished to reach Moscow his march was perfectly well directed as far as Smolensko, and his line of operations with Sweden and Riga was covered by the Dwina as far as the Borysthenes and Mohilov; but, if his design was to winter in the Ukraine and to induce a rising among the Cossacks, he ought to have passed the Niemen at Grodno and traversed Lithuania. So much for Charles XII. How is Your Majesty and what is the spirit of your troops?" And the Emperor turned to the King of Würtemberg.

"They are already animated with ardor for the great cause, sire, and I shall have them harangued frequently."

"I would advise you not to do so," said the Emperor, "it is not harangues at the moment of attack which render them brave; old soldiers dislike them and the young forget them at the very first fire. It is discipline which binds troops to their colors. There is not a single harangue recorded by Livy which was ever spoken by the general of an army, because there is not one which has the characteristic of an impromptu. Is it not so, Monsieur le Prince?"

The Prince of Mecklenburg-Schwerin, thus suddenly appealed to, flushed, looked down and stam-
mered, "Really, sire—I—never having read—I
should say——."

"And you would be quite right, too, Monsieur le
Prince," said Napoleon hastily, to extricate the
Prince from his embarrassment. "If harangues are
of any use it is during the course of campaign, to
dissipate false alarms, keep up good spirit in the
camp and furnish material for conversation in the
bivouac."

The Emperor took a pinch of snuff and turned to
the King of Bavaria. "I trust Your Majesty has
found little difficulty in collecting your supplies," he
said.

"On the contrary, I have had a good deal of difficulty," said the King of Bavaria. "Your Majesty
shall find, however, that the difficulties have only increased my zeal for the great cause. But sometimes
I wish that, like the generals of antiquity, we did not
have to pay attention to magazines."

"It is an error to suppose that the generals of
antiquity did not pay particular attention to their
magazines," said the Emperor. "It appears from
Caesar's Commentaries that in many of his campaigns
this subject occupied much of his attention. They
had only found out the art of not being slaves to, and
depending too much on, their supplies; an art which
has been that of all great captains,—Hannibal, Turenne, Condé, Prince Eugene. Frederick in his in-
vasions of Bohemia and Moravia, in his marches on
the Oder and on the banks of the Elbe and the Saale,
put into practice the principles of these great cap-

tains.   For commanders-in-chief are guided by their experience or genius; tactics, evolutions, the science of engineering and gunnery, may be learned in treatises like geometry; but the knowledge of other parts of war is only to be acquired by experience and by studying the history of the wars and battles of great leaders."

"And when did Your Majesty find time to study the campaigns of Caesar and the great Frederick?" . inquired the Austrian Emperor.

Napoleon glanced at the brilliant crowd before him, at the Kings, the sovereign Princes, Grand Dukes and Grand Electors, at the gold-embroidered uniforms blazing with diamond stars and crosses, and answered his Imperial father-in-law, "When I was sous-lieutenant in the regiment of La Fere."

CHAPTER XXV

THE TWENTY-NINTH BULLETIN

No pitying voice commands a halt,
No courage can repel the dire assault;
Distracted, spiritless, benumbed and blind,
Whole legions sink—and, in one instant, find
Burial and death.
　　　　—WORDSWORTH, *The French Army in Russia.*

ON the 24th of June, Napoleon crossed the Niemen with his Grande Armée, four hundred and twenty thousand men, seventy thousand horsemen and a thousand guns. And as we see him standing on the bank, watching that mighty host—French, Austrians, and Prussians—defiling before him over the three bridges, we may repeat the question put three years later by the bluff von Blücher, when with his muddy boots he tramped across the Apollo Gallery at Saint Cloud and looked about him: "Why should a man, who had all these fine things at home, go running off to Moscow?" Ah! let the grave historian answer; that is his affair.

It was the evening of December 20th, 1812, and a boisterous evening it was. The snow had been falling since morning, and the sharp wind had been whirling it about in thin, white clouds and driving it into every chink and crevice. There were banks of it about the front of the Hotel des Trois Dauphins, and the banks kept growing. For every hour old

La Barre would come and shovel it off the steps, throwing it to right and to left, and then he would stamp his big wooden shoes and shake his rough coat and go in to warm his wrinkled hands by the fire; for when the mercury stands at four degrees below zero and a sharp wind is blowing it is more pleasant indoors than out. Old La Barre was a harmless soul, and he had helped Philippe Courteau at the Trois Dauphins for many years. He was the best man in that quarter to bed a horse or wash windows. Henri Jodélle always used to say, when he went to the stable and saw La Barre bedding a horse, that "if he were the Crown Prince of Prussia he would have envied that horse."

So La Barre was a useful soul, and being a harmless one he was in nobody's path, and picked up many an odd sou, which he kept in a woollen sock in his garret, until one day the rats, being on campaign, and cut off from their base of supplies, and finding the country about them rather unproductive, ate the toe of La Barre's sock and spilled the money. There never was a man so distressed as La Barre, for two centimes rolled in a crack, where they could not be gotten out without taking up the floor, and Philippe didn't want that. So he gave La Barre two other centimes, and also a tin box for the balance of his money. La Barre got a rat-trap and put it at the foot of his bed, then he got a mouse-trap and put it at the head, and then he put the tin box under one end of his pillow. But he was not easily consoled for the loss of those two centimes, and often when he was in his room he would light a candle and place it by the crack and watch it carefully. No one knows

what he expected to see come out of the crack, but
that was what he did. So La Barre, like the rest of
the world, had his troubles.

Philippe Courteau and Henri Jodélle were sitting in
Philippe's room on the ground floor of the Trois
Dauphins. It was a comfortable room, but, as might
be expected, there was nothing gaudy about it. The
log fire was burning brightly in the fireplace, and
nearby was a pile of logs that La Barre had brought
in not long before and which were still moist from
melted snow. Philippe had stood some of the short
ones up on end about the fire to dry thoroughly before
he put them on. There were two pairs of Philippe's
boots beside the fireplace also, and over it hung the
sabre of honor which he had told Pierre he would show
him when he came to the Trois Dauphins. But Pierre
hadn't had time to come when he was getting married, and now he was with the Grand Army—at the
other end of the world, so Marie thought, and Heaven
knew when she would see him again, if ever. That
was not a cheering thought, but there were thousands
in France who had the same about others who were
charging the Russian guns at La Moscowa. Under
the sabre of honor hung a picture of the Little Corporal, with thin cheeks and long hair—a copy of one
of Gros's or David's pictures—and that was the way
Philippe remembered him, for he had not seen him
since the days in Italy and Egypt, when he led them
with Victory at his right hand, and Glory at his left.

About the round table in the middle of the room
sat Philippe and Henri. There were two bottles of
wine on the table, some cheese and a dozen slices of
thick, fine bread. There was also an empty chair at

the table, and that was a sign that they were expecting some one, for Philippe never put chairs about that table unless he expected to have his friends there to put in them. The fire burned merrily and Philippe and Henri drank their wine. Presently La Barre came in and sat down to warm his hands.

"Is it still snowing?" inquired Philippe.

"Worse than ever," said La Barre.

"The diligence will be late to-night," said Philippe. "Stout Matthieu will probably have his ears frozen, and the roan mare will be stiffer than ever. You must fix her up well, La Barre."

"They'll be lucky if they come at all," answered La Barre. "They'll get blowed over in a gulley, I'm thinking."

"Pish!" said Henri Jodélle. "Matthieu knows the road too well for that."

They heard some one stamping and puffing in the hall, and presently old Frédéric Bonneville put his head in at the door. His hat and his coat were covered with snow and there was snow on his eyebrows and on his mustache, but that was always white and so didn't look unnatural. His cheeks were red, and so was his nose—a nice bright red like a ruddy apple. "Dame!" cried Frédéric, shaking himself, "what weather! I thought I should never get here. The drifts are so deep that you are up to your knees. It's slow work wading and my wind isn't what it was once."

"Well, don't shake your snow all over us," said Philippe. "La Barre, take Frédéric's coat and hat."

Frédéric gave his things to La Barre, who carried them out of the room, and Frédéric coming before the fire stamped his feet and rubbed his hands, while Philippe brought out another bottle of wine. "Ah! that's the thing!" cried Frédéric, sitting down at the table. "Well, what's the news from Paris?"

"We don't know," said Henri Jodélle. "We're waiting to hear. What time does the diligence come, Philippe?"

"At nine o'clock, but it won't be here to-night at any such hour, you may be sure."

"I should think not," said Frédéric Bonneville. "I'm glad I'm not driving it to-night. I'll bet you five francs, Henri, that it does not come at all."

"Good," said Henri, "produce your five francs."

Frédéric laid it on the table, and Henri took five francs from his pocket and placed it also on the table.

"Now," said Philippe, "I'll bet you each five francs that it doesn't come before twelve."

"*Très-bien*," said Henri, "where are your five francs?"

"I won't do that," said Frédéric, "for I have bet it wouldn't come at all. If I take your bet, I bet that it does come before twelve."

"Well, I'll bet that it comes at twelve, or later, and you can bet it won't," said Philippe.

"All right," said Frédéric, and so the twenty francs were deposited on the table.

"Now, let us see," said the methodical Frédéric, "this five francs says to you, Henri, that it won't come at all, and your five francs says it will. And this five francs says to you, Philippe, that it won't come at twelve, or later, and yours says it will."

"Yes," said Henri, "and my five francs says to you,

Philippe, that it will come before twelve, and yours says it will not."

"*Très-bien,*" said Philippe, "there's no need for me to say what my five francs say, for that's been told. Come now, fill your glasses and drink with me this toast—To the success of the Grand Army!"

"Right," said Henri. So the glasses were filled and held aloft. Then they cried, "To the success of the Grand Army!" and emptied them.

"Just the same," said Frédéric, "the last news I heard wasn't very good."

"The Emperor has captured Moscow," cried Henri. "What more do you want?"

"Well, what the devil is he going to do now he has captured Moscow?" said Frédéric.

"Beat the Russians! fool," said Henri.

"But the damned Cossacks run away so fast that our men can't get at them," said Frédéric. "I was talking to M. Montfort only yesterday. He has been to Paris and every one there looks glum enough. That fellow Malet made a fine stir. Why, Montfort told me that his plan was all made to upset the government, and that he actually had the Duc de Rovigo under arrest for several hours."

"Parbleu! but what will the Emperor say to that?" said Philippe. "There will be trouble for somebody."

"There's trouble enough now," said Frédéric. "Funds are way down in Paris, and M. Montfort says there is a rumor there that Moscow has been burned."

"By whom?" said Henri.

"Oh! nobody knows; probably by Russians."

"But the Russians have been driven out of

Moscow," said Henri, "and the Emperor has beaten them thoroughly at La Moscowa, which was a glorious victory for us. You always imagine bad luck, Frédéric. You were that way in 1809; you thought they would never get back from Vienna, and yet the Austrian fools were licked out of their boots. Leave it to the Little Corporal. He'll come out all right, never fear."

"Yes, but Austria isn't Russia," said Frédéric; "and if the weather there is like this weather, I say— God help France!"

"You're right, Frédéric," said Philippe slowly, "Austria isn't Russia. There's no one in Grenoble that would stick by the Little Corporal more than I, unless it's you, Henri, but I've never thought well of this Russian business, and God knows I wish he were back in Paris this day, where he ought to be. Sacré! and cutting the heads off those Malet people too."

"I wish so too," said Henri, "but we can't know much about anything till we get news from Paris. Suppose we play vingt-et-un."

"Now that's a good idea, Henri," said Frédéric. "How did you happen to think of it?"

"Well, you old white-whiskered rooster, you needn't think you are the only one who has ideas," said Henri.

Philippe produced the cards and, as there was hardly room on the table for everything, he put the bread and cheese on the mantel. He left the wine, however; they would never have consented to have had that removed. Frédéric arranged the five-franc pieces carefully and placed the candle on the side of the table and the game began. The fire burned

15

cheerily, for La Barre came in from time to time and put on a log of wood.

"You better open another bottle, La Barre," said Philippe after a time. La Barre did so and placed it on the table and then, going out into the kitchen, he cut himself a slice of bread and a large piece of cheese. Then he came back and, sitting down before the fire, stretched out his hands, as usual, to warm them.

La Barre had the bread in one hand and the cheese in the other, and he looked first at the cheese and then at the bread. He decided to eat one now and take the other up to his room to eat later. Which would taste best first? La Barre thought the bread and then he thought the cheese. Then he remained some time in doubt, looking from one to the other. The cheese had the most tempting look, but if he ate the cheese he would have only the bread, which would not taste well without the cheese, and again, the cheese might be improved with the bread. La Barre decided that they should be eaten together. But if he ate them now he would have nothing to eat later in his room, which he desired. He might keep both until later, but he wished for some now, especially since he could no doubt have a sip of wine with which to wash it down. La Barre was perplexed. He held the cheese in one hand and the bread in the other, and thought. The fire was warm, it was very late, and La Barre grew drowsy. His eyes gradually closed, his head nodded a little, his fingers relaxed and—the bread and cheese fell into the fire. There never was a man so distressed as La Barre!

"What time is that?" said Philippe as the clock began to strike. They listened and counted the strokes—two, three, four, five, six, seven, eight, nine, ten, eleven, twelve.

"Ah!" said Philippe, "I win if it comes at all."

"But it won't come now," said Frédéric.

"Listen!" said Philippe.

"I can't hear anything," said Frédéric. "They wouldn't make any noise anyhow with all this snow."

Just then there came a loud rapping at the door of the Trois Dauphins. "There they are!" cried Philippe. "La Barre!"

But La Barre had already trotted out, and was soon opening the door.

"Well, Matthieu," said La Barre, "I was thinking you was blowed over in a gulley."

"Mon Dieu! I wonder I'm not," cried the burly Matthieu. "The black horse broke a trace and I my lantern, and God knows how we ever got on, for the roan mare is stiff in the knees."

"It's Matthieu's voice," said Philippe, "I win from you, Frédéric."

"I win, too, Frédéric," said Henri.

"Le diable!" cried Frédéric, "I lose all around."

"Have you any passengers, Matthieu?" said La Barre at the door.

"Passengers? No! They know better such days as these. I got the mails and papers from Paris."

"What news from Paris, Matthieu?" cried Philippe coming to the door.

"The worst!" said Matthieu. "The army's in an awful way, and what with this and what with that we're all going to the devil sooner or later. Dame! but I can't talk now. It's victuals I want."

"Bring in your bag and give us the 'Moniteur' and then La Barre will give you enough to eat after you've put up the horses," said Philippe.

Matthieu brought in the bag and handed Philippe the paper, and then went to the stable after La Barre.

"Here, Henri," said Philippe, "you can read best. See what you can find."

Henri took the paper, opened it, and sat down at the table. "Here it is," said he, "Twenty-Ninth Bulletin," and drawing the candle near him he began to read:

Smorgoni, December 3, 1812.

Until the 6th of November the weather was perfect and the movement of the army was carried out with the greatest success. The cold began on the 7th; from that time we lost each night many hundreds of horses which died at the bivouac. Arriving at Smolensk we had already lost many of the cavalry and artillery horses. The Emperor arrived at Smolensk on the 9th. He hoped to arrive at Minsk, or at least upon the Bérésina, before the enemy. He set out the 15th from Smolensk and the 16th slept at Krasnoe. The cold which had begun on the 7th increased suddenly, and on the 14th, 15th and 16th the thermometer marked 16 and 18 degrees below zero. The roads were covered with ice; the cavalry and artillery horses perished every night, not by hundreds but by thousands, especially the horses of France and Germany. More than thirty thousand horses perished in a few days, and our cavalry was on foot. The army, so fine on the 6th, was very different on the 14th, almost without cavalry, without artillery, without transports. Without cavalry we were not able to reconnoitre a quarter of a league, meanwhile without artillery we were not able to risk a battle. It was necessary to march not to be forced to a battle which the want of munitions prevented us from desiring; it was necessary to occupy a certain space not to be outflanked, and this without cavalry who should give information to the columns. This difficulty joined to the sudden and excessive cold rendered our situation perilous. Men whom nature had not tempered so strongly as to be above all the chances of fortune, became disturbed, lost their gaiety, their spirits, and dreamt of nothing but misfortunes and disasters. Those who were superior to everything preserved their gaiety, their customary manners, and found new glory in the difficulties to be overcome. The enemy, who saw upon the roads the traces of the dreadful calamity which had come upon the Franch army, sought to profit by it. They surrounded all the columns by Cossacks, who attacked like the Arabs in the desert. Meanwhile the enemy occupied all the passages of the Bérésina, and their general placed his four divisions in different points where he thought the French army would wish to pass. The 26th at daybreak, after having deceived the enemy by different manœuvres made during the day of the 25th, the Emperor went to the village of Studzianca and immediately had two bridges thrown over the river in spite of a division of the enemy. The Duc de Reggio passed, attacked the enemy and continued fighting two hours. The enemy retreated to the tête-de-pont of Borisow. General Legrand, an officer of the first merit, was severely wounded but not dangerously. All the day of the 26th and of the 27th the army passed. In the combat of the Bérésina the Duc de Reggio was wounded. The day after we remained on the field of battle. We had to choose between two routes, that of Minsk and that of Wilna. The road to Minsk passed through the midst of a forest and through untilled swamps. It would have been impossible for the army to support itself there. The route to Wilna on the other hand passed through a very good country. The army, without cavalry, weak in munitions, horribly fatigued after fifty days of marching, dragging in its train its sick and the wounded of so many combats, had need to arrive at its magazines. The 30th the *quartier-général* was at Plechnitsi, the 1st of December at Slaiki, and the 3rd at Molodetschino, where the army received the first convoys from Wilna. All the officers and wounded soldiers and the baggage have been directed to Wilna. To say that the army has need to re-establish its discipline, to refresh itself, to remount its cavalry, its artillery and its *matériel*, that is the necessary inference from the statement which has been made. Rest is its first want. In all these movements the Emperor has marched always in the midst of his Guard, the cavalry commanded by the Duc d'Istrie, the infantry commanded by the Duc de Dantzick. Our cavalry has been so totally destroyed that there was difficulty in collecting those officers to whom a horse remained in order to form four companies of 150 men each. Generals took upon themselves the functions of captains, colonels those of under-officers. This sacred squadron, commanded by General Grouchy under the orders of the King of Naples, has not lost sight of the Emperor in all his movements. His Majesty's health was never better.

There was silence for a full half-minute when Henri finished reading. Then Frédéric Bonneville said:

"Well, I told you Russia wasn't Austria. 'Leave it to the Little Corporal,' you said. Sacré! a fine mess he's made of it. To think of all those losses, all those soldiers, all those horses, and guns, and baggage, gone to the devil, and what's to show for it? Nothing! And now what, in God's name, will become of France? There isn't a town in France but will have widows and orphans howling, and where's more men to come from? And what makes me *mad!*"—and Frédéric brought down his fist on the table—"is to think that along with all this, when all these soldiers are dead and dying, and all these widows and orphans crying and howling, and all of us at our wit's end, and France going to hell, he sends us this message—'His Majesty's health was never better.' Oh! he was well looked after, no doubt. His Majesty's health, indeed!"

There was silence again for a quarter of a minute, then Philippe said: "No, Frédéric, that isn't it. There's much to be said about this going to Moscow, but that's done. He's gone, and he's had hard luck, and he's stood by us, and now we've got to stand by him. He hasn't spared himself. I know how it was in Syria and I'll bet it was the same in Russia—the carriages and horses for the wounded and the Little Corporal on foot. And now mark my words. They'll all come, Russia, and Austria, and Prussia, and England, and who's to stop them? Not you, Frédéric, nor Henri, nor me, nor the King of Naples, nor the Duc de Reggio, nor the Prince of Neufchâtel, nor anybody else, but only he—the Little Corporal—who can and will! And so he says to us —People of France, your Little Corporal has had hard luck, and they've tried to down him, but they can't. Keep up your courage, your Little Corporal is in the fight yet, and his eye is as bright as it was at Marengo, and his head is as clear as it was at Austerlitz, and what he was then he'll be yet!— *le conquérant toujours!*"

"That's it! that's it!" cried Henri Jodélle. "I didn't see it at first, but that's it. They'll all come now. Well, let them come. They'll find France ready and they'll find the Emperor ready, and His Majesty's health—thank God!—was never better. Join me now in a toast. Come, Frédéric, come, Frédéric! To the health of His Majesty! Frédéric! Vive l'Empereur!"

CHAPTER XXVI

THE LION AT BAY

And dar'st thou then
To beard the lion in his den?
—SCOTT, *Marmion.*

IT was the month of January, 1814. The year just past had been one of victory and disaster. The battles of Lutzen, Bautzen, and Dresden had again asserted the supremacy of the French Emperor's arms, but the disasters at Leipzig had rendered Lutzen, Bautzen, and Dresden of no avail. Bavaria had deserted France in her hour of need, Germany had thrown off the yoke, and Austria her neutrality, and, as von Sybel puts it, " Die Erhebung Europas gegen Napoleon " had begun.

Sergeant Pasquin had undergone much during the past two years, but, by a curious coincidence, his fortunes seemed to rise as those of his Imperial master appeared more and more to decline. At La Moscowa, where with André Marceau he captured a Russian standard, Pierre was made sergeant-major, and in that capacity entered Moscow. At the close of the Russian campaign he was appointed sous-lieutenant, and during the campaign of 1813 in Germany he rose two steps higher, being made lieutenant at Bautzen on the 22nd of May, and captain at Dresden on the 26th of August.

But, says the inquisitive reader, let us see about all this. Tell us about these campaigns, and let us judge whether in three years Sergeant Pasquin should have become Captain Pasquin or not. Good reader, this story is in one volume, not a dozen. Were it in a dozen there would be room to tell you of all these battles—Smolensk, Witepsk, La Moscowa, the Bérésina, Lutzen, Bautzen, Wurtchen, Dresden, Leipzig, Hanau, but after a while you shall see the certificate of the *Garde Municipale de Grenoble*, which states that these honors came to him just as you have been told; and as to whether he should have had them or not—well, you will have to leave that to the one who gave them to him, the Emperor Napoleon.

So at the beginning of this year 1814 Pierre Pasquin, *ci-devant* sergeant, has become Captain Pierre Pasquin of the Garde Impériale.

On the 25th of January, Napoleon set out to join the army, this time not to lead them to Berlin, or Madrid, or Vienna, or Moscow; not to fight on the banks of the Danube, the Elbe or the Rhine; but to defend France, invested, inroaded, invaded; to prevent the Austrians, the Cossacks, and the Prussians from riding in triumph down the Avenue des Champs Élysées. But before leaving Paris he said two things, and this is one of them: "*J'appelle les Français au secours des Français*" ("I call the French to the succor of the French"); and this is the other: "I shall conduct this campaign as General Bonaparte."

Along the Marne and Seine the armies of Silesia and Bohemia were advancing; the former commanded by the Prussian Blücher, the latter by the Austrian Schwartzenberg. On the 27th of January

the Emperor met the Prussians at St. Dizier. It was
a furious battle. When the enemy had been repulsed
and the French marched through the town, Pierre
counted thousands of bullets in the doors and shutters of the windows, and as for the trees they were
cut to pieces. The army of Silesia fell back to the
heights of Brienne and took up position there. From
this situation they received the French with a heavy
artillery fire, which seemed to render useless the
efforts of the Emperor's soldiers. To the right of the
road was a redoubt defended by eight hundred men
and four pieces of cannon, which cut the ranks of the
French as they advanced to the attack. The Emperor, who was on his horse near a garden, sent for
the Captain François Legrand with a company of
grenadiers of the Guard, and when "le grand diable"
presented himself His Majesty remarked, "What
have you in your cheek?"

"My quid, sire."

"Ah! you chew tobacco?"

"Yes, sire."

"Take your company and go and take that redoubt
which is doing me so much harm."

"It shall be done, sire."

They set off by the right flank on the double, and
when they were within a hundred feet of the barrier
of the redoubt François halted them. Then he ran
alone to the barrier. There was an officer there holding the bar of the gates. Seeing François advancing
alone, he may have thought that he was going to
surrender, or he may have thought something quite
different; but he had very little time to think of anything, for François ran that great sabre of his clear

through him, and opening the gates he shouted, "En avant!"

Did they come? They came in just three leaps! And the Emperor, who had watched the whole proceeding through his glass, said, "The redoubt is taken."

Again and again the French charged, but the ground had become cut up by constant manœuvring and it seemed as though they could make little headway. Night was coming on. "I must put an end to this business," said the Emperor. "I am going to sleep to-night in the chateau of Brienne."

He put spurs to his horse, and, galloping out before the first line, pulled up before the central regiment. "Soldiers," said he, pointing with his hand toward the slope and Prussian batteries, "I am your colonel. I shall lead you. Brienne must be taken."

There was one great shout of "Vive l'Empereur!" and then no more breath was wasted. They closed their ranks, they set their teeth and they pushed on—on past the staff, on past the Emperor, up the slope into the main street of Brienne, driving back the Russians, charging into Blücher's staff, capturing the nephew of the Prussian Chancellor de Hardenberg, and on past the chateau of Brienne—the Russians and Prussians flying before them even to Mezières. How was it done? Even as the simple chronicler of the event has told us. The Imperial word was spoken. "Each soldier became equal to four."

On the 31st of January the Prussians advanced again to the field of La Rothière near Brienne—that field of La Rothière upon which the young Bonaparte had drilled and played in his school days at

Brienne, and upon which he now stood, with twenty thousand French soldiers about him and eighty thousand Russians and Prussians before him, fighting in the death-struggle of his Empire.

The combat at La Rothière was disastrous to the French, and the Emperor was compelled to fall back on Troyes. So the month of February began, and gloomily enough. The French Emperor had been forced to retreat after a pitched battle, and the two immense allied armies, advancing along the Marne and the Seine, had almost united. Could they be stopped now upon their triumphal march to Paris?

Every one said, "It is impossible." Impossible, gentlemen? "Ce mot n'est pas Français," General Bonaparte had cried in the early days, and it is General Bonaparte who leads you now.

And so, on the morning of the 9th of February, the Duc de Bassano, coming into the Emperor's headquarters to bring the dispatches which had been drawn up during the night to urge forward the peace negotiations at Chatillon, found the Emperor lying on his maps and planning with his colored pins.

"Ah! it is you!" cried the Emperor. "There is no more question of that. See here, I want to thrash Blücher; he has taken the Montmirail road. I shall fight him to-morrow and the day after to-morrow. The face of affairs is about to change and we shall see. We won't precipitate anything; there will always be time enough to conclude such a peace as they propose to us."

An hour later the Emperor was on the march to Sézanne. En avant! soldats des Français! The lion has been crouching; he is roaring now!

On the 10th of February the Emperor beat the Russians at Champaubert, on the 11th he routed the Prussians at Montmirail, on the 12th he beat them again at Château-Thierry, and on the 14th he worsted Blücher at Vauchamps. Thus in five days the army of Silesia, advancing proudly along the Marne, was sent to the right-about, leaving five generals, four flags, 68 cannon, and 28,000 men in the hands of the conqueror. Messieurs les Prussiens, it is a hard road to travel—this road to Paris!

Now for the Austrians, advancing by Nogent, Bray, and Montereau to Nangis, commanded by von Schwartzenberg. On the 18th of February the Emperor drove them back at Montereau and, entering Troyes in triumph on the 24th, sent off to Paris fourteen flags—one Austrian, four Prussian and nine Russian. Messieurs les Autrichiens, les Prussiens et les Russes, it is a hard road to travel—this road to Paris!

Now for the Prussians again, who, led by Blücher, were descending the Marne toward Meaux. So the Emperor left the army corps of Oudinot and Macdonald to hold the Austrians in check, and advanced again, with diminished numbers but with undiminished *sang-froid*, to meet the Prussians, and reached, toward evening, the little village of Herbisse.

A learned man was Monsieur Valentine, the curé of Herbisse, and his house—the presbytery—a modest structure containing one apartment which Monsieur le curé used as kitchen, salon, dining-room and bedchamber, and which had adjoining it a bake-house. On the evening before mentioned, M. Valentine was seated in his apartment of many uses, toasting his toes by the fire, while his niece, the black-eyed Henriette, was cutting a pie in the bake-house. The candle on the table was lighted and supper was ready, and when the fair Henriette had finished cutting the pie, she would bring it in and they would have supper. Then M. le curé would smoke his pipe, or read his breviary until he grew drowsy, and Mlle. Henriette would wash the dishes and go to her small room over the bake-house. And, finally, M. le curé, divested of his cassock, would snore loudly in his bed in the apartment of many uses. Such had been the life for many evenings at the presbytery of Herbisse—such no doubt it would be to-night. But before Mlle. Henriette had finished the delicate operation previously alluded to, a great noise of galloping horses was heard in the village of Herbisse. Nearer they came and stopped with a tumult unprecedented before the presbytery door. Imagine then the surprise of the worthy Valentine when, upon going hastily to the door of his apartment, he found himself *vis-à-vis* to His Majesty the Emperor of the French, behind whom were Marshals, aides-de-camp and orderly-officers, a seemingly endless crowd.

"Monsieur le curé," said His Majesty, "we have come to ask your hospitality for one night. Don't let this visit alarm you. We will make ourselves very small so as not to crowd you."

M. Valentine, "perspiring with mingled eagerness and embarrassment," conducted the Emperor into the apartment of many uses. The supper-dishes were pushed away. His Majesty threw his hat and sword on the table. The attendants brought his maps and papers, the door was closed, and in five minutes the Emperor was busily at work planning his march against von Blücher. The staff went into the bake-house, for on campaign it was always *loge-qui-peut*. Well, the bustling and going and coming and running to and fro of M. Valentine and Mlle. Henriette! It would have made a sluggard active. Chairs were gotten for the Marshals, and as for the aides-de-camp they sat on the table, the window-sills and the floor. Then nothing would do but that Mlle. Henriette should sing them a song. So Mlle. made her best courtesy and sang them some verses of Chenier's " Le Chant du Départ," which begins thus:

> " La victoire, en chantant,
> Nous ouvre la carrière;
> La liberté guide nos pas;
> Et du nord au midi la
> Trompette guerriere
> A sonné l'heure des combats! "

And she would have received a round of applause that no doubt would have cracked the bake-house windows, had they not feared to disturb the Emperor. Then M. Valentine, rosy with joy and perspiration, came in, bringing the best bottles from his cellar.

" Pax vobiscum! M. le curé," cried the jolly Lefebvre. " I studied for the priesthood myself in my young days, but *mille tonnerres!* I've kept little of all that but the coiffure."

" And why did you keep that, Monseigneur?" inquired M. Valentine.

" Because it was the soonest combed," said the chuckling Lefebvre. The curé laughed. " Don't imagine I have forgotten everything, however," continued the Marshal. "You shall see. I will quote some Virgil for you:

"Tityre tu patulae—parbleu!—sub tegmine fagi,
    Recubans—deus ex machina—quid pro quo—sacré!—ad
    finem."

There was a burst of laughter, in which the worthy curé joined. "Monseigneur," said he, "if you had continued your studies for the priesthood you would have become a cardinal at the least."

"Dame! I confess my Latin is a bit rusty," said the Marshal, "but gentlemen"—and he looked toward the laughing aides-de-camp—"there is one expression I haven't forgotten. It is this—Dulce et decorum est pro patria mori—and by God's name that's what we've got to do now with the Cossacks only twenty leagues from Paris!"

"Bah! Monseigneur," cried the aide-de-camp Letort, "we shall chase them back."

"Yes," said the Marshal, setting his teeth, "we shall see if they come."

At this moment the canteen mules arrived. A long table was made by placing a door on four casks. The Marshals sat down while the aides-de-camp ate standing. The worthy Valentine placed upon the table his bottles of cherished wine, and was quite overcome with surprise and delight at hearing the good-natured Lefebvre say, "Come, M. le curé, sit down here and take pot-luck with us."

Imagine then the worthy Valentine, sitting in his bake-house at the table of boards and casks, with Marshal Lefebvre, Duke of Dantzig, on his right, and

Marshal Ney, Prince of the Moscowa, on his left, and opposite him the Marshal Berthier, Prince of Neufchâtel and Wagram, while in a semicircle about the table stood the Imperial aides-de-camp, booted, spurred, embroidered, laced and plumed. Surely the star of Valentine was in the ascendant. The worthy curé felt himself enrolled among the gods.

Smile on, joyous Valentine! You are the lucky one in that party. In little more than a year he who sits at your left, Ney, Marshal of France, Duke of Elchingen and Prince of the Moscowa, will have been shot like a common malefactor. And he who sits opposite you, Berthier, Marshal of France and Prince of Neufchâtel and Wagram, will have committed suicide; and many of those high-spirited aides-de-camp about you will have laid down their lives at Mont St. Jean; and he—the great one—who sits yonder in your apartment of many uses, will have become England's captive, and the Empire with its crowns and its thrones, its stars and its crosses, will have faded like a dream— but you will still retain your presbytery of Herbisse!

And, when the supper was finished, some straw was found in the barns nearby and each one made his couch for the night. The curé had also his bundle of straw, and after the excitement of the evening, he slept so well that he was still snoring when, at daybreak, the Emperor and his staff departed to pursue the Prussians. Great was the mortification of M. Valentine, curé of Herbisse, when he awoke and found them gone, but when he went again into his apartment of many uses he saw upon his table the purse of gold—the souvenir left in every peasant's hut in Europe upon whose pillow had rested the Imperial brow.

16

The next four weeks were hard ones for the Imperial Guard. On the 28th of February there was a battle at Sézanne. Then they pushed on to La Ferté-sous-Jouarre, where to his delight the Emperor saw the Prussians retreating toward Soissons. Blücher was now in a perilous position, the Aisne before him, the Marne behind him, Marmont and Mortier on his left and Napoleon on his right. The grenadiers said, "We have got that old fighter." And they pressed on, but, all at once, on the 3rd of March, Soissons surrendered, and Blücher made good his escape across the Aisne. Fancy the rage of the Imperial Guard after their days and nights of toil, fighting, and marching! Pierre and François Legrand were in such a temper that they forgot to eat their soup. "No matter," said François, "we will have them yet." The pursuit was ordered, and on the 7th of March they met the Prussians at Craonne, but Blücher had been reinforced by Bülow and Wintzingerode—it was 100,000 to 30,000 now.

No one stopped to think of that, however, and when the Imperial Grenadiers were ordered to storm the heights of Craonne they did it with a will. Captain Pasquin had his plume and scabbard shot away, but he fought so hard that he foamed at the mouth, and there were many more who did likewise. Blücher fell back, sullen but not defeated. Then the same thing was repeated at Laon on the 9th and 10th of March. The same display of valor, the same impetuous onset, the same bloody losses, but this time the Emperor was forced to retreat, conquered by numbers, leaving a fourth of his army dead at Laon and Craonne.

So they came to Rheims, and found it occupied by the Russians entrenched behind redoubts of casks and rubbish. Near the gate to Paris, on a level piece of ground upon which stood a windmill, the Guard built a fire, and the Emperor stretched himself near it on his bearskin, for he was very tired. It was the 13th of March and ten at night. Suddenly the Russians made a sortie, firing musketry on the left. The Emperor jumped up from his bearskin.

"What is that?" he cried furiously.

"It is a 'hurrah,' sire," said the aide-de-camp Letort.

"I will see about that," said the Emperor. "Bring me Captain Reubelle and Captain Pasquin." They were not long in coming.

"You," said he to Reubelle, "bring your pieces and fire on those gates, and you, Pasquin, be ready to enter the city. I must be in Rheims by midnight. You are fools if you do not go through those gates."

"We will go through them, sire."

The battery was brought up and the shells fell in the centre of the city. The cuirassiers of the Guard, meanwhile, were drawn up behind the guns, prepared to charge with the grenadiers. The Emperor ordered the firing to cease, then he gave the signal. The trumpets sounded, Pierre shouted "Forward!" and they went, carrying all before them.

The cuirassiers dashed through the Rue de Vesle and the Rue Libergier, sabring right and left, while the grenadiers followed with their bayonets. The people of Rheims, shut up in their houses, hearing the tumult, lighted their windows, and Rheims was illuminated on all sides. By midnight the Emperor was in the city and the Russians were routed. They had found their "hurrah" a costly one. But it could not go on for ever, this rushing from the valley of the

Marne to the valley of the Seine and from the valley of
the Seine to the valley of the Marne, this fighting
Blücher one day and Wintzingerode another, and Bülow another, and Schwartzenberg another. The French
forces grew weaker and weaker, and the enormous
masses of the enemy advanced nearer and nearer to
Paris—advanced slowly, though, and cautiously—so
cautiously!—for, though they outnumbered ten to one
the forces of their foe, they trembled lest at an unex-
pected moment they might see upon the brow of some
hill the eagle of France, the caps of the Guard, and the
terrifying cocked hat and greatcoat of the Little Corporal.

Then the Emperor prepared his *coup de maître* and
determined to march cn St. Dizier, leaving Paris tem-
porarily exposed; determined to rally his garrisons in
the fortresses of Lorraine and Alsace, to join Augereau advancing from the south, to cut the enemy's
lines of communication, and being in their rear with
150,000 men, compel them in self-defense to wheel
about and give him battle.

He set out, and his columns disappeared beyond
Vitry-sur-Marne. And then, while the Allies, astonished by the boldness of this manœuvre, paused in
surprise, hesitating between a further advance or a precipitate retreat, there came to the allied headquarters
Monsieur le Marquis de Vitrolles, bearing from the
Prince de Talleyrand—head, shoulders, body, legs and
arms of the plotters in Paris—this message: "You may
do everything and you dare do nothing. For once then
be daring." And when this assurance was given them,
Messieurs les Puissances Alliées tightened their sword-
belts, adjusted their plumes, counted their numbers,
and casting one frightened glance behind them,

sounded their trumpets and gave the word—"To Paris!"

On the 28th of March at St. Dizier the Emperor learned that he was not followed by the army of Schwartzenberg but by the corps of Wintzingerode, and more—the Allies were marching on Paris. Would it hold out until he could arrive? "Let us march! Let us march!" And so by St. Dizier, Vitry-sur-Marne and Doulencourt, on in breathless haste to Troyes, where they arrived in the night, the panting grenadiers of the Imperial Guard having marched forty miles in one day. But no stop here— on! on! If the grenadiers can do no more, on with the cuirassiers! And so the Emperor hastened on, his traveling-carriage rattling over the stones. But ere long the wearied cuirassiers could no longer keep pace with him, and he pushed on with only Caulaincourt and Berthier in his carriage. At every post-house he sent off couriers to announce his approach, at every post-house he learned news more and more disastrous. The Empress with the King of Rome had quitted Paris, and Joseph, after issuing proclamations very like the English skit of the period—

> "Brave lads of Paris! never fear,
>   Though Blücher's force be drawing near;
>   I, Joseph Buonaparte, am here."

Joseph had run off too! The enemy were before the walls!—they were at the gates!—there was fighting on the heights!

The traveling-carriage was abandoned, and springing into a light post-calèche, with Berthier and Caulaincourt, the Emperor dashed on. "Faster! faster!" he cried. The postillions plied the whip and spur, the horses galloped with bloodshot eyes and foaming mouths, the calèche swayed from side to side, the wheels struck fire from the pavements, but above the whirling of the wheels, the shouts of the postillions, the galloping hoofs and the cracking whips was heard the Imperial voice crying ever " Faster! faster! faster! "

And so, at ten at night on the 30th of March, covered with dust and foam, panting, trembling, terrified, hoping, doubting, mad with impatience, they dashed into Fromenteau, five leagues from Paris, and pulled up before the Cour de France to change horses. Up and down in the darkness strode the Emperor, counting the seconds till his horses should be put in. Then some straggling soldiers passing in the gloom shouted, " Paris has capitulated! "

" These men are mad! " cried the Emperor. " The thing is impossible! My carriage! my carriage! "

Too late! Napoleon. The Czar of all the Russias, lighted by the flames of Moscow, has found his way to the doors of the Tuileries Palace.

So ended the campaign of France. Nothing like it had been seen before. Nothing like it is likely to be seen again. In the hour of disaster the World-Conqueror disappears. There remains only the Champion of France, who might have saved his crown had he signed away her territory or her greatness.

" Peace at any price! " cried all about him—his ministers, his brothers, his marshals and his friends. " Sign! " cried the Allies, " and retain your crown."

What! sign a treaty that stripped France of provinces on every hand and left her less great than he found her? No! he would have none of it. And so he fell—game to the last—*le Français des Français* battling *pour la belle France!*

CHAPTER XXVII

Les Adieux de Fontainebleau

'Twas thus that Napoleon left us;
   Our people were weeping and mute,
As he passed through the lines of his Guard,
   And our drums beat the notes of salute.
     —THACKERAY, *The Chronicle of the Drum.*

"MARCH!" said General Petit, and the grenadiers of the Imperial Guard advanced across the palace park, through the great gates, into the Cour du Cheval Blanc and on to the foot of the Horseshoe Staircase.

"Halt!" said General Petit. There they stood motionless, those great grenadiers—those veterans who had faced the cannon in the marshes of Arcole, who had battled at the pyramids while "forty centuries looked down upon them," who had climbed the wall of St. Jean d'Acre, who had charged the Austrian centre on Marengo's plain, who had seen the sun rise on the heights of Austerlitz, who had fought with fire in the streets of Moscow. There they stood, hundreds of statues made of bronze and crowned with laurel. To reproduce them, France must have had again a twenty years of victory. The light breeze gently waved their plumes; the horses that stood harnessed to the carriage near the great curved staircase champed their bits. Thus they waited.

How many Kings and mighty men of France had gone up and down that Horseshoe Staircase! How many Queens and gilded favorites had swept triumphant through that courtyard! Francis the First, doing the honors to the Emperor Charles the Fifth; Catherine of Medici, and by her side her craven son, planning the Bartholomew; Henry of Navarre, with his white plume of Ivry and his "charmante Gabrielle"; Louis XIII and his scarlet-robed Prime Minister, Richelieu the omnipotent; the Grand Monarch and his stately court; "le Bien-Aime," and the Pompadour.

But the traveler who stands to-day in that courtyard of the Fontainebleau Château forgets the Valois and the Bourbon, forgets Francis of Angoulême and Henry of Navarre; for the old concierge who walks by his side does not tell him of the hunts and tourneys of the second Henry, or of the fêtes and pompous journeys of the Grand Monarque, but, stopping at the foot of the Horseshoe Staircase, he says these words: " Here Napoleon took leave of his Guard, April 20th, 1814. Since then this court has been called Cour des Adieux."

Twelve o'clock! The click of spurs was heard upon the marble floor of the palace vestibule. The Emperor appeared in the great doorway. The Garde Impériale presented arms.

He came rapidly down the staircase and advanced to where they stood, and then he said—but everyone knows what he said, for the words have been printed again and again. They mean little now—they are mere words. But it was different when they were first spoken on that April morning, by the Emperor Napoleon to the soldiers of his Old Guard, in the courtyard of the Palace Fontainebleau. They were his good friends, who had marched at his side and camped about his tent, had stemmed the tide of defeat and turned it into victory, and closed around him, like a brazen wall, when the Russian guns swept the icy plains at Moscow.

He was their Little Corporal, who, after twenty years of triumph and of glory, had come to say good-bye.

So they listened while he spoke, and they saw him kiss the eagle, and they watched him as he entered his carriage, and they followed the carriage with their eyes as it drove along the courtyard, out of the gate, and disappeared. Then slowly and sadly they marched to their barracks. And all was quiet in the courtyard of the Palace Fontainebleau.

CHAPTER XXVIII

"Vive le Roi!"

> "But what good came of it at last?"
> Quoth little Peterkin.
> "Why, that I cannot tell," said he;
> "But 'twas a famous victory."
> —SOUTHEY, *Battle of Blenheim.*

BRIGHTLY shone the sun on the 3rd of May, 1814. It was a lovely day, and surely if a day ought ever to be lovely that day should have been so. Why? Had not the sun and "Nec pluribus impar" been the emblem and motto of that wonderfully high-heeled and big-wigged grandiloquent monarch, King Louis Quatorze? And in the old days at Versailles was it not true that "the rain of Marly never wet one," and that when the king had planned to go a hunting it was *always* clear in deference to the royal will? What could be more appropriate, therefore, than that the sun should shine brightly on that 3rd of May, 1814, when the Grand Monarque's descendant, Louis-Stanislas-Xavier de Bourbon, after a somewhat extended foreign tour of twenty-four years, was to make, by the kind assistance of Messrs. George of England, Alexander of Russia, Francis of Austria, and Charles Maurice de Talleyrand-Périgord, his serio-comic *entrée* into his good city of Paris, and settle down in the Tuileries Palace for the rest of his natural life. Therefore shine brightly, sun; chirp gaily, little birds;

run quickly from the sky, clouds! And the sun, birds and sky, knowing that it was proper for them to shine, sing, and be clear, did so, and the day was lovely.

There had been great rejoicing a few days before at Compiègne, where the Marshals and Generals of the Empire had gone to welcome King Louis de Bourbon. How happy they all were to see him, and the old custom of kissing the royal hands could not be revived too quickly. But in this case it happened that the royal hands were scrofulous ones, and as people are not generally fond of kissing scrofulous hands, although they may be royal, His Most Christian Majesty kindly consented to put royal green gloves on the royal scrofulous hands, and the Marshals, Generals, Counts and Barons kissed the royal green gloves and were happy. Then they all sat promptly down to dinner, for His Most Christian Majesty was always punctual. "L'exactitude est la politesse des rois" (Punctuality is the politeness of kings) was his motto, and, by the way, the only thing he ever said worth remembering, for all those Latin sentences which he used to rattle off so glibly were cribbed from classic authors.

What a dinner it was!—four soups, four removes, four great dishes, four great *entremêts*, and thirty-two *entrées*. And when the Most Christian Majesty sent some vermouth to Marshal Macdonald, and Marshal Macdonald, who was much more at home facing cannon-balls than eating big dinners of Most Christian Majesties, forgot to rise and cry "Vivat," the kind King forgave him so gracefully and royally that it touched the hearts of everybody, and even the marble Apollo in the royal dining-room shed tears.

Then they came on to Saint-Ouen, leisurely enough, for there was no hurry, and it was just as well to let the good people of Paris get up on their tiptoes of expectation before their eyes were gladdened by the sight of a Most Christian and Royally Scrofulous Majesty.

But finally the 3rd of May came round, and the royal king was all dressed for the royal entry, with beautiful green gloves on the royal scrofulous hands, and bright red velvet gaiters on the fat, gouty legs, and a blue coat with gold epaulettes, and on the royal hat—and this was the most touching of all—a big white cockade, which had been pinned there, when the Most Christian Majesty was in London, by the fat hands of no less a personage than Beau Brummel's friend, that worthless rake and puppy the Prince Regent of England, alias " first gentleman in Europe," whom Thackeray, skilfully dissecting in the " Four Georges," found to consist mainly of scented hand-kerchiefs, padded waistcoats, oily wigs, and wind.

Now to get King Punctuality into the carriage. That was a trick indeed! And the Marshals and Generals pushed and tugged, and, as a combination of effort is generally successful, it was finally accom-plished, and the Marshals and Generals could take off their plumed hats and mop their brows and thank their stars that Louis-Stanislas-Xavier de Bourbon was not to get out again until he reached his jour-ney's end, and hope that there would be a derrick at the Tuileries Palace when he did so. And, in witness-ing the difficulties experienced by His Most Christian Majesty in mounting his coach to make his *entrée* into his good city of Paris, it is interesting to note the remarkable agility with which, a year later, this same two hundred and odd pounds of royal scrofulous flesh got into its royal traveling clothes, down the grand staircase, into the royal coach, and packed off to Ghent, when the cocked hat and *redingote grisé* of the Little Corporal appeared before the gates of Lyons.

But, says the candid reader, you are hard on King Louis XVIII. He was a stout king, it is true, but then he was old and infirm; you should have some respect for old age. Remember too what a hard time he had had wandering about over Europe, and what beautiful letters he had written to the First Consul, full of touching allusions to Francis I.

Good reader, any sympathy expended on Louis-Stanislas-Xavier de Bourbon would be a case of pearls and pigs. If, when he was Count of Provence, he had only eaten and grown fat he would have done no more than many another, but he tried to blacken the character of poor Marie Antoinette, and did it systematically too. And when the wind began to whistle and the storm to howl, he jumped into a traveling carriage, for he was more agile in those days, and hurried off to Coblentz, leaving brother Louis XVI, who had a good heart and an empty head, to get out of things as best he could. Now, however, since kind foreign friends had gotten brother Louis XVI's bed ready for him, and a good dinner was cooking in the Tuileries kitchen, he was naturally willing enough to come back and enjoy it all. And so, with punctual King *Cochon* in the carriage, the royal procession started at a trot.

At the right door of the carriage rode the Count d'Artois, who had made his entry into Paris some days before. On which occasion, when he had been

somewhat at a loss for something to say to the joyous
deputation sent out to meet him, the Prince de Talleyrand or Count Beugnot had kindly invented for him
the famous phrase, " Nothing is changed; there is only
one more Frenchman," which looked so nicely the
next morning in the " Moniteur." He rode along on
his prancing horse trained *à la Franconi*, looking as
gay as in the old days at Versailles, when his principal
occupations had been dancing on the tight rope and
seducing *femmes de chambre*.

By the left door rode the Duc de Berri, the worthy
son of his worthy father the Count d'Artois; and in
front of the royal carriage—and this might surprise
us if we did not know that, as the Duc de la Rochefou-
cauld said, " Everything happens in France "—rode
Marshal Berthier, Prince of Neufchâtel and Wagram,
the man who during twenty years had been, in cabinet
and carriage, by the side of the Emperor Napoleon.
He rode along with the gayest possible air, and,
en passant, the reference to the *Emperor Napoleon* was
quite a slip in this connection, for the Marshal Berthier, Prince of Neufchâtel and Wagram, at that
moment knew no such person. He had a slight ac-
quaintance with *Usurper Bonaparte*, but it would have
been most *mal à propos* for any one to have mentioned it.

But it was not all comedy, this *entrée* of Louis-
Stanislas-Xavier de Bourbon: there was tragedy about
it too. By the King's side in the royal carriage sat
the pale, melancholy Duchess d'Angoulême, the last
of the family of Louis XVI. She was entering again
this Paris of which she had such dreadful recollections,
this Paris where her little brother Louis had perished

at the hands of Simon the shoemaker, and her father, mother, and aunt Elizabeth upon the guillotine. There was no joy in her face.

And look on ahead of the royal carriage. There, lining the road on either side, dressed in their blue coats and great bearskin caps, scarred with the sabre-cuts and bayonet-thrusts of Marengo, Austerlitz, Jena, Eckmühl, Wagram, Moscow, Lutzen, Bautzen, Montmirail, stood the Grenadiers of the Garde Impériale. Among them were our old friends, François Legrand, Gustave Lébon, and André Marceau. Their great hairy caps were pushed down on their knit brows, their lips were curled in angry scorn, their teeth showed fiercely under their heavy mustaches; and when the royal procession passed they all presented arms with such a furious rattle of weapons that more than one spectator trembled.

The comedy was in the fat king, the grinning Count d'Artois, the foppish Duc de Berri. The tragedy was in the sad Duchess d'Angoulême and in those heroic, war-worn veterans of the Garde Impériale. And thus they reached the Tuileries Palace, and thus was Louis-Stanislas-Xavier de Bourbon installed—not *par la grâce de Dieu*, but by the grace of England, Russia, Prussia, Austria, Sweden and Dame Fortune —King of France—*pro tem.*

CHAPTER XXIX

A THUNDERBOLT

On a sudden open fly,
With impetuous recoil and jarring sound,
The infernal doors, and on their hinges grate
Harsh thunder.
—MILTON, *Paradise Lost.*

THUS they reached the Tuileries Palace, and how nice everything was! " Why, it must be confessed," said His Majesty, " that Bonaparte was a very good tenant. He has arranged everything excellently for me." Why, it was perfectly charming! There were a number of N's here and there, however, on the furniture and on the walls, but that was easily managed. A strip of velvet was pasted over them and the effect was fine; and as for the eagles beside the throne—why, they looked so well that it was decided not to take them down. Then there were some marble busts of the Emperor about the Louvre, but they were soon fixed. Clever workmen put some plaster of Paris on the nose and made a nice plaster of Paris wig for each, and there you were! The simplest thing in the world! Bonaparte? Not a bit of it—Louis XVIII! And now to business. The Imperial *chefs* were kicked out of the Tuileries kitchen and the Royal *chefs* put in, and the menus were carefully arranged for the royal breakfasts, dinners and suppers, and, this important matter being happily concluded, a

Charter was issued, dated "In the nineteenth year of our reign," which was quite right and proper from the point of view of His Most Christian Majesty, who, whether living at Hartwell or wandering about in Poland, believed himself always King of France *par la grâce de Dieu.*

Then *Monsieur* went smiling and bowing and caracoling along on his circus-trained charger to hold a review in the Champ-de-Mars. And His Majesty went in his wheeled chair to the opera to see "Oedipe," and beamed like a big round moon over the edge of the royal box at his faithful subjects And Madame la Duchesse d'Angoulême went up in the Tuileries attic and hunted for an old spinnet which had belonged to Marie Antoinette, and which had been left in the palace, and which Madame la Duchesse expected to find there in spite of all the moving and house-cleaning that had taken place in that establishment since 1792.

And then the Imperial Guard was cut up and made Royal Grenadiers of France and Royal *chasseurs à pied* of France, and Royal cuirassiers of France and Royal *chasseurs à cheval* of France and Royal Light-Horse Lancers of France and several other royal things. And six companies of Royal *gardes-du-corps* were instituted just as they had been in 1789, and more companies of *gardes-du-corps* were made for Monsieur and also some *compagnies rouges.* And the old ones were kicked out and the new ones were put in. The *émigrés* and old noblesse got stars and ribbons and were made captains and colonels and generals and what-not. And if you had fought at Austerlitz or Wagram you were nobody, and if your grandfather

17

had held the king's shirt or tied the king's garter at the *petit lever* you were a great man. And Napoleon's profile was wiped off the Legion of Honor and the profile of Henry IV was put in its place. Now Henry IV was a jolly king and a brave one, and the French have always been glad to sing his praises and those of his " charmante Gabrielle," but no doubt you will agree that his piquant physiognomy was as much out of place on the Cross of the Legion of Honor as it would have been upon the pyramid of Cheops.

And as may be supposed, with all this eating, and prancing, and bowing, and kicking-out and hoisting-in, and theatre-going, and proclamation-issuing, and bust-decorating, the government of His Most Christian Majesty was much too busy to pay any attention to the Treaty of Fontainebleau, or send to Bonaparte the sums of money guaranteed him by that Treaty to pay his bills in Elba. And so, before very long the people of Paris and Lyons and Marseilles and Grenoble and Boulogne and Orleans and numberless other places, witnessing the grand transformation scene arranged by the royal company, under the stage direction of M. de Blancas and His Most Christian Majesty, began to ask themselves this question, " Where are we at?" Good people, you are coming out of your trance. You have been laboring under the absurd delusion that you have had a revolution, a republic, and an empire. No such thing! You are in the nineteenth year of the reign of His Most August, Most Serene, Most Glorious, Most Robust and Most Scrofulous Majesty, Louis XVIII of France and Navarre, King by the grace of God!

It was a gloomy winter for our friends in Grenoble,

the winter of 1814-15. Marie was busy caring for the little Josephine, who was three and a half now. She wrote often to Pierre, and she wondered when she would see Pierre again, for Pierre had been among the 600 grenadiers chosen by the Emperor to accompany him to Elba. It was hard to leave France and all there after the years of separation that had already passed, but Pierre had written, " It is hard, but I must go. I owe him all." And Marie had written, " Go, it is your duty."

So Marie cared for the little Josephine, and the garçon Gaspard assisted the père Henri at the Café Jodélle. As may be supposed it was not a joyous winter for the père Henri, or for Philippe Courteau, or for old Frédéric Bonneville. They met often at the Hotel des Trois Dauphins, and when the papers came from Paris and they read of some new act of the Royal Government which overturned the existing state of things and threw contempt upon the old soldiers of the Empire, Philippe would look at Frédéric Bonneville and say with a grave face, " Well, you wanted peace. You've got it. What do you think of it? I observe you don't go to the *mairie* to get your pension any more."

Frédéric's pension had been cut off, and so had Philippe's and Henri's likewise. Thus the winter was gloomy, for trade was bad, and each had to look closely at his affairs or he would have found the hungry wolf snuffing at his door. They formed a club, Philippe, Henri and Frédéric; they called it " Club Violette," the Violet Club, and this was the sign of membership. When they met one who they thought was of their party they said, " Aimez-vous la

violette?" And if the answer was "Oui," then the
one so answering was not with them; but if the answer
was "Eh bien," then the one so answering was of their
party. And they met often at the Trois Dauphins,
and while La Barre stood by the door and looked up
and down to watch who came, they toasted "Caporal
Violette" who lived on the island of Elba. And
there were many more in France who did likewise.
And so the winter passed.

One evening in the early days of March, 1815, the
diligence from Voreppe came clattering into Grenoble.
Burly Matthieu was still driving, but the black horse
and the roan mare—the one having gone blind and
the other having broken a leg—had been succeeded
by two shaky bays. There was only one passenger in
the diligence, a tall man with black hair and mustache
and keen dark eyes. He wore a round hat, boots
and gloves, and a long blue overcoat, and as he looked
out of the diligence window and saw the houses and
dimly-burning lamps of the Rue Montorge, his face
assumed a hard and bitter expression. So then, after
six years, Jean Deteau was in Grenoble once more.
And where had he been all this time? Oh! in Spain
fighting under Soult, Jourdan and Joseph Bonaparte,
where little had been experienced but disaster, and
where the Anglo-Portuguese army commanded by
Lord Wellington had been steadily driving them back
toward France, until finally after the battle of Vittoria
they had been compelled to cross the Bidassoa. Then
they fought to keep the enemy out of southern France
until the Empire fell, when, after the king's return,
Deteau found himself on half-pay and with no very
pressing call for his services either. So that his ex-

pectations for a great military career, expectations
which had assumed gigantic proportions in 1809,
could now all be put in a thimble, and not a very
large thimble at that. He had quickly discovered
during a two days' stay in Paris that his former
patrons could do nothing for him, so he became at
once a zealous supporter of the Bourbons and a reviler
of Bonaparte. But there were so many others doing
the same thing that he attracted no attention and was
given no opportunity to show his newly-acquired zeal.
Therefore he set out for Grenoble, nursing his disappointment. And did he know of Marie's marriage
and Pierre's honors? Oh, yes, he knew all about it,
for at the time of the wedding stout Robert Bovard
had sent him full particulars, being totally ignorant
of what had occurred on the road to Tudela and sup-
posing that as he had known Pierre he would be glad
to hear. Thus he was sufficiently posted, and thus he
rode down the Rue Montorge, the hard look in his
eyes and rage in his heart. Jean Deteau, beaten in
love and defeated in war!

When they reached the Trois Dauphins old La
Barre came out. "Got any passengers, Matthieu?"
said he.

"One," said Matthieu.

Deteau opened the coach door and stepped out.
"I'm here for the night," said he to La Barre, "and
I want supper."

"*Chenument* (very well), Monsieur."

"You may bring in my luggage."

"Yes, Monsieur."

Deteau walked into the hall of the inn and sat
down. "Where do I lodge?" he inquired, without
getting up as La Barre came in with the luggage.

"You can stop in this room on the right," said La Barre, depositing the bags and lighting a candle.

"Now," said Deteau, "I want supper."

La Barre bustled off, leaving Deteau to his own meditations. At the end of twenty minutes he came back and said, "It's ready, Monsieur."

Deteau found the dining-room comfortable, a good fire was burning, and the supper was not unpalatable—it never was at the Trois Dauphins—and so when he had finished half a bottle of wine he felt more cheerful.

"And how are the times?" said he, as La Barre came in with a fresh log for the fire.

"Malheur! very poor," said La Barre. "Trade's none too good, and people in this house ain't over-glad when they reads of the doings in Paris."

Deteau saw which way the wind blew. "Ah!" said he, sighing, "no doubt they, like me, regret the downfall of the Emperor."

"Indeed they do," said La Barre. "I've often heard M. Courteau and M. Jodélle tell that we was all going to hell with the d——d Bourbons."

"*Mon oeil!* Have you indeed?" said Deteau. "And is M. Jodélle a friend of M. Courteau?"

"Yes, oh, yes, they are great friends. They drink often to Caporal Violette."

"And who is Caporal Violette?" inquired Deteau.

"Well, seeing as how you're one of us who is grieving because he ain't here, there's no harm in saying it's the Little Corporal—him as is at Elba."

"Bring another glass, good fellow," said Deteau, "we must both drink to Caporal Violette."

La Barre did so and they drank. Then Deteau plied him with questions and they drank again. La

Barre's tongue worked so beautifully in a short time that Deteau was not long in learning all about the " Club Violette " and its members.   Then as La Barre discovered that the stranger took a real interest in him and in his statements, he grew eloquent and began to pour forth his personal views on the state of France.   Deteau rose abruptly.   " It is late," said he.

" *C'est renversant!* (wonderful).   So it is," said La Barre, looking around at the clock.   " I must get the mail-bag ready for morning.   Parbleu! but I've forgot the letter M. Jodélle give me to put in it."

" M. Jodélle gave you a letter? " said Deteau.

" Yes, it's to M. Pasquin—him as is with Caporal Violette—him as we've been drinking to."

" And where is your letter? " said Deteau quickly.

La Barre was fumbling in his pocket.   " Here it is," said he, examining it by the candle.   Then he laid it on the table.   Deteau picked it up.   " Yes, it is to M. Pasquin," he said, " fortunate M. Pasquin who is with Caporal Violette.   My friend, we must drink again to Caporal Violette."   And so they drank.

" Go and get your mail-bag," said Deteau.

La Barre went out with steps somewhat unsteady. Deteau drew an envelope from his pocket and laid it down beside the letter.   " Not quite the size but near enough," he said quietly, and slipping Henri Jodélle's letter into his pocket, he left the envelope lying on the table.   Presently La Barre returned, mail-bag in hand.

" Mon ami," said Deteau, " open your bag.   Give me the pleasure of starting on its way this letter to the brave M. Pasquin who is so near him we both honor—Caporal Violette."

So La Barre hiccoughed and opened the bag, and Deteau gracefully dropped the envelope within.

"There are quite a good many letters in it, are there not?" said he.

"Yes, it's heavy," said La Barre.

"Fasten it up," said Deteau. "When does the diligence go south in the morning?"

"Eight o'clock," said La Barre, swaying from side to side.

"Foutre! Stand up there, you fool!" cried Deteau. "You'll knock over the candle."

"D——n candle!" said La Barre. "Hé! Hé! We're pretty great friends, ain't we? We drink often to Caporal Violette."

"Yes, yes, of course. Now see here, you are *paf*" (drunk), and Deteau shook his arm. "I am going at eight in the morning and shall want breakfast before. Do you understand?"

La Barre hiccoughed. "We're pretty great friends, ain't we?" said he smiling placidly.

"Malheur! What's to be done with this ass?" cried Deteau in disgust.

"*Je suis paf*," mumbled La Barre. "*Hé! Hé! je suis paf!*" He tripped over the rug, fell down on it, curled himself up, and began to snore.

"Well, he may lie there for all I'll bother with him," said Deteau, and blowing out the light he went to his own room. Then closing his door he sat down by the candle and opened the letter carefully. "I don't know that anything will come of this," he said casually, "but I thought I would find out what was going on." So he began to read, and as he read he smiled, a sneering smile, and then his eyes glittered.

He rose and waved the letter in the air. "I have him! I have him!" he cried softly. "I can't get at that diable Pasquin, but I can get at you, M. Henri Jodélle. This will be good reading for M. de Vaudre-court, *procureur-du-roi*, and then we shall see if I who bring to light Bonapartist conspiracies am not entitled to something from the Government."

In the morning Deteau stood on the steps awaiting the diligence. It came, and so did La Barre, a trifle the worse for wear, with luggage and mail-bag.

"My good fellow," said Deteau, after paying his score, "when does M. Courteau return?"

"To-day," said La Barre. "He's been to Vizille."

"Well," said Deteau, with a sarcastic smile, "you fill his place superbly. Here in this envelope you will find something I wish to give you."

Old La Barre, overwhelmed with gratitude, stood hat in hand by the diligence door.

"Monsieur," said he, "how can I ever thank you?"

"Oh! don't mention it," said Deteau, looking out over the top of La Barre's head. "Come, postillion, *en avant!*"

The diligence started, but before they had proceeded far Deteau put his head out of the window. "I have changed my mind," said he. "I am not going south. Stop at the Hotel des Ambassadeurs, Rue Montorge."

La Barre, meantime, had gone into the Trois Dauphins. He was much excited about the mysterious envelope. What could it contain? It was not very heavy, still there was something in it. What a fine man the stranger was! Suppose he were some famous person in disguise, some Prince of the Empire. La Barre had heard of such things. It was rumored that

the King of Naples had come disguised into France.
Suppose this were the King of Naples. Well, if that
were so the gift would be large, for the King of
Naples was a generous giver. And if the gift were
large La Barre would purchase a pig; he had always
wanted one, and there was a convenient stall in the
stable which could be made into a pen. He would
buy a sow and then he would raise young pigs and
sell them, and the tin box under the pillow would
become quite full. This was a happy thought and a
pleasant one. La Barre opened the envelope. There
was a good-sized piece of paper in it folded several
times, and upon unfolding it La Barre read these
words—*you are a fool.* There never was a man so
surprised as La Barre!

On the morning of the 6th of March, M. de Vaudrecourt, *procureur-du-roi*, was seated in his office on the
Grand Rue, Grenoble, preparing a document to send
to the Hotel de Ville, when his servant announced a
visitor, " M. Jean Deteau."

" Bon jour, monsieur," said Deteau as he entered.
The *procureur-du-roi* bowed.

" I am a military man, Monsieur, and desire to go
briefly to business. Here is a letter that chance has
put in my way. You know the parties, or know of
them. Read it and you will see why I am here."

M. de Vaudrecourt took the letter and read:

Mon cher Pierre.

I am writing from the Trois Dauphins. Marie is well
and Josephine also. Things in France as you know are no
better. What could one expect? Do you know what I
heard? It was whispered that before long the time for
violets will have come. " Elle reparaitra au printemps," they

said. God grant it may be so. Who has been appointed *procureur-du-roi* in Grenoble, do you think? Vaudrecourt! the biggest fool and the biggest scoundrel, too. He would be glad to break up the Club Violette, but he shall not. Once he sang the Little Corporal's praises, now he licks the hand of the Bourbons. He is a *chien hargneu.* But no matter, we shall continue to toast Corporal Violette and one day we shall see.

Votre beau-père affectionné,

5 Mars, 1815. HENRI.

"Ah," said M. de Vaudrecourt, placing the letter on his desk, "as it is directed to M. Pasquin, the signer is, I fancy, M. Henri Jodélle."

"Exactly," said Deteau.

"Monsieur, you have rendered me a service," said the *procureur-du-roi.* "I have been trying to get hold of some of the members of the Club Violette. Thanks to you, they shall not escape me now."

"I can tell you all about them, Monsieur," replied Deteau.

"*Très-bien,* you shall do so, but in my carriage. We will pay a visit to M. Henri Jodélle. If, as he says, I am a ' snappish cur '—*le diable!* he shall feel my teeth."

The *procureur-du-roi* ordered his carriage, and when it came there was a gendarme on the box beside the coachman. M. de Vaudrecourt and Deteau entered.

"Tell him to drive to the Café Jodélle, Place Grénette," said the *procureur-du-roi* to the gendarme.

Gaspard had gone to the Trois Dauphins that morning, and this is how he came to go there. After breakfast Henri had said, "Gaspard, go to the Trois Dauphins and find out if Philippe has come back from Vizille." So Gaspard set out, and as the morn-

ing was bright he felt happy and occasionally looked
in the shop-windows as he went along. At the same
time that the carriage containing M. de Vaudrecourt
and Deteau reached the Café Jodélle, Gaspard reached
the Trois Dauphins, where a moment later the diligence from Vizille came rattling up to the door and
Philippe Courteau jumped out. His arrival occasioned
the wildest excitement and demonstrations of joy on
the part of La Barre, who probably felt that the re-
sponsibility of the Trois Dauphins was too much for
him alone, or why should he have made such an ado?
As for Gaspard he set off for the Café Jodélle as fast
as his legs could carry him. Probably he was in
such a hurry because he thought he had wasted time
on the way thither.

"The little Gaspard is a swift runner," said dame
Bovard as she saw him speeding down the Rue Montorge.

Ah! swift indeed! Run, little Gaspard! There are
some at the Café Jodélle whose safety is in danger.
There are some at the Café Jodélle who need you
and your message. Run, little Gaspard, run!

M. de Vaudrecourt and Deteau entered the Café
Jodélle with the gendarme. They passed to Henri's
sitting-room and knocked. "Come in," said Henri,
and they entered. Marie sat near the window sewing,
the little Josephine was playing on the floor and Henri
writing at the table. He looked up in surprise when
he saw the *procureur-du-roi*, and then rising he leaned
on his crutch and said briskly, "Well, sir?"

"M. Henri Jodélle, I believe," said Vaudrecourt.

"Of course," said Henri, "you know me well
enough. What do you want?"

Henri had been looking intently at the *procureur-*

du-roi, but Marie had been looking elsewhere, and before M. de Vaudrecourt could answer she cried out, " Father! father! it is Jean Deteau! "

" Le diable! " cried Henri, " so it is."

" I am flattered to think that Madame Pasquin remembers me," said Deteau, bowing. Ugh! what a bow, and what a sneering accent on the words " Madame Pasquin."

" So *Rosbif de rat d'égout!* (you skunk!) you've come back, have you? " roared Henri. " They must have damn-fool cannon-balls in Spain since they knock over honest men and leave curs like you."

" You shall pay for that," snarled Deteau, advancing.

" Stop! " cried M. de Vaudrecourt, " stand back! This is my affair."

The gendarme had meanwhile closed the door, and little Josephine was regarding him with wondering eyes.

" M. Jodélle," said the *procureur-du-roi* in a bantering tone, " I have reason to believe that you are not satisfied with the blessings showered upon you by the Government of His Majesty. And more, that you have in Grenoble talked in an outrageous manner regarding His Majesty's representatives. And in short, sir, you have conspired and are conspiring with the agents of the Usurper. Of this I have proof."

" What proof? " cried Henri.

" A letter of yours to M. Pasquin."

" Well, bring it out."

" Mon Dieu! I am not fool enough to give it you now. It shall be seen at the proper time."

" And how did you get it? " demanded Henri fiercely.

"No matter how I got it. Let it suffice that I have it."

"Well, what if you have!" cried Henri. "I have never conspired. No letter of mine can prove it."

"Do you mean to say that you don't belong to the Club Violette, and that you don't drink to Caporal Violette, which is only another name for the Usurper?"

"Yes," said Henri, "I belong and we drink to him. We've fought under him and we wish him well. There's no conspiracy in that. My God! if you are going to arrest people for that, you will have to arrest three-fourths of France."

"Indeed," said the *procureur-du-roi*. "We shall see."

"Ah!" cried Marie, coming forward, "he has never conspired. Believe me he has never conspired. He has fought for the Emperor, and my Pierre is with him, and he writes to him and wishes the Emperor well. Oh! surely, surely, that cannot be wrong."

"Get out of the way," said the *procureur-du-roi*, sternly. "Now mark me, Henri Jodélle. You've reviled me long enough. I'm a 'snappish cur,' am I? You shall feel my teeth. I 'lick the hand of the Bourbons,' do I? You shall feel the weight of their hand. I am *procureur-du-roi* in Grenoble, and by the King's name I'll have you tried for abetting the Usurper, and if we catch you, as we shall, you'll hang on a gallows in Grenoble forty feet high."

And then something happened, for the door burst open, and Gaspard, his big brown eyes blazing with excitement, sprang into the room and cried with all his little might: "What do you think? Napoleon has landed in France! He is on the march to Paris!"

CHAPTER XXX

The Eagle with the Tricolor

The imperial ensign, which full high advanced,
Shone like a meteor, streaming to the wind.
—Milton, *Paradise Lost.*

THE *procureur-du-roi* turned pale, Marie uttered a joyful cry, and Henri Jodélle stood erect and tossed his head.

"You lie!" cried Jean Deteau, striding toward Gaspard.

"Chiche!" cried Gaspard, "no I don't. The diligence brought the news this morning. He's coming and everybody is coming with him."

There was no doubt that something was up now, for they heard shouts in the street, and through the window they saw a company of the 7th of the Line marching toward the Place Grénette.

M. de Vaudrecourt had grown terribly nervous. He had other matters to think of now beside revenge on Henri Jodélle. "I don't believe a word of it!" he exclaimed, but his face showed he lied. "Deteau, come with me to the Hotel de Ville." And the *procureur-du-roi* rushed to his carriage, followed by Deteau and the bewildered gendarme. "To the Hotel de Ville, *à toute bride!*" cried M. de Vaudrecourt, and they went at a gallop, but as they left the Place Grénette they heard ominous shouts of "Vive l'Empereur!"

Poor Marie! the excitement of the last half-hour had nearly upset her. She didn't faint, but, dazed by her conflicting emotions of fear and joy, she sank into a chair. Why, if the Emperor was coming, Pierre was coming too! Could it be true? Could it be true?

"What did they want here?" cried Gaspard.

"No good, you may be sure," said Henri, "but I've no time to talk now. Fetch my hat. I must see Philippe." Gaspard brought it. "Now Marie, my dear," said Henri, kissing her, "don't worry. We'll lead them a dance! Parbleu! I wish I had two legs!" And old Henri thumped hastily out of the café.

"Mamma," said the little Josephine, coming to Marie's side, "is papa coming with Emperor?"

"Yes, dear," cried Marie, "papa is coming with Emperor. Papa is coming, Josephine."

"Oh! nice! nice!" cried Josephine. "Gaspard! Gaspard! Papa is coming with Emperor! Papa is coming with Emperor!" And seizing Gaspard's hands, she danced up and down through the room. And thus into the Café Jodélle, so lately filled with rage and terror and anguish, came joy and hope and rejoicing—brought by the Imperial name!

And now, Authorities of Grenoble, what means have you of resisting the Invader who is rapidly advancing? Let us see. You have the 5th, the 7th and the 11th regiments of the Line, the 3rd engineers, the 4th artillery and the 4th hussars, several thousands in all, and he has but eleven hundred. Yes, you have enough, place your men, load your cannon, fortify your redoubts, you will crush him yet—if your men stand firm. So during the afternoon and evening of the 6th of March the redoubts were strengthened, the cannon loaded, the city gates shut, and the 3rd engineers and 4th artillery placed in position on the ramparts. During the night of the 6th and 7th, the 5th regiment commanded by Lessard was sent to meet the enemy. They advanced beyond Vizille and took up a position where the road was narrow—on the right a partly frozen lake, on the left a high hill. Behind them lay the little village of Vizille, its inhabitants even at that early hour gathering in the streets with joy and wonder depicted on their faces, and farther north was Grenoble, its ramparts bristling with cannon, its gates shut, its redoubts bright with bayonets. And still farther north was Lyons, all commotion with regiments entering it from all directions and plumed Marshals hastening from Paris to take command. And Dijon was in consternation, and Chatillon uproarious, and Troyes wild with excitement, and beyond all was Paris, seething like a volcano, and in the Tuileries Palace a Most Christian Majesty asking advice to right and to left. Surely if *Messieurs les Autorités de Grenoble* do their duty there is little need for troops in Lyons or anxiety on the part of His Most Christian Majesty. A usurper with eleven hundred men!—bah! You shall see. Thus with all France behind them in uproar and before them the road to Gap quiet and deserted, stood the soldiers of the 5th of the Line, looking with fixed gaze ever to the southward—silently waiting.

So the hours of the morning passed, and near noon, over the crest of the hill toward Gap, they saw the eagle of France and the bearskin caps of the Imperial Guard. Nearer and nearer they came; the white cross-straps that held the knapsacks could be distinguished now, and the plumes in the bearskin caps. And there was Marshal Bertrand on his horse, and who was that riding beside him dressed in the gray overcoat and the plain cocked hat? It was he, the Little Corporal! Not a sound was heard but the tramp of the grenadiers and the ring of the horses' hoofs. Thus they advanced, and when they had come within a hundred paces of the sphinx-like wall that confronted them, they halted. "Mallet," said the Emperor, "tell them to put their guns under their arms." Then dismounting, and with his overcoat unbuttoned showing his green uniform of the *chasseurs à cheval* with its star of the Legion of Honor, he advanced alone, facing that phalanx of silent soldiers, those serried rows of sharp, bright bayonets.

Do you see him, soldiers of the Fifth? That is Bonaparte. He comes to raise civil war in France, they say. He comes to drive the Bourbon Louis from his *par la grâce de Dieu* throne. He is an outlaw. *Les Puissances Alliées* have set a price upon his head. Which one of you now will pull the trigger of a well-aimed musket, give the Usurper here a brigand's death, and put an end to this Return from Elba? And for the soldier who kills him, what reward? Why, gold and glory! The cross of honor from the hand of His Most Christian Majesty at the Tuileries Palace! Fêtes and decorations from *les Puissances Alliées!*

He comes nearer. Yes, it is Napoleon! It is the Emperor! On his head the little hat he wore at Jena and at Wagram, on his back the gray greatcoat of Montmirail, by his side the sword of Austerlitz! About him the glory of his victories, behind him the grenadiers of his Garde Impériale, above him the flag of France!—torn by balls, blackened by powder, proudly fluttering, ever advancing, ever victorious! Thus in the deathlike stillness he approaches, nearer and nearer, step by step, step by step. See! he is here! Now, soldiers of France, between Louis-Stanislas-Xavier de Bourbon and Napoleon Bonaparte—choose!

"Well, how are you all in the 5th regiment?" said the Emperor cheerfully.

"Quite well, sire," answered the soldiers.

"I am come again to visit you. Are there any among you that would wish to kill me?"

"Certainly not, sire!" shouted the soldiers.

Up went the shakos on the bayonets, and on the clear frosty air rang out the shout—the old shout of Austerlitz and of Wagram—"Vive l'Empereur!"

The Bourbon commander put spurs to his horse, the band struck up the "Marseillaise," the broad folds of the Imperial banner fluttered in the breeze, the 5th of the Line wheeling about formed the van, and on they marched—bands playing, flags flying, people cheering, soldiers shouting—in triumph to Grenoble!

And when they reached Grenoble it was nine at night, the drawbridge was up, the gates fast barred, the brazen guns frowning from the ramparts, and all about was inky darkness. Small chance to enter Grenoble to-night. And in the blackness the Emperor went and stood alone before the drawbridge, facing the walls of Grenoble and the death-dealing batteries. But none could see him in the darkness, and there was silence. Then the brave Labédoyère came and stood beside him, and out of the gloom and the silence he cried to the soldiers on the ramparts, "Soldiers, it is I, Labédoyère, Colonel of the 7th! We bring you—*Napoleon!*"

There was a great shout from the soldiers, lights flashed on the ramparts, the drawbridge was lowered, the gates fastened by the authorities were beaten in twain by axes, and Grenoble with its walls and its bastions, its redoubts and its ramparts, its guns and its bayonets, fell—before the Imperial name!

The garrison and the people came rushing out, and on all sides were shouts and flaming torches. So they went in triumph through the city—a vast mass of frenzied soldiers and vociferating people and waving lights and strains of music, and in the centre the Emperor on his white horse. And the people sang the *chanson à l'air Charles VII:*

> " Il faut combattre; l'Empereur l'ordonne,
> Nous obéirons à ses lois;
> Pour conserver sa couronne,
> Nous chasserons tous les rois.
> Allons, enfants de la patrie,
> Jurons tous à notre Empereur,
> De lui bien conserver la vie,
> Avec lui n'ayons jamais peur."

When they reached the Place Grénette all the houses were bright with lights, but brightest of all shone the Café Jodélle, with all its windows ablaze from floor to roof, while in the door stood Marie, Gaspard, and the little Josephine. And all at once from the crowd of soldiers and people there came running a stalwart, decorated Captain of the Imperial Guard, who threw his arms about Marie's neck and kissed her and the little Josephine, and that was the happiest night the Café Jodélle had seen for many a year.

"And where will Your Majesty lodge?" said Marshal Bertrand.

"I will go to the Trois Dauphins," said the Emperor. "It is kept by one of my old soldiers."

So they went with all the crowd following. And while the Emperor was getting supper, the crowd in the Rue Montorge grew larger and larger and the shouts redoubled. For there came forty workmen of Grenoble carrying the gates of the city, and at their head old Henri Jodélle, his eyes flashing, and his wooden crutch pounding the cobblestones. And the people cried with a thousand voices, "Vive l'Empereur!"

"Sire," said Marshal Bertrand, "the people want you."

So the Emperor came out and stood on the steps of the Trois Dauphins, and beside him stood Marshal Bertrand, and beside him Philippe Courteau. And surely a Czar of all the Russias, when he put on his crown in the Cathedral of the Assumption, never looked more imposing than did Philippe Courteau that night. And there too was old La Barre dancing for joy, and there too was Gaspard, cap in hand, and there too were Marie and Pierre holding the little Josephine, and there too was old Frédéric Bonneville beside them. And the Rue Montorge was packed with people, and every window of the Trois Dauphins was full of them, and every window in the Rue Montorge was illuminated. And when the Emperor appeared, there was a great shout and then silence. And before them all old Henri Jodélle advanced to the steps of the Trois Dauphins, and while all held their breath to listen, he said:

"Emperor, we could not bring you the *keys* of your good town of Grenoble, but here are the *gates!*"

CHAPTER XXXI

IN THE PLACE BELLECOUR

The ruling passion, be it what it will,
The ruling passion conquers reason still.
—POPE, *Moral Essays.*

ON the 9th of March the Emperor set out for Lyons. That city was full of troops and Monsieur le Comte d'Artois had come from Paris to take command of them, but he did not find their temper to his taste and when, at ten at night on the 9th of March, the Marshal Macdonald reached Lyons he found Monsieur in a despondent mood.

"There is no reliance to be placed upon these soldiers, Monsieur le Maréchal," said the Count d'Artois, as Macdonald entered the dining-room of the Governor's house with the Count des Cars. "I have given orders to evacuate the city in the morning."

"Abandon Lyons!" cried the Marshal Macdonald. "Where then will you stop after quitting the barrier of the Rhone?"

"The troops have declared that they will offer no resistance," said the Count d'Artois.

"Let us try something before giving up," replied the Marshal.

"Well, take command," said the Count d'Artois, "I give you full powers."

"Let us suspend our retreat, Monseigneur," said

Macdonald. "We can always come back to that if necessary, for, if Napoleon is within a march of the town, let him make as much speed as he likes he cannot arrive until between one and two o'clock in the day, as he has to lead wearied soldiers. Let us assemble our men at six in the morning, see them, speak to them; we may gain something by it. We will try to change their opinion by attacking them on the subject of their honor, always a delicate point with a Frenchman. We will explain to them the misfortunes that must result from a civil war, and the danger to France, no less great, of seeing all Europe raised in arms against her for the second time."

To this the Count d'Artois agreed, so the Marshal Macdonald ordered the Morand and la Guillotière bridges to be barricaded and summoned all the garrison to assemble next morning in the Place Bellecour. Between three and four in the morning General Brayer was announced at the Marshal's hotel. He found Macdonald seated in his apartment at a table upon which lay his hat and numberless papers and about which pieces of torn paper were strewn on the carpet. The Marshal was writing an order. He looked weary, for he had been up all night.

"Monsieur le Maréchal," said General Brayer, "I come to tell you that the troops have refused to be reviewed by the Count d'Artois, but they will be delighted to see you, their old General."

"Who can have put that idea into their heads?" cried the Marshal in surprise. "Are we on the eve of a fresh revolution? Is every bond of discipline relaxed?"

"No," replied General Brayer, "but they have been

excited by speeches and their officers are not less excited. So many follies have already been committed, so little interest has been taken in the soldiers, and so much injustice has been done to make places for the *émigrés* upon whom rank, honors and distinctions have been showered."

"From your manner, sir," said the Marshal curtly, "I gather that you share these opinions."

"I do. I agree with them. But, Monsieur le Maréchal, it is getting late. It is more than time to warn Monsieur not to appear before the troops, to prevent him from being insulted."

"True," said the Marshal. He took his hat and accompanied by General Brayer set out for the Governor's house.

"His Royal Highness is asleep," said the Count des Cars when the Marshal was ushered into the antechamber of the Count d'Artois.

"That makes no difference," replied Macdonald, "my business admits of no delay."

The Count d'Artois, therefore, was awakened, the Marshal was announced, and the Count sat up in bed.

"Well, Monsieur le Maréchal?" said he.

"Monseigneur," said Macdonald, "the reports I have received during the night, regarding the state of mind of the men, are no better. It is possible that the presence of your Royal Highness may be a constraint upon them. Perhaps it would be better if I saw them alone, for I am accustomed to war and, as it were, one of themselves. They can express their opinions more freely to me, and I will let you know the result as soon as possible."

"As you please," answered the Count d'Artois.

At six in the morning, therefore, the Marshal Macdonald rode alone to the review. The rain was pouring, and the troops drawn up on parade filled the great Place Bellecour, in the centre of which stood an equestrian statue of the Grand Monarque, looking haughtily down upon these soldiers of France who had just refused to do honor to his descendant.

"Vive le Maréchal Macdonald!" shouted the soldiers as the hero of Wagram rode into the Place Bellecour. The Marshal ordered them to form a square and rode into the middle of it that he might be better heard.

"My friends," said he, "I thank you for this reception. I flatter myself that it arises from a recollection of the care, which from a sense of duty and of attachment, I have always taken of your comfort. I recognize your loyal services and your devotion in good and bad fortune. Though we have succumbed at last it has been with honor at any rate, and it has required all the armies of Europe, and some great blunders on our side, which cannot be imputed to us, to put us down. You all know I have been the last to submit. We have fulfilled our obligations, and released by the will of the nation we have contracted others not less sacred. To these the Royal Government will find us equally loyal. The invasion that has collected us here at Lyons will let loose upon *la belle France* even greater misfortunes than those of last year, for then ancient France remained intact, but now the Allies will make us pay dearly for a fresh appeal to arms. I think too highly of your patriotism to believe that you will refuse to do as I do, who have never deceived you, and I am sure you will follow me along the path of duty and honor. And now, my friends, the only guarantee that I ask of you is to join with me in crying, Long live the King!" And rising in his stirrups the Marshal Macdonald waved his hat in the air and shouted three times as loud as he could, "Vive le Roi!" Not a single voice joined him. The Marshal Macdonald shouted alone.

Well, what was to be done now? The troops had suddenly turned to stone. The Place Bellecour had become a square of sphinxes. The Marshal sent for the Count d'Artois, hoping, all reports to the contrary, that he would be received, if not with cordiality, with respect at least. His Royal Highness soon came followed by his staff, but there was the same stony silence. Then dismounting, the Marshal and the Count d'Artois walked down the lines, exhorting the troops, but the soldiers stood motionless, impassive and silent. There was a battalion of the Garde Impériale on the right of the Place, and as they reached it the Count d'Artois went up to a " vieux moustache " decorated with the Legion of Honor. It was André Marceau.

"Surely a brave soldier like you," said the Count d'Artois, placing his hand on André's shoulder, " will cry Vive le Roi! "

"No I won't!" said André bluntly. " I've only one cry, and that's Vive l'Empereur!" And he shouted it out with all his might. In an instant it was taken up by regiment after regiment, and in the face of His Royal Highness the Count d'Artois, standing at the foot of the statue of his proud ancestor Louis le Grand, was hurled again and again that world-conquering shout, Vive l'Empereur! The Count d'Artois grew crimson with rage. "Monsieur le Maréchal," said he, "it is as I told you. Nothing can be done with them. Send them away." There was therefore no march past, but the troops were sent at once to their barracks.

"We may be more successful with the officers, Monseigneur," said the Marshal. "I will try them by themselves. They may have felt some awkwardness before their men."

"Do what you can," said his Royal Highness. "I am going to see M. Girouette at the Hotel de Ville."

CHAPTER XXXII

MAYOR GIROUETTE

Manners with fortunes, humors turn with climes,
Tenets with books, and principles with times.
—POPE, *Moral Essays.*

THE Hotel de Ville at Lyons faced the Place des Terreaux, and on the morning of the 10th of March,
1815, the Mayor's study upon the second floor had
as its occupants a stout gentleman with a very bald
head who was busily engaged in writing at a desk,
and a small black poodle which was stretched com-
fortably before the fireplace. The stout gentleman
was no other than the most worshipful Mayor of
Lyons, M. Jacques Girouette, and the black poodle
was his dog Fidèle.

Nothing was heard in the apartment save the crack-
ling of the fire and the squeak of M. Girouette's pen
as it ran rapidly over the paper. The worshipful
Mayor was engaged in drawing up two proclamations, one of which, already nearly finished and lying
beside him on the desk, began as follows: " Citizens of
Lyons, the invader Bonaparte having been beaten
back and the legitimate authority of our glorious sovereign Louis XVIII having been firmly established,
it behooves us to show our loyalty to His Majesty."
The other proclamation upon which the worthy Mayor
was working had this inception: " Citizens of Lyons,

once more our august sovereign the Emperor Napoleon arrives in triumph! Let us rally round the tricolor, that glorious flag under which France has so often marched to victory."

From time to time the honorable M. Jacques scratched his head or pulled at the high black stock about his neck. The honorable M. Jacques was evidently in some perplexity, and well he might be, for here was a trying situation truly! With, on the one hand, a Most Christian King going but not yet gone, and on the other a Most Imperial Emperor coming but not yet come, what was the proper course to be pursued by a most prudent Mayor who desired to save his official head? Why, like the Austrian eagle, look both ways. And so, with a large and elegant white cockade on his hat and an elegant and large tricolored one in the drawer of his desk, M. Jacques Girouette, Mayor of Lyons, was prepared for any freak of fortune.

Presently the door was opened and the gendarme Laserre appeared. "Monsieur le Maire," said he, "the Count des Cars brings you a message from His Royal Highness the Count d'Artois."

"Admit him instantly," cried Mayor Girouette, slipping into his desk the proclamation beginning "Once more our august sovereign the Emperor Napoleon." A moment later the Count des Cars entered, and the worthy Mayor, who had advanced to the centre of the apartment, made him a low bow.

"Monsieur le Maire," said the Count des Cars, "His Royal Highness will be here shortly. He wishes to have a conference with you."

"I am entirely at the service of His Royal Highness," answered the Mayor, bowing again.

" Do you know the result of Marshal Macdonald's review of the troops?" inquired the Count.

" No, Monsieur."

" Well, they refuse to march against the rascal Bonaparte."

" The more fools they," said Mayor Girouette.

The noise of a carriage was heard before the Hotel de Ville, and the Count des Cars stepped to a window and looked out upon the Place. "His Royal Highness has come," he cried. And the Count and the Mayor hurried down the staircase.

For a few moments the Mayor's study was deserted, only the black poodle Fidèle lay before the fire. Then Monsieur le Comte d'Artois entered, followed by the Mayor and the Count des Cars. Monsieur, aged and faded, was greatly changed from the dashing Count d'Artois of former days who played the part of Figaro to Marie Antoinette's Rosina in the "Barbier de Séville," and was the gayest of the gay among the brilliant cavaliers of Petit Trianon. Still he was rather tall and slim, and with his gold-laced uniform and blue ribbon was altogether the most presentable male member of the Bourbon family. He sat down in an armchair, while M. Jacques Girouette and the Count des Cars stood respectfully before him.

" Monsieur le Maire," said he, in a tone that attempted to be gracious, "you have heard no doubt that the troops are not disposed to carry out our wishes. I have just come from reviewing them. They manifest a most unaccountable attachment to the Usurper, and in this emergency we must look to the good people of Lyons to do their duty to France and to the King. Can I rely upon you, Monsieur le Maire?"

"Upon me? Girouette?" cried the Mayor, "can Your Royal Highness doubt it! Never have I swerved from my loyalty to my legitimate King, even when I was compelled to take my bread from the hand of the Usurper. The villain! he dragged us about over Europe and slaughtered us in endless numbers to gratify his vile ambition. Now the wretch would come again, but we have enjoyed peace for a year and have seen once more our glorious and legitimate King. The dastard Bonaparte will find that the people of France will never again submit to him."

"Such sentiments do you honor, Monsieur le Maire," answered the Count d'Artois, "but from what I have seen I am frank to say I do not think they are shared by the inhabitants of the city of Lyons."

"The more fools they!" cried the Mayor. "If the Brigand ever approaches the walls of Lyons—which pray God he never may!—I would be willing to take a sword myself and go against him."

"I will not require such a proof of your devotion, Monsieur le Maire, but can you find me twenty loyal men who will disguise themselves as National Guards, go to the Guillotière bridge and fire upon the enemy? If we can get some one to make an attack when the Usurper's advance-guard appears, we may gain something yet."

"I will find them, Monseigneur, be assured I will find them, and I will lead them myself if there is need," cried the worthy Mayor.

"I shall not fail to inform His Majesty of your loyalty, Monsieur le Maire," said the Count d'Artois as he rose and left the room.

The Mayor, bowing obsequiously, followed him to

his carriage, saying in earnest tones, "Assure His Majesty, Monseigneur, that Girouette was at his post."

The Count d'Artois entered his carriage and motioned M. des Cars to take the opposite seat. "To the Place Bellecour," said His Royal Highness, and the carriage rolled away.

As Mayor Giroutte returned to his study, he encountered his wife upon the landing of the staircase. Madame Girouette was a quick little woman, with bright black eyes that snapped vivaciously.

"Well, Jacques Girouette," she cried, "what have you been telling His Royal Highness?"

"I have promised to find him twenty men to go to the Guillotière bridge and resist the Invader."

"Idiot!" cried Madame Girouette. "Where will you find them? Don't you know that everybody is going over to Bonaparte? Don't you know that the troops on the Place Bellecour refused to follow Macdonald? Don't you know that the Invader is carrying all before him? What are you and your twenty men going to do? You will lose your post by your foolishness, Jacques Girouette."

"Simpleton!" cried the Mayor. "How do you know I am going to find twenty men? That's what I told His Royal Highness. Am I not Girouette the politician? Have I not lived under a Monarchy, a Republic, a Directory, and an Empire? I was not born yesterday. Keep your eye on me, Madame, and, in a crisis like the present, be thankful that you bear the name of Girouette."

"Well, don't be a fool," answered his wife. "Manage affairs as you please, but come out of it with a whole skin and keep your post."

By this time they had reached the Mayor's study. "You may be sure I'll do that," said M. Jacques, as they entered. "Whichever wins, heads or tails, Bonaparte or Bourbon, Girouette will keep his post." The Mayor put on his greatcoat and his hat with the white cockade, and opening the drawer of his desk drew out the tricolored one and slipped it into his pocket.

"And now," said he, "I'll go and try to find those twenty men."

"You better not try too hard, Jacques Girouette," said his wife. "You will get into trouble."

"Never fear, Madame," replied the Mayor. "The twenty men will *not* be found, but none shall say that Girouette failed in his duty to his King."

The stout Mayor bustled down stairs and out into the street. Never had he felt so fully the importance of his position. Lyons was now the point in which the great events would culminate. He—Girouette—was Mayor. A Royal Prince had come to ask his aid. If all went well a Most Christian King would recognize his loyalty. And then? Why then he might become the *Royal* Prefect Girouette. Happy thought! If on the other hand Bonaparte should triumph? Well, he would know how to give him a joyous welcome too. He would know how to display his unswerving fidelity. And then? Why then he might become the *Imperial* Prefect Girouette. Again a happy thought! Oh! these great Kings and Emperors. They were clever and acute, no doubt, but they were no match for Girouette the politician. He had always felt that he was the man for a crisis. Fortunate town of Lyons to have him—Girouette—for Mayor!

19

While reflecting upon these and other pleasant thoughts of a kindred nature, he reached the corner of the Cours du Midi. There he saw his friend M. Pourchot, running toward him.

"Great news, Monsieur le Maire!" cried Pourchot. "The Count d'Artois has left the city. Marshal Macdonald met him in the Place Bellecour, told him that nothing could be hoped from the officers as well as from the soldiers, and insisted on his immediate departure to prevent his falling into Bonaparte's hands. So the Count's carriage set off at a gallop, escorted by some of the 14th dragoons. Everyone is now preparing to welcome Bonaparte."

"Mon Dieu!" cried Mayor Girouette, "I must lose no time," and he set off for the Hotel de Ville at a trot. As he hurried along he pulled off his hat and thrust the white cockade into his pocket, and put in its place the tricolored one. On the Rue du Plat he met a crowd of workmen carrying their picks.

"Vive l'Empereur!" bawled M. Girouette as loud as he could.

"Vive l'Empereur!" shouted the workmen tumultuously.

The Mayor, breathless and panting, came in sight of the Hotel de Ville. Heavens! there was the white flag of the Bourbons flying from its top. This would never do. Up the stairs hurried M. Jacques Girouette, ran into his study and pulled the bell violently. The gendarme Laserre entered.

"How dare you?" cried Mayor Girouette as soon as he could get breath enough to speak, "how dare you leave that vile white flag flying? Take it down!"

"But, Monsieur le Maire," cried the bewildered

gendarme, "you yourself told me to have it raised only two hours ago."

"Ass! dolt! idiot!" roared Mayor Girouette. "Don't you know that the Bourbon Prince has fled in terror? Don't you know that our glorious sovereign, the great Napoleon, is approaching in triumph from Grenoble? Get out, you fool! Put up the tricolor at once."

Little Fidèle, bounding forward from the fireplace, barked joyfully, and stout Mayor Girouette sat down to recover his breath. Suddenly some one was heard running along the Place des Terreaux and shouting "Vive le Roi!"

"What! what! what!" cried M. Girouette, springing up and thrusting his tricolored cockade into a small blue vase upon the table beside him. "Who cries Long live the King?"

The Mayor hurried to the window, threw it up and stuck out his head. "What news?" he yelled.

"Bonaparte is beaten back," cried the breathless messenger. "His advance-guard has been repulsed in the direction of La Tour du Pin."

"Long live the King!" shouted the Mayor, drawing in his head. M. Jacques hastened across the room and rang his bell, and soon Laserre entered.

"The Invader Bonaparte is beaten back," cried Mayor Girouette, adjusting the white cockade in his hat, "Down with the tricolor! Hoist the white flag of our glorious sovereign King Louis XVIII!"

And now, after so much exertion and such unparalleled activity, surely stout Mayor Girouette was entitled to a few moments repose. He stretched himself in his armchair, and his double chin soon acquired an extra fold by pressing down upon his high black stock. Little Fidèle lay again before the fire, and the ticking of the clock alone disturbed the stillness of the room. The worthy Mayor had not slept more than half an hour, however, when the door burst open, and Madame Girouette, pale and excited, rushed into the room and seized him by the arm.

"Up! up, man!" she cried, "Bonaparte is here!"

"Long live the King," said M. Girouette drowsily.

"Bonaparte! Bonaparte! man!" shrieked Madame Girouette, shaking him violently, "Bonaparte is here! His advance-guard has passed the suburb of la Guillotière. They have appeared at the bridge. The officers, the soldiers, the people are raising deafening shouts. The shakos are on the bayonets. The barricades are thrown down. Everyone is rushing forward to welcome the new arrivals." Little Fidèle barked joyfully.

"Long live the Emperor!" cried Mayor Girouette, starting up, seizing his hat and ringing his bell.

"Down with the white flag and up with the tricolor!" he roared to Laserre as he met him in the hall.

Down the staircase hurried the stout Mayor and Madame his wife. The people were rushing from all quarters crying "Vive l'Empereur!" In the distance could be heard the strains of the "Marseillaise."

"Mon Dieu! man," shrieked Madame Girouette as they reached the doorway, "your cockade!"

The Mayor snatched off his hat. Heavens! there was the white cockade of the Bourbons. Up the staircase three steps at a time ran stout Mayor Girouette, dashed into his study and sprang to his desk. The tricolored cockade was not there! Whisk went the papers flying in all directions as M. Jacques rummaged his desk. The strains of the " Marseillaise " sounded louder and nearer. They were coming!

" Mon Dieu! Mon Dieu! my official head!" cried Mayor Girouette, careering about the apartment. In came little Fidèle barking joyfully and ran against his legs. " Le diable!" roared Mayor Girouette, giving poor Fidèle a terrific kick that sent him flying across the room. Crash went the dog into a little mahogany table, over it fell, and the vase upon it was broken into a thousand pieces, and there on the floor lay the much-sought-for and ardently-desired tricolored cockade! " God be praised!" cried Mayor Girouette, seizing it and rushing down stairs. Was he in time? Yes, there they were! The band playing the " Marseillaise," the people shouting, the Emperor on his white steed. And Mayor Girouette, panting, perspiring, waved above his head his hat with the tricolored cockade and frantically shouted—" Long life to the great Napoleon! Long life to the great Napoleon!" Up in the study, under the overturned table, among the broken glass little Fidèle lay dead.

CHAPTER XXXIII

PARIS AT LAST!

Hail to the Chief, who in triumph advances!
—SCOTT, *Lady of the Lake*.

His Majesty King Louis XVIII held many confer-
ences during the early days of March, 1815, and he
asked much advice from Generals, Ministers, Marshals
and Princes. And some that he got was bad, some
good, and some indifferent. But upon one occasion
he heard a plain truth, and this was the nature of it.

"M. Fouché," said His Majesty, "I know you are
a man of great ability. Nobody knows France better
than you, and no one ever conducted the police with
greater vigor. Tell me, frankly, what is your opinion
of the system of government I have followed?"

"My opinion, sire," replied Fouché, "is that Your
Majesty, on coming to the government of France,
ought not to have changed anything but the bed-linen
of the Emperor." Unfortunately for himself, His
Most Christian Majesty had changed that and much
beside.

At eleven at night on the 19th of March the royal
traveling-carriages rolled into the courtyard, and His
Majesty left in haste the Tuileries Palace, where
four days before he had sworn, in presence of the
Senate, to die upon his throne. He did so in the

end, but through no merit of his own. As soon as
the King had taken his departure, the servants in
livery removed the portraits of the Bourbons from the
private apartments, rolled the stout Louis's chair out
of the Imperial study, stripped the fleurs-de-lis from
the hangings in the Salle de Maréchaux and replaced
the bees; the National Guards in the Place du Carrousel tore off the white percale from their tricolored
cockades; the Imperial chefs, chamberlains, ushers
and valets donned their uniforms and resumed their
places; Excelmans raised the tricolor above the Tuileries dome; the crowd in the courtyard shouted "Vive
l'Empereur!" and all was ready for triumphant
Caesar.

There is a curious old house in Paris at No. 2
Rue Jean Jacques Rousseau. It is four stories high.
Over the windows on the ground floor hangs the
sign, "Vins, Liqueurs"; over the windows on the
second floor the sign, "Aux Petites Caves du
Louvre," and over the windows on the third, in larger
letters than the rest, "Hotel de Bernay." In this
house, on the second floor, Jean Jacques Rousseau
once lived and wrote, and so for him the street
was named Rue Jean Jacques Rousseau. Well, on the
20th of March, 1815, this curious old house stood just
as it stands to-day, save that it was not called "Hotel
de Bernay," but Hotel de Marbette. It was a great
resort for hussars and grenadiers, and as in Grenoble,
if you had asked a soldier who it was who kept the
best liqueurs, he would have told you Henri Jodélle at
the Café Jodélle, so in Paris, if you had asked a
dashing hussar or jack-booted cuirassier where the
best drinks were to be had, he would have directed

you to the jolly host of the Hotel de Marbette. And a lively business was done by the Hotel de Marbette on the 20th of March, 1815. From morning till night the wine-room, on the ground floor, was filled to overflowing with veterans of the Grande Armée, all drinking, gesticulating and talking at once. And as may be surmised, there was but one topic of conversation—the Emperor's landing at Cannes and his triumphal march to Paris.

There was terror in the Tuileries Palace, there was alarm in official circles, there was uneasiness in Paris and in many parts of France, there was dismay in Berlin, there was consternation in Vienna, but there was only joy in the Hotel de Marbette. The old veterans knew but one thing—the Little Corporal was coming back. With him they were everything; without him they were nothing. They had been reduced in pay, degraded in rank, politely spit upon and kicked out of doors by the royal government. Their deeds and their scars were forgotten, and they had been compelled to stand aside and see prance before them the scions of a defunct nobility, who looked at all the world through the " Hartwell telescope," and wore lightly on their embroidered breasts that cross of the Legion of Honor to earn which they had simply taken the trouble to breathe, and for which these scarred warriors had shed their blood at the Vistula, the Niemen, the Danube, the Elbe and the Rhine.

But now—wonder of wonders!—he was coming back again. *Les journées de la gloire reveniraient!* Once more the tricolor would wave, the sabres would flash, the trumpets would sound, the white horse would come galloping down the lines, and they would

go, *au pas de charge*, to give them all—Bourbon, Hapsburg, Romanoff and Hohenzollern—as François Legrand put it, "a d——d good licking." What wonder, then, that they were joyous. What wonder that
the jolly host of the Hotel de Marbette was joyous
too, for as fast as he opened a bottle it was emptied,
the silver clinked on the table, and rolling off, lodged
swiftly in the pocket of the jolly host. Under such
circumstances he would be a queer host who would
not be joyous and pray for a "Return from Elba"
every day.

So they were a merry company. There were hussars in their brilliant uniforms, great shakos and trailing sabres; grenadiers with their white leggings, belts
and bear-skin caps; cuirassiers with glittering breast-
plates; carabineers, *chevaux-légers* and artillerymen.
And they clinked their glasses and laughed and drank
and talked, telling stories and anecdotes of deeds that
were done in camp and trench and at the cannon's
mouth at Jena, Eckmühl, Moscow, Marengo, the
Pyramids and Aboukir. If you had been there with a
note-book and had written down all you heard, you
would have had stories enough to write books for a
lifetime.

François Legrand was the centre of an admiring
group, for few had seen so much as François. Before
him on the table was an enormous bottle of strong
red wine, from which he filled his glass from time to
time. He was in the midst of a story. It had come
by the last post, and was an excellent one too, judg-
ing by the expressions on the faces of the crowd about
the table.

"Yes," cried François, "Macdonald did his best,

but he couldn't get one word out of them—not one.
So what does he do then? He sends for d'Artois to
come and talk too. Parbleu! he might have known
if they wouldn't cheer for him they wouldn't cheer for
d'Artois."

"D'Artois wouldn't even come to see the Guard
when he came to Paris," said Gustave Lébon, setting
down his glass.

"He won't want to see us soon again, I'm thinking," said old Barcoeur. There was a shout of assent
to that.

"So d'Artois comes," continued François, "you
know how, all smiles and bows and feathers and lace,
his horse jumping up and down and playing God
knows what circus tricks. Not a cheer did he get.
Sacré! you bet your biscuit he was mad. So he tries
it on foot, up and down the lines. But he couldn't
get noise enough out of them to scare a gazelle, and
finally he comes to the Guard. What does he do
then? He goes up to one soldier and slaps him on
the back. 'Surely you, a brave fellow, will cry Long
live the King!?' says he. And who did he ask that of,
think you? Who in God's name did he ask that of?"

"Who was it?" cried the crowd.

"André Marceau!" roared François, striking the
table a blow that made the bottle and glasses jump.

"Mille tonnerres!" cried stout Benoit, the lieutenant, "I'd give a month's pay to have seen André's
face."

"Well, d'Artois got his answer," said François,
"'To hell with the Bourbons,' or words to that effect,
and then they cried 'Vive l'Empereur!' Ah, the fellow who was at Lyons that day and saw that sight was

a lucky dog! Imagine André's face when d'Artois says, 'You will cry Long live the King!?' By my sabre! imagine André's face."

"Vive André Marceau!" shouted the crowd.

"That's right," cried François, "Vive André Marceau! But there's others here who would have done the same if they had had the chance. Come now, fill up and drink this toast, Long live the Imperial Guard!"

"Oui! Oui!" cried all the rest, jumping up. Old Barcoeur, who was so stiff in the knees that he could hardly stand, didn't rise, but he waved his glass in the air and drank as much as the next. When he had finished, he lowered his glass and said solemnly, as though he had reached the conclusion after profound meditation, "D——n d'Artois and all the other Bourbons!"

"That's it!" cried a ringing voice, "D——n d'Artois and all the other Bourbons, and the Prussians and the Austrians and the Russians, too! La France toujours!"

It was Pertelay, Captain of the Bercheny Hussars. He was a big fellow, Pertelay, and well put up. He wore his shako over one ear, his florid countenance was marred by an enormous scar, his mustaches, half a foot long, were waxed and turned up to his ears, his hair, plaited in two long locks, fell from under his shako upon his breast, his sabre trailed on the floor. A typical hussar was Pertelay—a hard drinker, a brawler always ready to fight, a fellow ignorant of everything that did not concern his horse, his accoutrements and his service in the field. But brave?— he would ride à toute bride at the cannon's mouth and think no more of it than you would of eating a hard boiled egg.

"That's it!" cried Pertelay, who had just come in, elbowing his way to the table and slapping old Barcoeur on the back, "D——n d'Artois! Long live the Imperial Guard! *Mes amis*, the Emperor is at Fontainebleau. He is expected in Paris by night."

François Legrand threw his arms about Pertelay's neck and danced up and down. "By night? by night?" he cried, "To-night? This night?"

"This night!" cried Pertelay, and, freeing himself from François' embrace, he filled a glass from the big bottle, then jumping on a chair, he beat with his sabre on the table to silence the din of voices. "Pertelay! Pertelay!" they roared, "Vive l'Empereur! Vive Pertelay! Vive la Garde Impériale!" Pertelay continued beating the table with his sabre, and finally there was quiet. Then standing erect on the chair, he held his glass above his head and cried, "My friends, I have a toast for you. The health of him who comes to-night—the Little Corporal!" At that they roared with delight for five minutes. At last, when they could roar no more, the toast was drunk all standing, even old Barcoeur, who managed in some way to get upon his legs—and then they roared again. God help the Bourbon royalist who put his nose in at the Hotel de Marbette at that minute!

"Come, Pertelay, we want a song," cried François Legrand. "We want to hear your sweet voice, Pertelay."

It was perhaps excess of courtesy to call Pertelay's voice "sweet," for it was a great thundering bass, but it was sweet to the ears of those who listened, and, after all, they were the judges.

"And what will you have?" said Pertelay. He was as jolly as brave, and his stock of songs knew no end.

"Partant pour la Syrie," said an old grenadier with black hair and white mustache—Floibert, I believe they called him.

"No, no," cried François, "we want a song with a good chorus. We all want to come in. Sing the song we all know well—The Captain Tarjeantirre."

So Pertelay stood on a chair and beat time with his sword, and the others crowded about him. And Pertelay sang the verses in his own matchless way, but when it came to the chorus they all drew their swords and held their glasses high and made the rafters ring. And so they sung the martial song, The Captain Tarjeantirre.

"To horse! to horse, away! To horse! to horse, away!"
  Then up we sprang, while the trumpet's clang
    Was sounding deep and clear.
  The month was May; the world was gay;
    We rode with Tarjeantirre.
"Come, fill us up a stirrup-cup,
    We'll quaff it with a tear;
  Farewell, fair maids of Chenonceaux,
    Our hearts stay with you here;
  Farewell, best loved of Chenonceaux,
    We ride with Tarjeantirre!"

A roving, roaring, rollicking blade was the Captain Tarjeantirre,
  With his waxed mustache and his sabretache,
  And his laughing black eyes clear;
  With his handsome face and his martial grace,
  And his heart that knew no fear.
The beau sabreur of the Grande Armée was the Captain Tar-
  jeantirre.

" To horse! to horse, away! To horse! to horse, away!"
  Our squadrons came, like lines of flame,
    With thund'ring rush and roar;
  Carabineer, and cuirassier, and gleaming-gold hussar.
  The bridles.rang; the sabres' clang
    Was music to our ear;
  And proud were we, that day, to be
    Behind our leader dear.
  Yes, proud were we that day to be
    The train of Tarjeantirre.

A roving, roaring, rollicking blade was the Captain Tarjeantirre,
  With his waxed mustache and his sabretache,
  And his laughing black eyes clear;
  You wonder why we longed to die,
  And faced death with a cheer?
We knew our captain loved his men, and we loved Tarjeantirre.

" To horse! to horse, away! To horse! to horse, away!"
  Ah! ne'er again shall sound that strain
    Upon my eager ear;
  I've had my day; the world is gray;
    Alas for Tarjeantirre!
  In Jena's dell he fighting fell,
    But still I hear his cheer:
  'Twas " En avant! Vive l'Empereur!
    My snow-white plume is here! "
  'Twas " En avant! Vive l'Empereur!
    Who dies with Tarjeantirre? "

A roving, roaring, rollicking blade was the Captain Tarjeantirre,
  With his waxed mustache and his sabretache,
  And his laughing black eyes clear;
  With his handsome face and his martial grace,
  And his heart that knew no fear.
The beau sabreur of the Grande Armée was the Captain Tar-
    jeantirre.

The chorus ended in one mighty roar, and I ven-
ture to say the old house in the Rue Jean Jacques
Rousseau never heard anything like it before or since.

Then they gave three cheers for the Emperor, three for the Imperial Guard, three for the Bercheny Hussars, three for Pertelay, and there is no knowing how long they would have continued, but they saw Gautier of the 13th cuirassiers coming in, and they cried out for news. Gautier was gruff and of few words. "Ma foi," said he, "you read the 'Moniteur,' don't you? The news is short. The Tiger has escaped from his den. The Monster was three days at sea. The Brigand has landed at Cannes. The Invader has arrived at Grenoble. General Bonaparte has entered Lyons. Napoleon slept last night at Fontainebleau. His Imperial Majesty enters the Tuileries this day."

So it was. And on the evening of the 20th of March the façade of the Tuileries was lighted from the Marsan Pavilion to the Pavilion of Flora, while in the Salle de Maréchaux the Queen Hortense, the Archchancellor Cambacères, Count Regnault de Saint-Jean d'Angely, ministers, prefects, generals, colonels, court-ladies, senators and officials of one kind or another awaited the Emperor's arrival.

At a quarter to nine a carriage came at a gallop along the Quai of the Tuileries, surrounded by hundreds of officers from all the cavalry corps, riding *ventre à terre*, waving torches and shaking the night with thunder-pealing vociferations. Across the Place du Carrousel they dashed, under the Arch of Triumph, and halted with snorting horses, flashing bridles, jingling spurs, clattering sabres and peals of exultation before the Tuileries Palace. The carriage door was flung open, and the ministers, senators, prefects, generals and marshals, pouring down the grand staircase, beheld Napoleon, borne aloft above the heads of the

excited throng, who, to his repeated exclamation,
" Gentlemen, gentlemen, let me walk! "—returned no
other answer than " Vive l'Empereur! "   And so up
the grand staircase, through the Salle de Maréchaux
and the Gallerie de Diane, wearing his petit chapeau
and his travel-stained gray greatcoat, surrounded by
tumultuous shouts and glittering uniforms and waving handkerchiefs and wreaths of flowers, the great
Imperial Conqueror was borne to the doors of his
apartment.   And thus was fulfilled the prophecy of
the Imperial bulletin: " La victoire marchera au pas
de charge.   L'Aigle avec les Couleurs Nationales
volera de clocher en clocher, jusqu'aux tours de Notre
Dame! "   And thus was Louis-Stanislas-Xavier de
Bourbon dethroned, and thus was the Emperor Napoleon re-established, to reign—one hundred days.

CHAPTER XXXIV

À WATERLOO

To arms! to arms! ye men of might;
  Away from home, away;
The first and foremost in the fight
  Are sure to win the day!

—BENJAMIN, *To Arms.*

CAPTAIN PIERRE PASQUIN had followed the Emperor
on his surprisingly triumphant march from Grenoble
to Paris, and then, after the Guard had been reorgan-
ized, he was stationed for a time in barracks at Courbevoie. There were three battalions at the barracks
and every month a battalion took its turn on duty in
Paris. The duty was an active one too—eight hours
on guard, two hours on patrol, and the grand rounds
at night. But as may be surmised, a captain did not
have all that.

On the 4th of June they were ordered to Avesnes,
and on the 13th they advanced to Charleroi. It was
a glorious morning when they left Avesnes, one of
those mornings when the blood leaps lightly, the heart
beats hopefully, and nature sings her pæans. The
grenadiers wound along the road, a long blue line
checkered by white belts and shaded by tassel-tossing
shakos. The crests of the cuirassiers flared crimson
and their corselets burned and blazed; the white-
horsed artillery racked and rumbled; the *chevaux-légers*
with light hoofs champed the highway; while in the

20

van, rubricking the green horizon with a dash of gold
and blood, rode those glorious, dauntless braggarts,
the Bercheny Hussars. Pierre watched their fluttering pennons, now lost amid the boughs and branches
of the ravine, now war-welcoming upon the white
road of the ridge. From time to time their song
swelled to him, and his heart caught the cadence:

Strap the saddles! bit the bridles! toss the fetlocks in the sun!
Let the clarions loudly clamor! let the bugles sternly stun!
Like the banging, bellowing bison now we roaring ramping
    run,
And we'll fight for fame with fury for the great Napoleon.

En avant the voltigeurs! en avant the grenadiers!
En avant the chevaux-légers! en avant the cuirassiers!
For our mighty monarch militant bids us dashing daring don,
And we'll glut our graves with glory for the great Napoleon.

Strap the saddles! bit the bridles! toss the fetlocks in the sun!
Let the clarions loudly clamor! let the bugles sternly stun!
Like the banging, bellowing bison now we roaring ramping
    run,
And we'll war with hell or heaven for the great Napoleon.

"François," cried Pierre, "the Bercheny have it!
The Emperor or death!"

"Yes," said François, shifting his quid, "we want
the Little Corporal. Europe says No. To hell with
Europe!"

A statesman would have expressed it differently, but
François was no statesman.

Thus these brave fellows, one hundred and twenty
thousand hearts, epic in fidelity to the man who spent
their lives, marched—to Waterloo. Plain of Belgium
near Brussels, the deeds done on you upon the 18th of

June, 1815, have made you world-famous through all ages. For England you are a synonym of glory, triumph and "king-making victory," and they call you—Waterloo. For France you are a synonym of ruin, rout, annihilation, and chaos universal, and they call you—Mont St. Jean.

> " And while, in fashion picturesque,
>   The poet rhymes of blood and blows,
> The grave historian at his desk
>   Describes the same in classic prose."

And so of you great men have writ and poets sung. And through the pages of Sibourne, Charras, Chesney, Jomini, Alison, Ropes, Thiers, and Dorsey Gardner—through the mighty Hugo's " Les Misérables," and the " Childe Harold " of that great " Napoleon of the realms of Rhyme," George Gordon, world-thrilling as Lord Byron—the earthquaking shouts of your contending hosts resound. Read them, good reader, if you would see Napoleon on the heights at Ligny, or Ney at Quatre-Bras, or Jérôme's battalions battling at Hougomont, or the Scotch Grays charging, or the brave Picton Brigade under fire, or the " Iron Duke " holding his wavering lines, or the wildly-dashing onsets of the Imperial cuirassiers, or the Old Guard, with their " Ave! Caesar Imperator, morituri te salutamus," making their " vainly-glorious charge."

Waterloo! Who thinks of it as a victory? It has become a synonym for defeat, because the vanquished was greater than the victor.

CHAPTER XXXV

Face to Face!

La fortune est toujours pour les gros bataillons.
—Sévigné.

WHAT has become of Jean Deteau whom we last saw in the carriage of M. de Vaudrecourt, *procureur-du-roi?* He had transformed himself into a Bonapartist again by the time he reached the Hotel de Ville, and through the influence of two friends in Paris—MM. de Vilette and de Romontte—he got himself appointed to the staff of General de Bourmont, an ancient royalist, who had been vouched for by the Marshal Ney. The Marshal found himself mistaken in his protégé, however, for at the opening of the campaign, de Bourmont deserted to the enemy, carrying all his staff with him.

"Eh bien! Monsieur le Maréchal, what have you to say for your General de Bourmont?" said the Emperor when he heard the news.

"I would have vouched for him as for myself, sire."

"Blue is always blue and white is always white," replied His Majesty.

Nor did de Bourmont and his staff receive a cordial greeting from the Prussians, for the blunt von Blücher, when an aide-de-camp called his attention to de Bourmont and his white cockade, exclaimed, "Einerlei, was das Volk für einen Zettel ansteckt, Hundsfott bleibt Hundsfott!" ("All the same, whatever ticket one stitches on him, a scoundrel stays a scoundrel!") And this remark of the plain-spoken Blücher applies not only to de Bourmont, but to Jean Deteau as well.

After the battle of Ligny on the 16th of June the Marshal Grouchy was sent with 30,000 men to follow up the Prussians, while the Emperor Napoleon with the balance of his army pursued the English on the 17th to the heights of Mont St. Jean, where they halted to give him battle on the morrow, Sunday, the 18th day of June. At half-past one the battle began when the Emperor from his position at La Belle Alliance ordered forward the corps of D'Erlon. Then the action became general, and erelong Hougomont was torn and riddled by balls, La Haye Sainte and Pape-lotte the scenes of bloody conflicts, and Mont St. Jean a hill of fire. But at three o'clock, instead of Grouchy whom the French Emperor expected, came the Prussians whom he did not, and the corps of Bülow attacked Planchenoit on the right and rear to cut the French line of retreat. The Prussians drove back and forced out of Planchenoit the 6th corps of Lobau and the Young Guard with its three batteries. Then His Majesty sent three battalions of the Old and Middle Guard with two batteries to retake the town. He could send no more, for the rest of the Guard was forming for the great attack on the English lines— those lines which had not been broken despite the furious charges of the now foaming, bloody, breathless, *hors de combat* Imperial cuirassiers. The three battalions advanced on Planchenoit and it was a quarter to seven in the evening. Pierre was at the head of his company, sword in hand, and at the head of the second company marched François Legrand with his sword in his hand likewise. And so they charged on, their batteries advancing before them and answering the Prussian fire with a storm of shot and shell. They drove the Prussians out of Planchenoit and supported the Young Guard, but the Prussians, reinforced by the corps of Pirch I, advanced· again. The farmhouses of Planchenoit were burning now, the cannonade shook their foundations, and the Prussians came in force, shouting madly through the smoke and flame.

And if you had been in Planchenoit that night you would have seen blazing timbers, smoking roofs, loading, firing, bayoneting, slashing, stabbing, charging; you would have heard noises, air-filling, sky-rending, clangorous, thundering, deafening, piercing, trumpet-tongued, multisonous; you would have witnessed sights terrible, terrific, tremendous; you would have beheld deeds shocking, revolting, appalling, gallant, courageous, intrepid, valorous, high-spirited, chivalrous, magnificent, homage-compelling, world-inspiring!

And as they fought thus, those grenadiers of France, they heard a shout which swelled ever louder and louder from the plain of Waterloo until it was distinguishable amid the thunder of the cannon and the shock of charging hosts—"The Guard recoils! the Guard recoils!" And then another even more terrific, "Sauve qui peut! Sauve qui peut!"

Did they know what it meant for them, those grenadiers in Planchenoit? Yes, they knew. If they would prevent the Prussians from rushing in upon the rear of the French army as it fell back from Waterloo, there they must stand, there they must fight, there and there only must they die!

" Mille tonnerres!" roared François Legrand, his cap gone, his hair singed with fire, his eyes bloodshot, " En avant! en avant!"

" Forward! Forward!" cried Pierre, his uniform torn and rent, his scabbard gone, his forehead bleeding, his eyes flashing wildly, " Charge them, I say! Charge them! Sacré! but they shall rest in hell before we go!"

So they dashed on, but at every step the Prussian fire cut their ranks and strewed them like leaves— bloody leaves indeed!—upon the ground. They foamed and fought, but the fire raked them and raked them clean. They were only a handful now, but they stood shoulder to shoulder, and through the drifting smoke the Prussians saw their eyes gleaming and heard, weaker in volume but with the same ring and awe-compelling power of days long passed by, their defiance—" Vive l'Empereur!"

Mark them, good reader, as they stand there, that little band—Pierre Pasquin, François Legrand, André Marceau, Gustave Lébon, Gérard Etienne and forty more—coarse, rough men the most of them, it is true, but in their eyes is courage, in their mouths truth, in their hearts loyalty! Of how many, more refined than they, can you say that?

Then a cannon-ball came, tearing away François Legrand's right arm so that it hung only by bleeding, quivering shreds. But as the Prussian cavalry charged he wrenched that mangled limb loose from his bloody shoulder and hurled it at the Prussians and cried, " Vive l'Empereur!" They came with a dash, that

Prussian cavalry, and among the first, on a proudly galloping horse, rode an officer who waved his sword and shouted, " No quarter for these wretches! " And as he spoke, he drew rein and plunged his sabre through the brave heart of helpless François Legrand. Pierre saw him as he came and he gave a great cry— " My God! it is Jean Deteau! " With a bound and a spring he seized that horse by the bridle.

" Do you know me? " he roared. " It is Pasquin! Pierre! "

" D——n you! " the black eyes blazed defiance.

At the same instant Pierre struck him with his sword with such force that Deteau's head, half cut off, fell forward, blood gushed from his mouth, and his cocked hat rolled on the ground. Then a shot struck Deteau's horse and it fell, bearing Pierre down with it, and all was darkness.

Along the road to Genappe, on the panting, foam-flecked steed Marengo, with Montholon on one side and Bertrand on the other, in the midst of a howling mass of fugitives, fled Napoleon. With him, more truly than with Francis I at Pavia, " All was lost but honor." For France the Heroic Age had ended; the Reign of the Commonplace had begun.

CHAPTER XXXVI

GRENOBLE

Parlez-nous de lui.
—BÉRANGER, *Souvenirs du Peuple.*

TWENTY-FIVE years have passed away. The turf grows green on Waterloo, and the Belgian Lion on the Memorial Mount stands the silent guardian of an "Empire's dust." And kings have come and kings have gone. Louis XVIII has ended his career in his state bed at the Tuileries Palace, and Monsieur, the once gay d'Artois, has had his day also as Charles X, and been forced to abdicate and flee in the July days of 1830. And now we are in the reign of the *ci-devant* Duke of Orleans, at present the "Citizen King," Louis Philippe I. "C'est le treizième!" ("It is the thirteenth!") said M. de Talleyrand as he took the oath to Louis Philippe. And no doubt the Devil thought that was a good number with which to stop, for he gathered M. de Talleyrand in, not long after. And so M. de Talleyrand departed this life, leaving behind him a large fortune and an unpleasant odor.

And what has become of our friends in Grenoble? Come, then, to the Café Jodélle and see. Who is that old man seated by the fire, holding that bright-eyed little girl upon his knee, and with that plainly-dressed but fair-faced woman standing beside him? That old man is grand-père Pasquin, once Captain

Pierre Pasquin of the Garde Impériale, once the boy Pierre of the Rue Montorge. Old man? you say. Why, he is not so very old; he is about fifty now. True, but he is old before his time. The years gone by have been hard ones and their marks remain. He lost a leg at Waterloo. The horse which fell on him, in that wild night of ruin and Empire-destroying convulsion, crushed it, and when he was found a day later and brought in by the peasant Piramme, who returned to his ruined home in Planchenoit, the leg had to come off. There was a bayonet wound which he received in the chest that left its mark also, and for years he could not use a hoe or spade without coughing fits. And yet he wanted so much to use the spade and hoe, for there was a garden in which he was much interested.

And who is that fair-faced woman beside him? That is Josephine, the little Josephine, grown to be a woman now, and such a helpful one. And the bright-eyed child? Ah! that is the best of all. That is Susanne, the little Susanne, who looks just as Josephine did in the days gone by. And why should she not? for she is Josephine's daughter and her father is Gaspard—no longer the little Gaspard, but Gaspard the vigorous, Gaspard the hard-working, Gaspard the devoted, Gaspard the prosperous, who cares for the garden in which grand-père Pasquin takes such interest, and sells vegetables from it in the Pasquin *épicerie* in the Rue Montorge, and manages also the Café Jodélle upon the Place Grénette.

And Marie, why is she not here? Ah! that is the sad part of the story. Marie is yonder in the cemetery of Grenoble, with the mère Pasquin on one side

of her and the père Henri on the other. And at her
head is a white stone which has but one word,
" Marie," and at her feet are flowers placed there every
Sunday by the little Susanne, and at her side the turf
is worn away where the old grenadier is wont to come
and kneel. So Marie has gone, but her picture above
the mantel has a wreath of flowers, and her influence
lives with them always, and will till life shall end.

And on the wall of the sitting-room in the Café
Jodélle hangs the sabre of honor which was once
brave Philippe Courteau's; for Philippe, when he
passed away, left it by his will to grand-père Pasquin,
and these were the words with which he left it, " To
him who is worthy of it—Pierre Pasquin." Now that
was a kind thought and a fitting one. And under the
sabre of honor hangs the certificate of the *Garde
Municipale de Grenoble*, and to this the old soldier often
turns his eyes. And you were promised long ago
that you should see it, and here it is.

GARDE MUNICIPALE DE GRENOBLE

Services de M. Pasquin (Pierre), Capitaine.

Né à Grenoble (Departement de l'Isère) le 2 janvier, 1791,
fils d'Amand et de Jeanne-Louise.

GRADES SUCCESSIFS	CORPS DANS LESQUELS IL A SERVI	DATES DES PROMOTIONS à CHAQUE GRADE
Enrôlé volontaire	115e rég. de la ligne.......	5 janvier, 1809
Sergent	3e rég. de la Garde Impériale	2 février, 1810
Sergent-major ...	Id.	8 septembre, 1812
Sous-lieutenant ..	Id.	28 décembre, 1812
Lieutenant......	Id.	22 mai, 1813
Capitaine........	Id.	20 août, 1813

CAMPAGNES DANS CHAQUE GRADE

ANNÉES	ARMÉES	GENERAUX EN CHEF QUI LES COMMANDAIENT	ACTIONS D'ÉCLAT OU SERVICES SIGNALÉS
1809	Espagne...	Maréchal duc de Montebello......	Blessé d'un coup de feu à Saragosse.
1809	Allemagne et Autriche	L'Empereur	Blessé d'un coup de baionnette à la bataille d'Essling, 22 mai, 1809.
1812	Russie.....	id.	Il sauva le colonel Hulot à la bataille de Wagram, 6 juillet, 1809.
1813	Saxe et Prusse...	id.	A pris un drapeau à l'ennemi en septembre 1812, à la Moscowa.
1814	France	id.	Blessé d'un coup de feu à la bataille de Dresde, 26 août, 1813.
1815	Waterloo..	id.	Blessé d'un coup de baionnette à la bataille de Waterloo, 18 juin, 1815.

Observations, Titres et Décorations.   Légionnaire, 2 février, 1810.

So it hangs, in its official dryness, a record of self-sacrifice, fatigue, privation, courage, valor, loyalty; a record of which he who made it and they who look daily at it may feel justly proud.

Now if there is one thing which children enjoy more than another it is a story. And who could tell stories like grand-père Pasquin?—wonderful grand-père Pasquin who had been everywhere and seen everything, they thought, and had spoken to kings and queens, and had been in the great wars and at the famous

battles, which were printed in large letters in the
school histories, and, best of all, had been decorated
by the great Emperor whose picture was in every
house in Grenoble, and whose glass and the cup
which he had used at the Trois Dauphins were still
preserved there by the good M. Fontlebelle who
owned it now. So in the winter evenings they would
gather about the white wooden fireplace in the Café
Jodélle—little Susanne and her friends, Louise,
Adolphe, Jules, Octave and Jeannette—and they
would come and stand about grand-père Pasquin's
chair and say, like Béranger's children in the " Souvenirs du Peuple," " Parlez-nous de lui," (" Tell us of
him ").

Well, grand-père Pasquin was always ready to tell
them, for he was fond of them all, and so he would
take the little Susanne on his knee, and while Louise
sat upon a stool and Jeannette stood beside the chair
and Adolphe and Jules sat upon the floor, looking up
with large, interested eyes, and young Octave now and
then poked the fire, the grand-père Pasquin would live
his past again. One night when they were all so
gathered, this was the story he told them.

" Now, mes enfants," said he, " do you all remember
André Marceau? "

" Oh, yes, we do remember him," said Susanne,
" he was a nice man."

" And who was other nice man with big mustache,
grand-père? " said small Louise.

" Oh! that was François Legrand! " cried Octave.
" I remember him well. He went with grand-père
over the walls at Essling."

" That is right, Octave," said grand-père Pasquin.

"It is fine that you all remember so well. Now you shall hear of André Marceau. You must know that André and I marched side by side for a long time, and we ate soup out of the same pot, and there is nothing like that for friendship, for the Emperor used to say that those soldiers who stood shoulder to shoulder the best in battle were those who had eaten their soup together for a long time. Now, one day my friend André Marceau got into trouble, and this is how it was. We were in Germany, and in one of the towns we had captured was a fine avenue which was nearly ruined by our cavalry. Now, to prevent more damage being done, the Emperor stationed guards with orders to allow no one to pass. One of these guards was André Marceau."

"Did André Marceau have large mustache like François?" inquired Louise.

"Be quiet, Louise," said Susanne, "André Marceau was a nice man."

"Pretty soon along came General Vandamme. 'Halt!' cried André. 'Sacré!' cried General Vandamme, 'what do you mean?' 'No one can pass,' said André. 'Indeed!' cried Vandamme, 'Learn, fool, that General Vandamme passes anywhere. Take that for your impertinence!' And General Vandamme struck André with his riding-whip."

"Oh! I do not like General Vandamme," cried Louise. "He was not a nice man."

"Be quiet, Louise," said Susanne. "You shall hear."

"Now as soon as General Vandamme had done that," continued grand-père Pasquin, "André Marceau, who was big and strong, knocked him down, and there was the great General Vandamme with his plumed hat and all, lying on the ground."

"Good! good!" cried Adolphe.

"Be quiet, Adolphe," said Susanne.

"Well, you may imagine that there was trouble then. Poor André was arrested and shut up in the citadel, and General Vandamme was going to hold a court-martial and have André shot, for when one strikes his superior officer it is no slight matter which two days in the guard-house will rectify. Now it so happened that the Emperor returned that night to the town, and on passing the citadel he saw a string hanging out of a window with a piece of paper on which was written 'Pardon! pardon!'"

"Now, who had written that?" cried small Louise.

"Why, André Marceau, of course," said Octave.

"Be quiet," said Susanne.

"So the Emperor said, 'Find out what that means and have the man brought before me on parade.' There was a parade next day, and when the Emperor came walking along to our company, André Marceau went down on his knees and remained there. The Emperor stopped short and asked the meaning of this. Our colonel said it was the soldier who had asked pardon in the citadel, and that when intoxicated he had struck a superior officer. You see the colonel was a friend of General Vandamme, and so he said André was intoxicated and did not give the real cause."

"He was a bad colonel," said Louise.

"Now, as you know, André Marceau was not intoxicated, for though he often drank, he was not drunk then, nor ever that I know of, and on this

occasion I have told you just why he struck his general. This, however, the Emperor did not know."

"But, grand-père, why did not you shout out, 'He
is not drunk! he is not drunk!'?" cried Jules.

"Écoute s'il pleut! (be quiet), Jules," said Susanne.

"Now have patience, mes enfants, and you shall
know all. The Emperor stood before our line and
said to us all, 'Is he a gallant fellow?' 'Yes, yes,
sire,' we all cried, 'he is an excellent soldier. We
know him well. He will never remain behind when
any fighting is going on.' Then the Emperor came
up to André, who was still kneeling, took him by the
ears and shook his head, saying, 'How is it that you,
who are a good soldier, could be guilty of such im-
proper conduct? Tell me, what would have become
of you if my arrival had been delayed a single day?'
Then he slapped him on the cheeks and said, 'Go
back to your regiment and never forget this lesson.'"

"Très-bien! très-bien!" cried Adolphe, "then he
was not shot! Oh! the Emperor was a nice man."

"But, mes enfants," said old Pasquin, "the best is
yet to come."

"Good! good!" cried Octave.   "Do you hear that,
Louise, the best is yet to come."

"Best is yet to come," repeated Louise gleefully.

"That night the Emperor found out why André
struck his General, for some one told M. Savary and
he told the Emperor. What do you think the Emperor did then?"

"What did he do? What did he do?" they cried.

"Patience, and you shall hear. Next morning the
Emperor sent for André Marceau, and André, all fear
and trembling, went up to the Emperor's tent. There

was the Emperor, looking stern enough, and there too were four or five Marshals and as many aides-de-camp, and, if you had seen as many of them as I have, you would know, by my simply saying they were there, what an imposing lot they were, all stars and plumes and gold. Then General Vandamme came forward, and with a very pale, set face he said to André, 'I apologize for having struck you. I am sorry for it.' Think of that! A great general apologizing before them all to a common soldier, and *the Emperor made him do it*, and he was the best friend the common soldier ever had! Now, children, give a cheer for the Emperor!" And old Pierre, fired by his recollections, was up on his legs of flesh and wood. So they gave it—old Pierre, little Susanne, and Louise and Jeannette and Adolphe and Jules and Octave. And through the Café Jodélle, as it had rung in days gone by, sounded again the shout—"Vive l'Empereur!"

Long live the Emperor? How can they cry that?—when beneath the willows at St. Helena, under a plain white stone, rest the ashes of a mighty dead, gone and forgotten.

Forgotten? Listen to what follows.

CHAPTER XXXVII

LA FRANCE DEMANDE

Home they brought her warrior dead.
    —TENNYSON, *The Princess.*

IN the year 1840, the Duke of Orleans, the eldest son of King Louis Philippe, was sent with the French army into Africa to check the growing power of Abd-el-Kader, and with him went his younger brother, the Duke d'Aumale. It was with much chagrin that the Prince de Joinville, third son of Louis Philippe, saw his brothers depart to this new field of glory to "break their lances right brilliantly." And then he fell ill with the measles and disappointment, for he too had hoped to have a mission of honor and renown. You shall have one, Prince de Joinville, and one far greater than your brothers. Their African campaigns are long ago forgotten, but the memory of your mission endures, and will endure while time shall last. And so, as he lay in a high fever, there came to his bedside his father, King Louis Philippe, and M. de Rémusat, the Minister of the Interior, and the King said these words: "Joinville, you are to go out to St. Helena and bring back Napoleon's coffin." On the 2nd of July the Prince de Joinville left Paris, and on the 6th he embarked at Toulon on board his frigate, the "Bellepoule," and set out for St. Helena.

Well, the news of this mission was known before

long in Grenoble and it created no little sensation there. The old veterans who met at the Trois Dauphins talked it over and arranged to go in a body to take part in the procession in Paris. They came also to the Café Jodélle to see grand-père Pasquin and to know if grand-père Pasquin was going too. Yes indeed! grand-père Pasquin was going. So they all remained with him during the afternoon, the best bottles in the Café Jodélle were opened, and they talked over the days gone by.

"Ah," said old Pasquin, looking up at the sabre of honor, "if only brave Philippe Courteau could have lived to see this day, and Henri Jodélle, too, for during many years they would not believe him dead, but said always, 'It is false rumor to deceive us. He will come again.'"

So the summer passed, but in the last days of November the grand-père Pasquin fell ill and this was the way of it. He had been to the cemetery one Sunday, for he went often on Sundays to see the three white stones bearing the names, "La Veuve Pasquin," "Marie," "Henri Jodélle." And on this Sunday it was late when he came, and after he had remained some time beside the stones, he went slowly to the gates, but they were fastened and there was no one near them. He shook the gates and cried, "Open!" But no one came, for the custodian had gone away to eat a supper with his friend Le Rolle at the Place St. André. Then old Pasquin tried to climb the wall, but he slipped and fell. The wall was not low, so the fall stunned him and he lay on the ground. It was dark now, and the wind blew more strongly and shook the leafless trees. Presently the rain came, a sharp, cold rain, that fell hard and chill and made the water run in rivulets along the sides of the path. After some hours the rain stopped, but the night was damp and cold, and through it all the grand-père Pasquin lay upon the ground. When morning came the *jardinier* Simon Benoit found him there, close to the wall, soaked with water and stiff with cold. Benoit in haste gave him some brandy and had him taken home to the Café Jodélle, where Gaspard, Josephine and Susanne soon arrived, for they had been to Vizille. Worried enough they were, you may be sure, and he was rubbed and warmed and put to bed. But he grew very ill, and the skilful doctor, M. Sardique, who was summoned, shook his head and said, " He is very sick, Josephine, he is very sick."

Then fever set in; he was often delirious and he would cry, " Doctor, Doctor, shall I live to go to Paris? Shall I live to go to Paris? "

" Yes, yes, grand-père, you shall go to Paris," said M. Sardique, to quiet him. When the fever left him he was very weak, but when the doctor came again he repeated his question, " Doctor, shall I go to Paris? "

" Grand-père," said M. Sardique, " you have been very ill, you are very ill now. You must not think of that."

Old Pasquin was silent for a moment, then he looked fixedly at M. Sardique and said, " Doctor, I will go to meet the Emperor. I will go to Paris."

He grew somewhat better after that, but it was all in vain that Josephine and Gaspard strove to show him that he was not strong enough to travel. He let them say what they thought right, and then he said briefly, and each time with more determination than before, " I will go to Paris! "

So in December they set out; Josephine, Susanne and Gaspard, watching and tending the old soldier. He stood the journey better than they anticipated, and when he saw once more the towers of Notre Dame, the dome of the Tuileries Palace and the Arc de Triomphe, the fire came again into the old soldier's eyes.

Paris was all expectant when they reached it, for on the 29th of November the royal frigate " Belle-poule " had arrived at Cherbourg, bearing the Emperor's remains. And when on the 8th of December the Imperial barge started up the Seine, Cherbourg saluted with one thousand guns. Gaspard took them to the Café Bovard, on the Avenue des Champs Élysées, for Jules Bovard who owned it was a son of stout Robert Bovard who had been at Pierre's wedding feast, and they knew him well.

The 15th of December drew near. All day the workmen labored on the decorations of the city, and all night they worked, too, by the light of torches, for the " Bellepoule " had come ten days sooner than she was expected, and there was need to hurry. The weather was bitter cold, but the sturdy workmen labored on by day and by night.

The 15th of December came, and on either side of the Avenue des Champs Élysées were statues of victory, eagle-topped standards and tripods and arches. About the Arc de Triomphe were masts bearing banners inscribed with the names of all the armies of the Republic and of the Empire; garlands of flowers hung from the top of the Arch to the basement, and upon the summit was a statue of the Emperor in his Imperial robes, at his right hand an equestrian statue of Glory, at his left an equestrian statue of Victory, and all about tripods of colored flame. Over the Pont de la Concorde were statues of Wisdom, Justice, Strength, War, Commerce, Agriculture, Eloquence, while before the portals of the Chambre des Deputes Palace loomed a colossal statue of Immortality. On the Esplanade des Invalides were statues of Kings and famous Captains of France, who had given their country honor and renown, from Clovis to Macdonald. Between them all were tripods sending forth bright flames, and they stood thus, in long white rows, awaiting the great one soon to pass before them.

The Avenue des Champs Élysées was lined with National Guards on either side, and behind them were five hundred thousand people, and there were forty thousand more upon the great stands on the Invalides Esplanade and thousands more within the Invalides Church and upon every housetop, while in a window of the Café Bovard were Gaspard, Josephine, Susanne, and, in a chair, the grand-père Pasquin, and so the march began.

At the head of the procession came the Gendarmerie of the Seine with their trumpets and their colonel, then the *Garde Municipale à cheval* with trumpets and standard; two squadrons of the 7th Lancers, the Commandant of Paris and his staff, a battalion of infantry of the Line, the *Garde Municipale à pied* with flag and drums and colonel, the General of Division and his staff, the École Militaire of St. Cyr, the École Polytechnique, the École Etat-Major, battalions of infantry, cavalry and artillery, squadrons of cuirassiers of the National Guard, a carriage containing M. l'Abbé Coquereau, chaplain of the St. Helena Expedition, the white horse covered with violet crape embroidered with the golden bees and bearing the amaranth velvet and gold-embroidered saddle used by the Emperor when First Consul, and then the banners of the 86 Departments of France borne by mounted cuirassiers. Thus they passed on with pealing music, a blaze of variegated color amid tricolored balconies, funereal urns and golden eagles. Ah! what was that shining in the distance, high above all? The old soldier sat erect in his chair. Down the Avenue des Champs Élysées, crowned with flags, surrounded by gleaming bayonets, amid waving plumes, enveloped by clouds of incense, girt by a sea of upturned faces, rolled the great Imperial Car, golden-glittering, awe-inspiring, memory-awakening, glory-recalling, triumph-typifying!—bearing the ashes of Napoleon!

The old soldier trembled; his sight grew dim, and his blood, with a rush of recollection, leaped to his brain. Faint, yet clear, and heard by him alone, sounded the battle-song of other days:

> En avant! En avant!
> The conqueror goes to war;
> The cannons loudly roar;
> The eagles proudly soar.
> En avant! En avant!
> The conqueror goes to war.
> Behold advance the flag of France,
> Triumphant tricolore!

"See! grandpa, see!" cried little Susanne, as the veterans of the *Vieille Garde*, in their faded uniforms passed by, " the Guard!   Your Guard, grandpa, the Old Guard!"

There was no response, and Josephine turned quickly from the window. He had sunk back in his chair, one hand lay in his lap, and the other hung listless beside him. On his breast was the Cross of the Legion of Honor. Pierre had followed the Emperor.

THE END.